DECEPTION TRAIL

Also by Fred Grove:

BUFFALO SPRING
THE BUFFALO RUNNERS
WAR JOURNEY
THE CHILD STEALERS
WARRIOR ROAD
DRUMS WITHOUT WARRIORS
THE GREAT HORSE RACE
BUSH TRACK
THE RUNNING HORSES
PHANTOM WARRIOR
MATCH RACE
A FAR TRUMPET
SEARCH FOR THE BREED

DECEPTION
TRAIL

FRED GROVE

A Double D Western
Doubleday

NEW YORK   LONDON   TORONTO   SYDNEY   AUCKLAND

All of the characters in this book
are fictitious, and any resemblance
to actual persons, living or dead,
is purely coincidental.

A Double D Western
Published by Doubleday, a division of Bantam Doubleday Dell Publishing Group,
Inc. 666 Fifth Avenue, New York, New York 10103

A Double D Western, Doubleday and the portrayal of the letters DD are trademarks
of Doubleday, a division of Bantam Doubleday Dell Publishing Group, Inc.

Library of Congress Cataloging-in-Publication Data

Grove, Fred.
Deception trail/Fred Grove.
p.   cm.
ISBN 0-385-23920-3
I. Title.
PS3557.R7D4   1988
813′ .54—dc19 87-19853
CIP

OG

CONTENTS

1   All Comers at Any Distance   1

2   Best Against the Best   20

3   Honors for a Great Horse   31

4   A Member of the Family   40

5   All Brag and No Bottom   51

6   A Lead or a Setup?   60

7   The Owl Person Comes   70

8   Another Dead End?   80

9   Sounds in the Night   92

10   When Fast Horses Always Lose   111

11   Odds and a Courtly Manner   120

12   Race Against the Fix   135

13   The Cowboy and the Lady   149

14   The Mystery Horse   157

15   The Other Side of the River   171

DECEPTION TRAIL

CHAPTER 1

ALL COMERS AT ANY DISTANCE

My name is Dude McQuinn. With my wife, Blossom, I run a little horse ranch and a few head of lean cows on the Salt Fork of the Brazos—that's in Texas.

Now, I have been known to keep the double doors swingin' at the Lone Wolf Saloon in town when I feel the onset of a cough, and some folks say I've got more lip than a muley cow. I don't deny that. A fact's a fact. But I remind you that palaver is what matches horseraces. That and difference of opinion. Like, my horse can outrun your horse at any distance. In a match race, you always try to get the advantage, if you can, and odds, if you can. As the poet fella said, all's fair in love and war and horseracin'. It's do unto others, because the other side will sure do it to you if you're not on the lookout. See what I mean?

Let's say you're passin' through the country with a little outfit on the lookout for fresh money. If your horse's best distance is long, you match him long. If he's a short sprinter, match him short. This, after you've eyeballed the other horse. All the while, from your roundabout palaver, the other fella figures he's got the advantage. See what I mean?

When you come to a little town, it's cagey to carry several horses. A saddler or two, maybe a trade horse. That way you can cover up your real runnin' horse. Make him look like an ol' packhorse or maybe have him harnessed to the wagon. Peroxide rubbed on a dark bay hide will make streaks, like the horse spends most of his time in harness. Maybe you stick some cockleburs, which we Texans refer to as cuckleburs, in his mane and tail. I always keep a sack of burs handy in the wagon. But you always want one horse to look like a sure-enough scorpion. Almost too fast to match, but not quite. Slick him up good. As you drag through town, trail him behind the wagon on a halter rope for everybody to see. That's the honey that draws the bees. And remember, just about every little town has a runnin' horse. By this time, you have caught the eyes of the local loafers, and word gets around fast.

Well, you make camp at the wagonyard or go on to the edge of town where there's water and grass. Maybe you bought feed at a livery stable as you came in. Cold cash is always a cinch ice-breaker in a new town. Also loosens the tongue. Most livery proprietors would rather lean on the blister end of a pitchfork and talk than muck out a stable. We're all human. He obliges with a few particulars about the local champion which you file away for reference.

That afternoon or next morning you'll likely have a caller.

"A friend happened to see you boys come in and said you might be carryin' a racehorse," he says. Or, "Was just goin' by and happened to notice that slick bay over there. Looks like a runner."

Now, a word of caution. The first rule in the match-race game is never appear eager to run. So you roll a smoke and with a nod in the direction of your slick horse say, "Texas Jack over there can run a little when the wind's behind him and his shins don't hurt, but he's off his feed and not up to snuff. Doubt if he could outrun a fat man today. But if he takes to his vittles in a day or so, I might harken to a match-up. All depends."

He takes that in with an "I see."

You palaver some more, visit about the weather, and inquire how range conditions are as to water and grass and what fat steers are bringin' in Fort Worth. If you're in a sodbuster town, like up in Kansas, your talk is likewise heavy on the weather and extra heavy on crops. You are always sympathetic if times are hard, which is easy for a cowman like me who's gone broke three times, so broke I almost sold my saddle once. It's surefire to grease the conversation if you throw in some cusswords against the government. Never fails. After a while, your man leaves. Says he might drop back in a day or two, which you figure he will.

Along toward evening you drift in to the main water hole. You ask for the best whiskey in the house, say Old Green River, like that's your "usual" and you're a man of good taste. After a time, you have another. You pay as you go, careful not to forget friend barkeep. You offer to buy him a drink. Most times he'll decline, bein' on duty, but will have what he calls "a mild cigar," which is the "house cigar," frazzled and used over and over, which he will put back in the box at the end of his shift. By now he notices that you're not like the local tightwads and he begins to cotton to you. Aside, he tells you one about the Traveling Salesman. Instead of Pittsburgh, the salesman, bein' out West, is from Kansas City or Denver. Or the barkeep tells one about the Farmer's Daughter.

You say, "That's a good 'un—never heard it before," and let go with guffaws and pound the bar and shake your head.

He beams appreciation. Furthermore, now that you've given the house some trade, he fans flies away from the free lunch and gestures for you to help yourself to the pickles, bologna, sausages, rye bread, and baked beans. A fork sticks out of a murky glass of water by the bowl of beans. Leery of the fork, you pass up the beans and have a sausage. It's so salty, you have to have a beer. Free saloon lunches are loaded with salt to make you drink more. Remember that.

When you let drop that you carry a racehorse, he obligingly furnishes some crucial details on the local scorpion. Like best distance, two hundred and fifty yards, and best time. Is sore-legged and likes a soft track. It had just rained the day before. Get it? Also, the local horse has one bad and dangerous habit: lunges left at the break, which means you will insist on a toss of the coin for post position in hopes you get the right side. That little morsel of fact right there could mean the horserace, because the horse that takes the break generally wins these short sprints.

Next morning the local horseman shows up at camp again. "Your horse any better?" he asks, eyeballing Texas Jack.

"No better," I say as I lay on a worried look, which I'm good at.

"I had kinda hoped we might agree on a little set-to," he keeps on. "My horse is matched big two weeks from now at the county fair and needs a sharpener."

"Well," I say, "if you feel you just have to run, I might oblige you with my ol' packhorse over there, Hoot Owl."

"Him?" The man is amused.

"He can run a little if the distance is right."

"How do you mean?"

"He's a slow starter. Takes a distance of ground for him to get loosened up, old as he is and muscle-bound. That's why, the few times I've run him—just for fun, mind you, against cow ponies—I've never matched him under three hundred yards. He just begins to take hold of the track at two-fifty. Needs time to pick up his feet, loosen up them muscles. Not fair to the horse. It takes him a while."

He tries to hide it, but a look like a coyote in the henhouse comes over his face. "Guess it won't hurt to lengthen my horse out a little." He figures he's got the advantage. At two-fifty his horse will be on the lead and long gone.

"But I'll have to have odds," I say.

"Odds?" He backs off.

"I'm doin' this just to oblige you," I remind him.

He agrees to two-to-one odds. And even though I don't win the flip for post position, my horse outbreaks his horse a full length. At the finish there's enough daylight between the horses to drive three hay wagons.

"Thought you said he's just an ol' packhorse that can run a little," the loser grumbles.

"I didn't say that's all he is," I reply. "He is a packhorse. Also pulls the wagon. Also would make a good kid horse. Today he was a racehorse."

But I'll say this, he pays up like a man and don't hedge and whimper like some. I don't want him to feel any worse, so I don't tell him that my "ol' packhorse" is Judge Blair, fastest horse in the Southwest, short or long. Well, there's been a wad of local money bet on the race, and before anybody can get tanked up and come on the prod, I am on the way out of town, makin' far-apart tracks.

You prob'ly don't know that Judge Blair scored big back in Kentucky. That he won the main handicap at Churchill Downs—that's where they run the Kentucky Derby—and to this day holds the record for the mile run at the old Kentucky Association track there in Lexington at Fifth and Race. Burned that mile in one-thirty-four and change. It was a thousand-dollar match race. Beat Sir Roderick, the top handicap horse in Kentucky, by a head. They said it was the greatest match race ever run in Kentucky. Back there, you see, against Thoroughbreds, we had to run the Judge as the Duke of Dexter, which sounds pretty fancy, though a true name, because we didn't have any papers to show that he was registered as a Thoroughbred with the Jockey Club, which is another story. It happened the Duke of Dexter was recently deceased and also a dark bay like the Judge, though his conformation lacked a heap of matchin' the Judge's. We got the Duke's papers through a connection, you might say. I reckon my horse has been run under more aliases than an Oklahoma outlaw on the dodge, all because no horseman wants to go up against Judge Blair any more. Why lose money? Truth is, the Judge is a mystery horse—or was, which is still another story, and which I'll get to directly.

How did I come to own the Judge? Well, I won him in an all-night poker game in San Antone. My lucky night. The cowman who put up the Judge claimed he was by Buck Shiloh, a son of the legendary Shiloh —now *there* was a boss stud horse who knew where the finish line was! —and out of the great Mexican track burner, Lolita. I soon found out that all the claims amounted to was hot air. Same for the name of Judge Blair, which the cowman made up to make the horse sound like quality folks and worth a wager. Like them scorpion colts sired by the great South Texas runner, Traveler, who established a strain of lightning-fast short horses. Traveler colts like Judge Thomas and Judge Welch.

But it didn't matter. Because I soon discovered I had me a sure-enough runnin' horse, pedigree be damned. Apparently, the Judge had never been run and the cowman had won him in a poker pot just the night before off a cowman as much in the dark as he was. . . . Right here I want to put in a few regretful words, the bad with the good. You see, some fool with a knife and no judgment who called himself a horseman had gelded Judge Blair, prob'ly because he was a little spirited, gelded him so he could handle 'im. My, as a sire what he could have passed on to his get: heart, intelligence, conformation, toughness, looks, temperament, that long stride which enables him to go a distance of ground, and burning speed. Not to forget his ability to change leads goin' into a turn, then to change back on the straightaway. You see, every time a horse changes leads, he rests the other front leg. I said heart, above all, heart. "Even if a horse comes down from kings and queens but lacks heart, he can't outrun a three-year-old turtle." That's a sayin' by an old pardner of mine, which I'll tell you about as we go along.

Some fellas who've rubbed on a horse or two and cleaned out some stalls figure it's easier to make a livin' as trainers. So they buy a big Stetson and a loud shirt and a belt with a big, shiny buckle and call themselves trainers, and maybe they get a couple of horses that have started a few times, so the horses have already been broke to run. But when they get a colt with spirit and go, they don't know how to handle him properly. So they geld the colt. Believe me, it takes a heap more horseman to handle a stallion. . . . Well, after the Judge had won a few races by daylight, and I mean broad daylight, nobody would match him. So I took to the road. But travelin' around didn't help, because the grapevine telegraph was always ahead of us: *Don't match Judge Blair. He's forked lightnin'.*

One afternoon at Uvalde—that's in Texas, too—I watched a dark bay gelding with no white markings run fifth in a five-horse race. He was called Rebel. He was smooth for looks, but he couldn't or wouldn't run much. His heart wasn't in it. I could see that. After the race, a keen-eyed old codger with a white bib of a beard and the face of a saint moseyed over to me and suggested that I buy Rebel.

"Buy him?" I started to laugh. "Son of a gun, that horse ran last."

"He's a dark bay, like your horse. That's one reason. Another is his conformation. In my judgment they'll weigh within twenty-five pounds of each other and each stands about fifteen hands. Except for Judge Blair's blazed face and white-socked feet, they'd be spittin' images."

"Don't believe I savvy you, old-timer."

"Haven't matched Judge Blair yet, have you?"

"Nope."

"You won't around here. Your horse is too well-known."

"I still don't savvy why you say I should buy Rebel."

"Have a drink with me and I'll tell you all about color. In a way it's simple, in a way it's not. Takes a certain finesse." He winked as he said it.

Well, that afternoon while the bourbon fumes rose around us, he told me all about the "switch" and how it worked. The idea was simple, but required a certain finesse for certain and which he possessed. You take two horses of look-alike color and conformation. One is slow, one is fast. You match the slow horse; of course, he loses. You hang around town a few days, careful to set up the drinks now and then, and opine that you know your horse can run better than he did. That he was just off his feed, or gettin' over the colic. You'd match him again, you say, if you could get odds. Is the other man for that! Here is where the finesse comes in. The night before the race you paint the fast horse to look like the slow horse, the slow horse to look like the fast horse.

The fast horse wins at odds, you collect the bets and get on out of town. It'll work every time, but you'd better have a fast horse and never run in the rain. If it even looks like rain about post time, just pay the forfeit and say your horse is off again. A man can get shot if the paint's runnin' when his horse crosses the finish line. The cagey old-timer told me his name was William Tecumseh Lockhart. No put-on titles. Just that. Before long I would call him Billy and Uncle. He had clear blue eyes set in a roundish, puckish face that at first glance made you think of a saint. His hands were small and deft, like a woman's. Later, more than once when our little outfit was threatened, I'd see a six-shooter suddenly bulge in those quick hands as fast as a gambler could flip an ace. Who was this mysterious old gent? Had he been a professor back East? Was Lockhart his true name? Was he wanted somewhere? However, to his credit I never saw his saintly features on the wall at the post office.

He could sound like a schoolmaster when he lectured a crowd of country yokels about horses, as full of facts as a mail-order catalogue. In frock coat, white shirt, string tie, flat-topped gray hat and benchmade boots, he could be a courtly gentleman of the old school around women, or you might take him for some dignitary on a visit. Then he could rip out a string of cusswords that would make a mule-skinner take cover, and never once repeat himself. Most times he was in good humor except when his joints hurt. When that was the case, he could be as tetchy as a grizzly.

When he happened to let slip a hint of his mysterious past, which was rare, and I pried with a question, he would answer, "Now, did I say?" and no more was said. So even now I know little more about Uncle Billy than I did in the early days. About all I knew for certain was that he didn't hail from the sunny South. Nobody did who always referred to the War Between the States as the Great Rebellion and whistled "The Battle Hymn of the Republic." That, and him knowing more about horses than any man I'd met, particularly about racehorses, his favorite breed. He loved horses and was more mindful of them than of the people who rode them. He could walk around a horse once and whisper to me to match him short or long. How did he know? Because he could tell whether the horse was short- or long-muscled. A glance told him if the horse toed in or out in front, or had that nice sloping shoulder, which most good runners have. Horses with shoulders set too straight generally don't run very far. You see, their reach is limited. They're not made for stridin' out.

To go along with his horse savvy and his talent with a paintbrush, Billy kept what he called his "medicine chest" in the rear of the wagon. It smelled like a travelin' drugstore back there: turpentine, white pine pitch, camphor, sassafras, Jamaica ginger, ointments and other medicines—you name 'em—the smells all blended together. He also kept a jug of sour mash whiskey back there with a cob stopper. I knew he put whiskey in some of his "potions," as he called 'em, because you could smell the sour mash when he doctored a horse in camp. He'd do that many times free of charge. He could mix up a quick cure for the colic or the blind staggers or the heaves, or whatever. In a bad case of the heaves, he might tell an old farmer, "Now, friend, this is not a permanent cure, but good to trade on when you meet a stranger." And they'd both laugh and nudge each other.

As we traveled around, I began to call him "Doctor" when I introduced him to a crowd of rubes, and he never objected, though I can't say I ever saw a diploma stuck anywhere on his medicine chest. The doctor title always impressed hick loafers; besides, he was a vet, the best I've ever known, then or now, whether he ever attended a horse doctor school or not. Except for the lack of a banjo player, our little outfit was almost like a travelin' medicine show, what with me the fast-talkin' front man on the match races, Billy and his lectures and potions, and—aboard the speedy Judge Blair—our educated Comanche jockey, Coyote Walking, whose father was the chief of all Comanches. When Coyote whooped, the Judge took off like the heel flies were after him.

How Coyote came to join the outfit was lucky for us and fatally unlucky for a Red River jockey called Hack, one in a series of pick-up boys we'd had to use. Still, despite the change in riders, Judge Blair had yet to lose a race as we campaigned across Texas to Indian Territory; in some instances, it was a case of where an exceptional horse made up for poor riding, or where the outfit and the horse together overcame raw skullduggery.

Like the time before a big match race in Fort Worth, when I and Billy happened to stroll behind the barns and spied the owner of the horse we'd matched in jaw-to-jaw conversation with our pick-up jockey. We saw our jockey nod and saw the man slip him a roll of greenbacks. I started to rush right over there and call off the race, but Billy checked me and, unseen, we eased back to our stall.

No, we hadn't left our horse unguarded. We'd hired a big, ugly deputy with two six-shooters, an old acquaintance of Billy's, to watch the Judge so nobody could slip in and fix him. That's how chancy the situation was there. The fix was on when you brought a good horse in, as we used to say, and you never left your horse alone. Another thing: You never let a stranger pet your horse or give him a tidbit. Sugar cubes loaded with laudanum was just one little trick used back then to throw a horse off, and sponges stuffed up a horse's nose. They'd do anything to win a race. The fix was so bad there, if you didn't have a guard, you'd lead your horse with you when you left the stall. At night you slept in front of your horse's stall with a forty-five.

"Remember the throat-latch wrinkle I told you I had to resort to one time back in the olden days?" Billy says.

Billy had told me so many wrinkles I had to ponder a bit. Then all at once it came to me, and I nodded.

"Well, don't say anything to the jock, and place all the bets you can. They'll give you odds now, figuring they have the advantage. We'll teach that slippery gent a lesson he won't forget. After this race he'll be so broke he couldn't buy a sack of Bull Durham."

First thing I did was to slip the throat latch out of our bridle. I don't think the jockey ever noticed the missing bridle piece, he was so intent on when he would pull the Judge. When I told the starter I was goin' to lead my horse up to the line, he reared back. "How come?"

"There's no rule against it," I told him, and started on. "Just don't holler 'Go!' unless the horses are lapped."

"Don't tell me how to start a horserace!" he jaws back at me. Lookin' back, I think he was halfway honest.

At the word "Go!" I jerked the reins out of the jockey's hands and stripped the bridle off my horse. The Judge broke a shade late, but he ran on down there like a hoop rollin'. He knew where the finish line was, that horse, jockey or no jockey, because he'd crossed a passel of 'em. He won by two lengths, with the fixed jockey clutched to his mane, one stirrup lost.

Like I said, we'd picked up this Hack fella along Red River. But before we reached Comanche country we knew he had three dangerous drawbacks: He craved whiskey, was a wolf after women, and when likkered up thought he was lightnin' with a gun, which he wasn't. All this can be a deadly powdersmoke mixture on Saturday night, when cowboys ride into town to whoop it up. Well, there was a pretty young saloon girl that Hack wanted bad; only problem was, so did a cowboy. By then the hour was late and Hack and the cowboy had tried to drink the place dry. Something was said. Both dug for their guns and Hack had a case of the slows and the outfit was immediately short a jockey.

We'd matched a Fort Sill major's stud at three hundred yards for five hundred dollars, with a hundred-dollar forfeit. I hated to give up that much money, and as post time neared, I went on the prowl through the crowd for a pick-up rider. Two young white boys looked the right size, but turned me down.

I was ready to throw in when I noticed this young Indian eyeballin' Judge Blair. He stood there like stone, his black eyes fixed on my horse in appreciation. I heard him say "Buffalo runner," then he came over and stroked the Judge's face and neck.

I didn't put off any longer. "Can you ride a racehorse?" Even though I wasn't impressed with this Indian. He was bandy-legged and short, but stout through the chest and arms, and he had good hands.

His eyes actually glittered. "Ride him I can."

"You win, I'll pay you twenty-five dollars. Lose, you'll just get ten." He didn't hesitate. "This thing I can do. The twenty-five dollars win I will." He wasn't cocky the way he said it; just confident, and I felt a mite better.

It was now post time. When I started to give the Indian a leg up the way I had Hack, he threw me an insulted look and leaped to the saddle, as nimble as a barn cat.

Still, I wasn't convinced. Was he all brag and show just to earn a few bucks?

That Indian didn't do a thing but jump the Judge out by a length at the break, and when the stud came to him at two hundred yards, the Indian let go the damndest screech I ever heard and the Judge opened up daylight. We won it right there.

Billy was with me when I paid the Indian off. "That was some ride," I says. "How would you like to come in with us as pardners? We'll split everything three ways. Share and share alike."

He seemed to simmer that through his mind for a long moment before he spoke. "My father, who is chief of all Comanches, has many relatives to feed. Camp they do, stay long time. Feed them he does, as they would feed him if stay long time he did. It is the old way, a way of honor. So my father the chief is poor. Come with you this Comanche will and send money home to my father the chief, who is generous, as all Comanches are."

Our lucky day. Later, we learned that Coyote was an honor graduate of Carlisle Indian School in Pennsylvania, with a hankerin' for the Bard of Avon's poetry.

With Billy around, it was like goin' to school every day, and likin' it. Another handy wrinkle I learned from him was the swingin' break. I can still hear Billy as he explained it to me and Coyote.

"What you do is turn your horse a little just before the break. Gives him momentum. You see, he pushes off and sorta swings into his get-away. First, a short step to pull on—for that key momentum—then a long stride and he's gone. That kind of break serves a double purpose. Let's say the starter is bought off to give the other side the advantage, and he sees your horse turned a little sideways, he'll holler 'Go!' every time. He'll figure he's got you beat. Only he won't know that a horse can break faster sideways than he can straight ahead.

"Most horsemen think if their horse is set straightaway and his feet are well under him, that's the ideal position. It's good, of course, but not the best. A horse trained to break sideways will soon learn to set himself. He sets his feet so he takes a short step first. He pulls with that one, then swings into that long stride. You see, while your horse is in his short step and pushin' off, swingin' into his break, the other horse is in his first step, which is a long step. First time I saw the swingin' break used, a country fella had this little-bitty bay mare matched at two hundred and fifty yards. He started her sideways and outbroke a big, strong horse over a length. She had the money won right there! Her tail was in that big horse's face all the way. I've learned more in match races and on small tracks than I ever did on big tracks."

That was an opening.

"Big tracks," I asks him. "What big tracks, Uncle?"

"Now, did I say?"

That ended the conversation.

I recollect only one time that Billy lost his confidence as a horseman. It was up in Kansas. We'd just pulled out of Missouri, kinda in a hurry, if you know what I mean? Billy saw this fast-drivin' horse and just had to have him, a trotter named Amos, which had been on the big tracks and could course the mile in two minutes. Amos was a powerful blue roan that stood sixteen hands, two inches, weighed fourteen hundred pounds. In full stride, he reminded me of a chaparral cock, the way he carried his head.

Well, Billy worked a trade with the farmer, also for a buggy and harness, and in the deal shuffled off a saddler with the chronic heaves— only to learn when we stopped in the next town that Amos was blind. That shook Billy up. For the first time he said he was gettin' old, that he'd lost his eye for horses. He said it was a disgrace to trade for a blind horse, and a greater disgrace to keep one.

He tried to trade Amos off, but something always seemed to nix the sale. Then one night a doper slipped into camp to fix the Judge before a race, and Amos gave the alarm and the doper had to run. Billy just couldn't trade him off after that, even when a preacher offered him three hundred dollars. By then, Billy wouldn't take a bottom-land farm for the old campaigner.

Oh, we had some close shaves. I recollect one in Indian Territory, the time we matched the Judge as Cheyenne Bob. No switch necessary. Everything went as planned. The Judge had daylighted the local favorite by eight lengths and I'd just collected the money, when a smart-alecky lightning-rod salesman I'd heard sound off in a saloon the night before hollered out to the crowd:

"You say that dark bay is Cheyenne Bob? Why, I'd know that blazed face and four white feet anywhere. Saw him run around San Antone. That's none other than the great Judge Blair—fastest hunk o' horseflesh in South Texas. You boys have just been taken!"

Well, you learn to take certain advance precautions sometimes. On this day to rendezvous across Red River as soon as we could. Billy had left town earlier, on the q.t., in the light camp wagon at the reins of our fast-steppin' sorrel team, with Rebel haltered behind. Coyote was to keep on ridin', like he couldn't control his runaway horse. He pretended to tug on the reins, then he'd look back for help. Some play-actor, that educated Comanche. All this put-on just before the drummer jerked the curtain on us.

With the money in my jeans, I hotfooted it to my Kentucky saddler, Blue Grass, tied behind the hotel, and took off down the alley. Them corn-fed townsmen didn't spot me till I was beyond town. They chased me till their fat horses played out. Then I made a little circle. That evening I and Billy and Coyote counted our money on the beloved Texas side of good ol' Red River.

Another time at Three Springs—that's in Texas, too—I thought we'd got ourselves in a box canyon for certain. We'd matched the mighty Hondo, who'd won thirty-three straight races. Shag Fallon owned him. Fallon, as nasty an *hombre* as I'd wished I'd never met, also owned the town of Lone Tree. It was town against town. Both towns bettin' crazy. One Three Springs fella bet his drugstore. Archer & Dodd bet their entire stock of general merchandise.

Well, Three Springs won the toss for the race site and the stage was set. Day of the race when Lone Tree hit town, every man was flashin' three-to-one money. We found out why soon enough. Seems Fallon conditioned his horse with a chain before each race. Then, when the jock rattled a few links of chain down the stretch, Hondo got wings in his feet.

We'd made the switch and were just waitin' around, when I was lured away and knocked in the head. By the time I came to and made it back to the barn, the race was about to start. A stable boy said while I was gone, and while Billy and Coyote had rushed out to watch a fistfight in the street, Wolf Garrity—an old acquaintance of Billy's but now with the Fallon bunch—had switched the horses. That meant only one thing: Garrity had switched Rebel for the Judge. We were sunk. Rebel couldn't outrun a hoptoad.

A light rain began to fall as the race started. To my amazement, Rebel took the break by a length. I knew that couldn't last long. But he still led after a hundred yards or so. I couldn't believe it. Then I saw Hondo's rider come down with that chain and the race tightened. Rebel would fade for certain. Just then Coyote whooped and Rebel took off. Glory be! It was like that, back and forth, as they tore for the finish. I heard Coyote whoop twice. Son of a gun, if Rebel didn't open daylight as they flashed past the judges' stand, Billy not far behind 'em on Blue Grass. But the rain was like buckshot and the paint would be runnin'.

I saw Garrity say something to the judges, then Garrity and Fallon and the judges rushed to our barn. Garrity ran over to where Billy and Coyote had a cooling blanket on Rebel. "This horse is a ringer!" Garrity shouts. "He's been painted. He's a ringer. He's not Rebel, the horse we matched."

"Prove it," Billy says, as cool as you please.

Sure of himself, Garrity rubbed Rebel's wet face. After a bit, Garrity looked at his hand in surprise. There was nothing on it. He sloshed a bucket of water on Rebel's face and rubbed again. Again there was nothing.

"There's another all-dark bay like this one around here somewhere," he says.

Billy stepped to the rear door and swung it open. Through the sheet of rain you could see our horses in the corral. "Take a good look," Billy says. "There's our sorrel team. A couple of trade horses—that dun, that buckskin. And there's that ol' blaze-faced cow pony we call Shorty."

After it was all over, I asked Billy how he did it.

He says, "You mean Garrity *thought* Judge Blair was in the barn. It was Rebel. I was afraid some Fallon man would slip in and fix the Judge, so I took him back to the corral and stabled Rebel in here. You see, I knew Garrity years ago. We worked the switch till I caught him holding out on me. That street fight was just a diversion that Garrity planned. It had moss all over it. So Coyote and I went out and pretended to watch the fight, while Garrity brought the Judge in and took Rebel to the corral. After the race, I switched the horses again, left the Judge in the corral for a face wash and brought Rebel in here."

Garrity went to jail soon after that on a bank robbery charge, and Three Springs won enough money to build a new schoolhouse.

Like I said, we'd draw good crowds in them little towns, 'specially the sodbuster ones, where entertainment was hard to come by. Even a stranger passin' through was cause for talk. Like, wonder who he is? Wonder where he's from? Reckon he's on the dodge? Suppose he stole that smooth sorrel? Yes, Billy loved to lecture on horses and equine ills, but sometimes he would stray off the subject and strike out on the Byzantine Empire, another favorite topic. Before long the crowd would begin to shuffle, a sign of boredom, and he'd call out for me "to fetch the bridle." All it was was about ten feet of cord, no bit or headpiece or cheekpieces. Just cord.

Everybody would stare at the cord, and the local smart aleck—every little town has at least one—would speak up, "You call that a bridle, Grandpa?"

"This," Billy would say, "is Professor P.D. Gleason's famous Eureka Bridle, devised after years of trial and error for the safety of mankind and to prevent cruelty to our four-footed friends."

"Who's this 'fessor Gleason, you call 'im? Never heard tell of 'im around here."

"An old and trusted colleague. The greatest horse tamer the world has ever known, now passed on to his just reward, weary of man's inhumanity to *Equus caballus.*"

"Eckus ca-what?"

Billy looks pained. "That is Latin for horse."

The smart aleck still scoffs. "Bet that little ol' piece of string won't hold my saddler, Dandy Dan. He's hard to handle."

"Would you like to bet a little on that, sonny?"

"I'll bet two bits."

"Two bits? I can see you're a big plunger. They'd love you at the county fair when you gamble for Kewpie dolls. We feed that kind of change to the chickadees where I come from."

"Then four bits, Grandpa."

"That's still birdseed, sonny."

"Then a dollar," the smart aleck comes back and winks at the crowd.

"Let's see your horse, sonny."

Already, I feel the approach of pity for the overmatched rube. By the time Billy gets through workin' him over, he'll be down to wart size. Callin' Billy "Grandpa" only sealed his doom even more.

Generally, the smart aleck would lead out a part draft-horse type with feet like dinner plates, or a high-strung hammerhead he considered a saddler. Maybe this one is a bay gelding that looks more outlaw than saddler. The way he walls and rolls his eyes, he sees about as much behind him as he does in front. He comes in on the lunge, the smart aleck yellin' and jerkin' on him.

"I can see that he hasn't been to school much," Billy says. "What does he do wrong?"

"Pitches with me every time I mount. Tries to run away, and kicks and bites."

"Have you tried kindness and patience?"

This strikes the wise guy as funny. "Sometimes, to get his attention, I have to quirt him between the ears."

"There's one rule that never fails when schooling horses," Billy says, with a frown. "The man has to be smarter than the horse. If not, the horse will train the man, as in this case. Dude, put a rope on Dandy Dan and remove the bridle."

"Remove the bridle?" the rube asks.

"Yes. You can't use two bridles at the same time."

I won't go into all the ties of the Eureka Bridle, but you start with a slip noose. The key is leverage against the upper lip.

"Now, mount up, sonny," Billy says.

Just as that's done, the horse humps his back and starts to pitch. Billy yells, "Hold his head up!"

The young man yanks on the reins and Dandy Dan settles down.

"Move him out!" Billy yells.

But as Dandy Dan starts off, he suddenly breaks into a run.

"Pull him up!" Billy yells.

The rube pulls hard and the gelding checks, fightin' the bridle.

"Now make him gee and haw!"

With the reins tight, Dandy Dan turns left, then right, not that he wants to. There's a look of wonder in the smart aleck's eyes as he rides back. "How much is this bridle?" No "Grandpa" this time.

"Why," answers Billy, unconcerned, "I don't know what they get at the general store for ten feet of cord one eighth of an inch thick."

The local wit, taken aback by now, dismounts and offers to pay his bet. Billy says, "You keep the dollar and the bridle. Just send Dandy Dan to school every day, and no more of that quirt between the ears to get his attention. Now, I'd better go through all the ties for you again."

The toughest go the outfit was ever up against was back in Kentucky, when we had to masquerade the Judge as the Duke of Dexter, like I told you, with papers from the dead Duke, a Thoroughbred, given us by a shifty old acquaintance of Billy's that Billy had saved from a crowd's hangrope years back when he'd pulled a horse in a high-stakes race.

Only reason we went back there was in hopes we'd learn the Judge's pedigree, which we figured we owed such an honest horse. We had clues, too, though they never amounted to much at first. But, as the old sayin' goes, everything comes full circle in due time. Well, the Judge won the Louisville Handicap at Churchill Downs, then the Jockey Club Handicap at Lexington, and then he beat that Sir Roderick, Kentucky's top handicap horse in the big match race I told you about when he set the mile record at the old Kentucky Association track in Lexington at Fifth and Race.

He was up against the top older horses in Kentucky, which proved his class at the longer routes, same as when he proved he could go short and outran the great Mexican speed queen, Yolanda, in Juárez. Gunned that quarter mile in twenty-one and one-fifth seconds, on a heavy track, too. "Like an arrow from a bow," Billy said. Most of Chihuahua went home broke that day. Texans still talk about that race. Because of that, and the races back in Kentucky, it was almost impossible to match him anymore.

Now, Sir Roderick's breeder and owner was Colonel Horatio P. Buxton, a red-hot Johnny Reb who had the Old Dominion Stud. His farm manager was Rube Vogel, as mean an hombre as ever stole a widow woman's egg money. But he was always nicey-nice around the colonel. Followed him around like a houn' dog. It was always "Yes, sir" to the colonel.

I'll pass up all the details, but the day of the big match race the colonel's two Glengarry colts were stolen. An old black man rode up right after the race and told the colonel. Instead of heading with the colts to the countryside as you'd expect, the thief had taken them into Lexington. It happened that, before this, I'd followed Vogel a couple of times into town because he always rode a red roan saddler, another one of our clues to the Judge's pedigree. I'd tried to talk to Vogel and try the other clue we had, which was a password; but he never bit. He was too cagey for that. One time I'd followed him and snooped around behind a saloon and found a warehouse where horses were stabled behind locked doors and there was a watchman on duty. A mite suspicious, it struck me.

So now I told the colonel and we all tore tail for the warehouse. It was the only lead we had. The watchman denied there were any horses inside and refused to open up.

It happened fast then. The black man rushed up on his mule and pointed at the watchman. "That's him, Colonel! The one that took your Glengarry colts!"

And in a flash there was Vogel, his mean eyes like pieces of flint, suddenly faced about on us with a six-gun. He had us for certain. The colonel was unarmed and I'd left my six-shooter in the wagon. I'm careless about that. But just then, and as fast, there was Billy on foot behind Vogel. Somehow Billy had run there from his buggy. I'll never forget what Billy said, in a tone I'd never heard before. "Raise your hands, Vogel, unless you want me to bore you a set of new button-holes."

And it was all over. We found the colonel's two fine Glengarry colts in the warehouse with other stolen stock, and the watchman confessed. He said Vogel was the mastermind behind a stolen horse ring, which operated from Kentucky through Indiana and Illinois and Missouri and down into Texas. This Vogel had a line of aliases as long as your arm. In Texas, he was known as Nate Thompson—wanted for bank robbery, murder, and horse theft. When he traveled about on ring business, he used the name of Si Eckert. He'd hid out at the Old Dominion as farm manager for five years. He went to prison in Kentucky, where horse stealin' is about as serious as murder because it's like stealin' a member of somebody's family.

If I ever saw cold hate in a man's eyes, a hate he'd never forget and I'd always remember, I saw it in Vogel's as he glared at me and Billy when the sheriff led him away. It's burned into my memory to this day. Vogel never talked, they said, which didn't surprise me. So we still didn't know the Judge's breeding. We thought our mission had failed.

The morning we made ready to break camp to head back west, Colonel Buxton rode up. He said he wanted another look at the Duke of Dexter. We led the Judge out and the colonel nodded to himself again and again as he walked around the horse; then he looked at us and said that except for one difference in markings, the Duke was the spittin' image of Sonny Stonewall, his fine colt stolen as a comin' two-year-old not long after Vogel had come to work for him. Sonny Stonewall, he said, had four white socks, whereas the Duke had white only on his hind feet. Billy, of course, had painted out the Judge's front white socks to fit the Duke's description.

Sonny Stonewall, the colonel said, was by Stonewall, a son of Lexington, 1850–75, the greatest distance horse of his day. Sonny's dam was the mighty fast Verona, a daughter of the imported Glencoe, who had both distance and burning speed. So you see now how the Judge could be conditioned to run either short or long.

By this time I knew we had to give up the Judge, and fair as that would be, I was sick at heart.

But before we could say anything, the colonel said that, since he was a breeder, he wouldn't want Sonny Stonewall back if he was gelded. That he couldn't stand the thought of all that great Lexington and Glencoe blood gone to waste because some fool was too quick with a knife. Then he thanked us warmly for the return of his Glengarry colts, which he had high hopes for, shook hands and rode away. But he knew and we all knew.

Like I said, it got to where we couldn't match Judge Blair anymore. That's why I was surprised when the stranger rode up to the ranch that early September day on the Salt Fork of the Brazos and challenged us to a match race.

CHAPTER 2

BEST AGAINST THE BEST

He rode up to the ranch on as fine a head-noddin' mouse-dun saddler as I'd ever seen. The mouse dun is a bluish-gray horse. What we Texans call a *grulla.*

"Sir," he says, as polite as a hungry preacher, "my name is Patrick C. Parker. I wish to speak to Mr. Dude McQuinn. I have been directed here from town."

"I'm Dude McQuinn." We shook hands. His soft grip told me he hadn't been on the end of a hoe handle in a long time or dug any post holes. "What can I do for you, Mr. Parker?"

A short-bodied man whose girth hinted that he had wintered well and held it, he had a round, beardless face that reminded me of a baby's skin, it was so smooth and pink, with baby-blue eyes to match. His voice was as obliging and cheerful as the baby face. He wore a black broadcloth frock coat and a checkered vest. Across the vest hung a heavy gold watch-chain which draped over a melon-shaped paunch. His black bowler bobbed as he talked and smiled. I gathered that he smiled most of the time. I figured he was about forty or so.

"Sir, I represent Mr. Matthew R. Vail, who happens to own a racehorse that knows where the finish line is. Mr. Vail has asked me to inquire as to the possibility of a match race with your vaunted Judge Blair." He handed me a little card. It read:

Patrick C. Parker, III
Attorney at Law
Fort Worth, Tex.

"Every man a king"
"Every man a fair trial"

"And who is Matthew R. Vail?" I says, surprised at the challenge.

"Mr. Vail is an entrepreneur, sir, constantly on the lookout for prospects. Denver, San Francisco, New Orleans, Kansas City, El Paso, St. Louis, Chicago, and my own Fort Worth. An impresario of the business world. A gentleman of many ventures. His active nature thrives on challenges. Having heard that your horse is unbeaten, he wired me to get in touch with you, sir."

"You've come far."

"Mr. Vail is a very generous client, sir, though not an easy man to please. He prods when he wants something. He's got his mind set on this race."

I'd never talked to a more polite man, him with his "sirs" and his fixed smile, like it was pasted on. When I didn't answer right off, he says with a worried frown, "Judge Blair is still unbeaten, is he not?"

I nodded. Yet, for the life of me, I couldn't feel excited about the match. Somehow it seemed too far-fetched. Also, the Judge was a shade past his prime, yet still sound and still a mighty fast horse. I planned to pension him in another year or two so he could take a deserved rest and finish out his days here at the ranch. Altogether, I figured we had run him some sixty times against all comers, from Juárez to Lexington, from one furlong to a mile, from paths on the prairie to the smooth racecourses of Kentucky. A once-in-a-lifetime horse. An honest horse. Easy to handle. A member of the family for certain. In time, he would be our kid horse. You may not believe this, but I quit poker after I won Judge Blair that night in San Antone. Never played another hand. I figure I've had all the luck one man is entitled to at cards. I quit when I was ahead.

I guess Parker figured I was playin' cagey when I didn't take up Vail's challenge, because he came back with, "My client is prepared to put up a sizable bet, Mr. McQuinn. Also forfeit money."

"I can see several problems in this," I says. "First place, I won't drag my horse all over the country. Not anymore. Even Fort Worth is a far piece."

Parker was all smiles again. "At my suggestion, and as a convenience for you, sir, Mr. Vail has agreed to race here in your county."

I took that in, sorting things out, before I answered. "It would be convenient for me to race sometime during the Stonewall County Fair, which is three weeks off. At the same time, I'd say it wouldn't be convenient for Mr. Vail."

"The railroad isn't far."

No matter what I said, he had a ready answer, same as if he'd thought it out beforehand. "There's another thing," I says. "I never match a race without a look-see at the other man's horse."

"That's easy. You can look over Mr. Vail's horse at the fair before the agreed date to run. If you don't want to run, you don't have to."

I gave him a look. "That would be a big expense for a man to bring in a horse on the train, then have to take him back without a race."

"Mr. Vail can afford it. The travel expense would be the same if he lost."

I'd never met a man so agreeable about a race and so eager to run it. I began to wish Uncle Billy was there to size up this Parker fella. Billy had pulled me out of many a bog hole when I'd failed to dally my tongue. There's no known substitute for an older man's judgment, which comes only with experience and age. I should have been wary from the first, but the money got bigger and bigger in my head.

"I won't race Judge Blair for peanuts anymore," I says. "None of that *I'll bet you thirty-five dollars my horse can outrun your horse to that big mesquite tree yonder.*"

He didn't hesitate. "How much would you like to wager, sir?" still pushin' "sirs" at me.

"I'd have to think about it."

"Would five hundred dollars be agreeable, sir?"

Five hundred bucks was a mound of money then. Times hadn't been on the prime side the past year. I was standing a Thoroughbred stallion named Little Dave I'd brought over from Arkansas, and a smooth quarter stud with Dan Tucker blood we liked, called Blanco. He had speed to spare and his get showed it. But you don't wear out the road to the bank with the fees charged on the Salt Fork, many times just to neighbors, and some can't pay. My studs covered many a good mare for twenty-five dollars, payable with a live foal. The horse farm business is like the cattle business; you're in it mainly because you love it. It's a way of life. You know you're gonna go broke some year, same as a jockey knows he's gonna get hurt sometime, no matter how good he is. It's the law of averages.

Still, I held off. I knew the Judge would be ready to run in a short time, if I didn't match him long. Mindful of what Billy had taught me, I'd never let him pick up much extra tallow. Coyote had worked him every few days. Not hard. Just enough to keep him fit enough to be conditioned in a short time for a race.

"Five hundred is fair enough, but still a little on the short side," I says, and rocked back and forth, the way Billy had schooled me.

"Would a thousand interest you, sir?"

"Might," I says, careful not to show surprise. Most horsemen would have raised the ante only a hundred or two.

"Well, sir, I have the authority to go that high."

I mulled that over; then, "But since you're the challenger, I'd have to have three-to-one odds." I halfway hoped he'd back out at that.

"Three to one?" That made him whistle and lose his smile. "I know Mr. Vail would never consent to such a disadvantage. But he might agree to two-to-one odds. I'd have to clear that with him, however." He was all smiles again.

"I'll run for that," I says. "Now, tell me about Vail's horse. Has he been campaigned in Texas?"

"High Eagle is a gelding campaigned mostly in southern Missouri and some down in Louisiana."

"High Eagle?" I ran the name through my memory. I'm like Billy about horses. I might forget a man's name, though never his face; but horses' names and a certain horse's overall looks stick in my mind like remembered brands. "I've never heard tell of him, but we're a long way from Missouri."

This Parker threw me a different sort of smile then. It was sly, like a horseman with the edge. "High Eagle is unbeaten, sir, same as your horse. Now you know why Mr. Vail wants this match race. The best against the best. The final challenge."

"Is High Eagle a Thoroughbred or a quarter horse?" You see, a fast quarter horse will outbreak most Thoroughbreds nearly every time. An exceptionally fast breaker even though he has all that Kentucky blood, Judge Blair would have the advantage in a short go.

Parker looked embarrassed for a moment. "To tell you the truth, Mr. McQuinn, I'm in the dark about that. All my work for Mr. Vail has been in the legal line, you know. Real estate deals. Ranch titles. Character references on loans and partnerships. Matters of that nature. This is the first time he's had me look into one of his horse ventures. He's a man of many varied interests."

"Do you happen to know High Eagle's best distance?"

"All I can tell you is that Mr. Vail informed me he would match you up to half a mile. No farther."

I turned that over in my mind. There wasn't time to condition the Judge for the longer routes, even the middle distances. Best to match him short. "Tell Mr. Vail I'll run him three hundred and fifty yards, if everything else is agreeable."

Patrick C. Parker actually beamed. "Mighty fine, sir. I'll wire Mr. Vail for confirmation on all this. Then you will hear from me by wire in town. Thank you, sir." He gave me that limp handshake and started to leave.

"Hold on," I says. "We didn't talk about weights."

Parker looked sheepish. "That slipped my mind. In Mr. Vail's letter, he did say something about wanting . . . what do you call it?"

"Catch weights?"

"That's it! Though I'm not sure I exactly understand the term."

"Means each side can use as heavy or light a jockey as they wish. Any weight goes."

"I see. I'm learning more all the time."

With that he was gone, even declined my invitation to stay for supper, and I wondered how wise I'd been to listen to such a quick match. But money talks and I knew the Judge would be ready to run. I had a hunch High Eagle was a Thoroughbred.

A few days later a telegram came for me in town. Everything was agreed on: the two-to-one odds, which would mean two thousand dollars banked for the ranch if the Judge won, and he always had; the distance three hundred and fifty yards; and the starter and the day of the race during the county fair to be decided when Vail arrived.

That same day I wired Billy at Painted Rock, Kansas, to punch the breeze for the Salt Fork. He lived on a horse ranch not far from town with his wife, Nancy Ann.

Billy looked a little thinner and older when he stepped off the train, but he still had sparkle in his eyes and spring in his step. I and wife Blossom (I'd dropped my rope on that sweet little Indiana girl the time we headed back East to trace the Judge's ancestors) and Coyote Walking staged a public huggin' match right there.

"What's all this about a big match race?" Billy says, embarrassed at so much attention.

I slid an arm around his shoulders as we ambled out to the buggy. "I'll tell you later, Uncle."

We had no more than reached the ranch when he asked to see Judge Blair and Texas Jack, the smooth look-alike gelding we'd used to work the switch after I'd retired Rebel; left him as a kid horse for a ranch family with five little young'ins. "It's not good for a horse's character to lose all the time," Billy had said. "It's a matter of memory, which is his strongest mental endowment. All he remembers is defeat. All he can see is that other horse or horses ahead of him as he crossed the finish line. Could lead to a nervous breakdown."

So we retired Rebel.

We all drifted out to the pasture near the house where I kept the horses, and I whistled and Judge Blair threw up his head and looked at us. But he didn't move toward us. It was a little game we played of hard-to-get. I whistled again and still he didn't come over.

"Looks like your own horse don't even know you," Billy says to guy me.

I whistled a third time, a shriller whistle. This time Judge Blair nickered and came on the trot, followed by Texas Jack. He always came on the third whistle, assured he would get some feed. Judge Blair with his handsome blazed face and four white-socked feet, Texas Jack likewise with all white socks, but no blaze. Except for the difference of the blaze, they were spittin' images. Both dark bays, heavy muscled, the Judge with that long slopin' shoulder that meant he had the long stride to cover a distance of ground. One time we taped his stride and it measured twenty-five feet! I fed them each a handful of oats, then dug into a sack for more.

Billy looked at them for a long time in silence, until his eyes began to fill, like he could see again all the races they'd run, all the skullduggery the outfit had been up against and still won—attempts to dope the Judge, and horses put in to bump him at the break; and the Judge, a balanced horse, as he righted himself with a change of leads and came on to win. For a little run of time Billy appeared to give in to the weight and memories of time. Then, all at once, the years seemed to fall away and he straightened and a wonderful smile spread across his white-bearded face that was all love, because he truly loved horses and understood them.

He eased through the wire fence and petted the horses and talked nonsense to 'em for a while, both horses as gentle as collies. "They both look good," Billy says, and examined the Judge's front legs for heat or swelling, and nodded to himself and circled the Judge twice, his eyes like probes. "We'll have him ready to run. You bet we will." He moved to Judge Blair's face and looked straight at him and nodded. "The eye of an eagle and the step of a deer. He's always had that, the mark of a true racehorse. A horse with brilliant speed and the heart to carry that speed far and beyond."

I had remembered to have a bottle of Old Green River, Billy's favorite sour mash, ready for him when he got there, and that evening Blossom put on a feed that drew the old gent's compliments again and again.

"There's only one item missing," he says to Blossom. "That's the cigaret butts I used to find in Dude's biscuits. They sure had a flavor."

"Yes, Grandfather," Coyote seconded, and Billy sent him a look and says, "Never could break you of callin' me that, could I?"

"No, Grandfather."

Billy threw up his hands in mock disgust, resigned.

"It's Coyote's way of showing respect for his elders," Blossom says.

"Yes, Grandfather," Coyote says.

After supper I told Billy all about the match race, how High Eagle was unbeaten, and I didn't hide my pride as I said how I'd rocked back and forth to get the wager raised, and described Patrick C. Parker III, and added the few details he had furnished on Matthew R. Vail.

"It's more than a little unusual," Billy says, "for a man to bring his horse this far for a match race. Make more sense if he traveled around with a fast horse, the way we used to."

"I think it's to satisfy Mr. Vail's ego," Blossom says. "Apparently, he can't stand for another man to have a faster horse than he has. From what Mr. Parker told Dude, Mr. Vail is a very rich man who lives on challenges."

"High Eagle." Billy repeated the name over and over, then frowned. "I've never heard of that horse, and I've heard of a lot of fast horses.

It's easier for me to remember a horse's name than it is a man's. Maybe it's my age."

"But you haven't been in Missouri in a long time," I says, "and only once in Louisiana, the time we campaigned the Judge in Cajun country. Unless," I pried, "you'd been there before?"

"Now, did I say?"

We all laughed at the old retort. Even Billy grinned.

"I can name you every horse we matched down there," he says. "Mississippi Belle, Scooter Boy, Buckshot, Gambling Man, and some we didn't match." He was as sharp as a jack-leg lawyer as he called the names. "No, High Eagle is unknown to me."

"You mean you're suspicious?"

"More curious than suspicious. But a match race is a match race. You've matched it on home ground, which is an advantage, and if this Vail fella's money is the right color, why be suspicious?" He turned thoughtful. "You're matched at three hundred and fifty yards. That means the Judge will have to take the break, if this unknown High Eagle is a scorpion. Starting tomorrow morning, let's work him every other day at a little over that distance—say four hundred. And I think it would be wise to send him back to school on the swingin' break."

He sounded like the salty Uncle Billy of old, set to bring the Judge to a peak on race day and not about to get outslicked.

I had cleared a long stretch on the prairie for a track and there we began to condition the Judge on alternate mornings and to school him again on the fast getaway.

Patrick C. Parker III rode up to the ranch a week before the Stonewall County Fair opened, mounted on the same head-noddin' saddler.

"Figured I'd better come a few days early to get High Eagle used to the track." He was almost apologetic as he said it, and then he smiled, like was it all right to arrive early?

"About when will Mr. Vail get in?" I says.

His baby face took on that sheepish look I remembered. "The boss is back in Chicago, down with a broken leg. Mad as a wet hen because he can't be here to see his horse run. Fell down a flight of stairs. Imagine that! He's put me in charge of High Eagle. Me—Patrick C. Parker— who knows about as much about racehorses as he does about how to raise tomatoes for the market. Let's see . . . you send a small boy up

the tree to shake 'em down, don't you?" He let go such a big belly laugh
that I joined in, too. Parker was quite a card, I could see that.

"Don't you have a trainer?" I says.

"Oh, yes. But I'm supposed to make all the arrangements the boss
was gonna make. How we'll start, who the starter and the finish judges
will be, and what time." He rubbed his forehead, a worried man off his
own range.

"We can work all that out at the County Fair office," I says. By now I
even felt sorry for this pilgrim in the match-race game. "Where's your
horse?"

"My horse?" He looked blank. "Oh, yes, my horse. The boss wired
me in Fort Worth that High Eagle and the trainer and jockey would
ship in here tomorrow from Kansas City."

"Well," I says, to be helpful, "I'd suggest that you go to the fair office
right now and be assigned a stall. There'll be plenty of folks around
eager to sell you feed."

He looked surprised and pleased. "I'm sure much obliged to you, sir.
I didn't know that. Mr. Vail didn't tell me how to handle all this. Just
said do it. That's Matthew R. Vail."

"You see, there'll be other races run the week of the fair, mostly
quarter horse races, so you need to have a stall for your horse." I felt
more neighborly all the time toward this greenhorn racehorse manager.

"Where is the fair office?" he asks, and gazes off, like it was some
faraway place.

"I'll show you. While we're there we might as well work out all the
details and conditions of the race, Mr. Parker." I couldn't have felt
more helpful if I'd just brought good news to some heathens.

"Call me Pat."

"And my name's Dude, remember?" I was close to liking this Patrick
C. Parker.

Well, the board chairman, Mr. Buck Young, was all for the big match
race. He told us he'd had in mind a Judge Blair Day for some time,
since the Judge was so well-known and unbeaten. He said why not stage
the race Saturday afternoon, the last day of the fair? It would be the
climax of the week and would draw folks not only from all over the
county, but beyond the county as well. I swelled up with pride for my
horse and agreed. In addition, he said, he'd now have time to get plac-
ards printed and posted to advertise the race far and wide. Further-

more, the owner and trainer and jockey of the winning horse would be honored with other fair winners at the awards banquet Saturday night.

By the time I and Parker left, all details of the race had been agreed on. Jeff "No Loan" Lawson, the local banker, who was tighter than the bark on a blackjack, would start the race, which would be lap-and-tap. The finish judges would be Hap Bud, Giles Margin, and Ted Wardlow. Having Lawson as the starter meant the break would come off even-Steven, no nose in front, exact to a hair, the same way you paid off a loan at his Lone Star Bank if you were lucky enough to get one. If your payment was late, look out. It was not unusual for "No Loan" to ride out personally and inquire why.

Outside the fair office, Parker sidled over to me and in an embarrassed tone says, "There's something I want you to clear up for me, sir. Didn't dare ask back there in front of Mr. Young for fear I'd look more like a tenderfoot horseman than I am. And that's what is a lap-and-tap start?"

"In the lap-and-tap," I says, "there are no gates. The jockeys ride their horses up to the line where the starter is and if they're closely lapped, that is side by side, with no horse ahead of the other, the starter taps them off. By that I mean he shouts 'Go!' or drops his hat or a flag."

He looked so relieved I started to feel sorry for him again. "Oh," he says, "so that's all there is to it? I thought maybe the horses went a lap before they started and the starter actually tapped a drum."

"You're not far off about the drum, Pat. Some years ago back in Kentucky I understand the signal for the start of the Derby was given by taps on a drum. But the timers didn't start their watches till the horses passed the official starting pole and the starter dropped the flag. Now they use a barrier."

"I'm sure much obliged to you, Dude. I mean Mr. McQuinn, sir."

"Call me Dude and forget the *sir.*"

"And you call me Pat. I'd better go now and wire Mr. Vail that I'm here to manage his racehorse."

I followed him with my eyes, and as I did a kind of curious thought took root. For a man who claimed he knew nothing about horse races, and who evidently didn't from his greenhorn's questions, why would he know about the starting drum? That was old Kentucky Derby style, never used in the Southwest that I knew. Then I shrugged. On the other hand, I guessed it was logical for a body to connect taps with a drum. And I realized I'd called him Pat back there. Well, he was a likable greenhorn, so apologetic and unsure of himself.

CHAPTER 3

HONORS FOR A GREAT HORSE

After we had worked Judge Blair on the track at the ranch and sent him back to school on how to step into the old swingin' break, Billy said it was important that our horse get the feel of the fairgrounds track before Saturday. So Thursday morning we saddled in.

We could hear the carnival long before we reached the fairgrounds, the calliope all snorts and whistles, the clank of machinery, and the hum of voices like a swarm of bees. We rode up and stopped to watch. A Ferris wheel already had riders at this hour. Same for the merry-go-round. On the midway a black man's catchy banjo music attracted a crowd to a medicine show, and when the music stopped, a fast-talkin' barker waved a bottle and hawked "miraculous" Kickapoo Indian Sagwa at "only a dollar." His hoarse voice rose higher. "A sure cure for corns, coughs, consumption—female weakness, St. Vitus Dance, vertigo —hysterics, insanity, apoplexy." Beside him, arms folded, all stern and noble, stood a dark-skinned man in a feathered headdress, fringed buckskin shirt and trousers, and a wide beaded belt.

I grinned at Coyote. "That a real Kickapoo?"

"White-man Kickapoo." He shook his head, amused.

Farther on there were game booths, and a bear danced on a chain while a smiling little man cranked a hand organ, and there was a skinny lion in a cage, and a stout hula girl shook her grass skirt while the barker invited the gawkers to see "the real show inside, for adults only. She shakes a mean haystack, boys."

Saturday the carnival and track would be swarming with fair-going, entertainment-starved ranch and farm families.

Beyond the midway, parked in two rows, stood large vans and freight wagons painted in bright colors, on their broad sides the name of the carnival: ADAMS BROS. SHOWS. Tied to the wagons were the pullers and movers of the shows, stout horses of draft breeding.

We rode on and drew rein at the track, which had a four-hundred yard straightaway with a half-mile oval of sharp turns, which we Texans call a "bull ring," though most bull rings don't have a long stretch that joins the oval.

The barns faced the backstretch. We wouldn't stable our horse there now. Instead, we'd bring him in the day of the race. The precaution traced back to when we had traveled around the Southwest and attempts were made to "fix" the Judge before a race. Then we learned never to leave our horse, day or night.

Riding to the head of the straightaway, I saw the track looked hard and fast, packed by weeks of dry weather and races run over the course during Fair Week. Stakes marked every common distance to the finish line: a hundred and ten yards, two-twenty, three hundred, three-fifty, and four hundred.

"Swing him into the break now, Coyote," Billy says, "and I'll set you off. The Judge looks drawn down and ready to run. Breeze him out four hundred yards, then I want a look-see at this unbeaten High Eagle." I beamed at the words. This was the old Uncle Billy on the match-race trail as the Judge took on all comers at any distance.

Coyote eased up to the line, swung his horse just right, Billy shouted "Go!" and Judge Blair broke like a shot. The Judge always ran in a straight line, unless bumped, "Like an arrow from a bow." He did so today. The long layoff hadn't hurt his speed.

"Dude," Billy says, full of enjoyment as he watched horse and rider, "this is what it's all about. If fast, well-bred horses don't go to heaven, then I don't care whether I make it there or not. Come to think of it, I'd lay three-to-one odds a good horse would have a far better chance than one William Tecumseh Lockhart."

Afterward, riding along the shed row, I spotted Parker lounging in front of a stall with two men. He noticed us at the same time and waved us over. We dismounted and I introduced Billy and Coyote.

Parker introduced his trainer, Vic Queen, who had thick shoulders and oversized, knob-knuckled hands and a battered bulldog face; and his jockey, Blondy Crider, a wizened, sun-wrinkled little stick of a man with a face the color of a saddle seat and who weighed even less than Coyote. They gave us a "howdy" and everybody shook hands. Both appeared middle-aged, both had the marks of men who had experienced hard times.

"So this is the great Judge Blair," Parker says, and eyed the Judge up and down. "I must say he looks like a great racehorse. Blondy, bring High Eagle out here for these gentlemen to see."

Crider led out a rangy gray gelding of about fifteen hands and a thousand pounds. Though he moved well, I saw nothing impressive about his conformation.

"How's he been doing?" Billy asks.

Queen shrugged. "He took the train ride pretty good comin' down from Kansas City, but can't say it helped him any. I don't like this track. It's too damn hard." He cracked a grin of broken, yellowish teeth. "Yet both horses run on the same track, so what the hell. Alibis don't win horseraces."

Billy nodded. "The track is hard. I'm glad we're only going three-fifty. Better, still, that neither horse has to negotiate the sharp turns on the half-mile oval." That was Billy, mindful of both horses.

Queen's response was another cracked smile.

His broken face comes before me now as I talk—pale gray eyes sunk deep into his skull, scars around the hooded eyes and the prow of a chin; the square hands like sledges, the hoarse voice.

No more was said and we rode away. When out of earshot, I looked in question at Billy and he reflected a bit before he spoke. "High Eagle is not a well-muscled horse. He looked sluggish in the eyes, and the eyes are the inner mirror of a horse. But he's unbeaten and he wouldn't be here if he didn't have the heart to run. I wish I'd seen him work." He reflected some more. "Ever go to a dance, Dude, and the best dancer wasn't always the prettiest girl? It all goes back to the heart to run."

Race day.

Although post time was three o'clock, we held off till two before we saddled into town and entered the fairgrounds. Sometimes crowds bother a racehorse and a high-strung runner will break out in a nervous sweat and lose his strength. Run his race in the paddock. Not that Judge Blair was ever washy, as the Thoroughbred folks say back in Kentucky. But why pressure your horse even a little?

The fair was an anthill of people, and as soon as we showed up a stream of racegoers followed us to the barns. By now the Judge was as well-known as a Texas politician and had a heap better reputation than most.

Patrick C. Parker was on the lookout for us and waved and hustled over with that ever-present smile. "For a while I was afraid you boys had backed out," he greets us, heavy on the banter.

"We pulled ourselves together," I says, "and decided we had to run you as a matter of Texas honor."

He went on. "I've turned down enough bets to start a bank. Figured I'd better hold back some money to get home on in case High Eagle fails to fly."

I shrugged. The agreement was that the loser would pay off right after the race. I and Blossom, with help from Billy and Coyote, had scraped up enough *dinero* to have on hand in case the Judge lost. You never can tell about a horserace, how things will go. I've seen a beautiful day turn into a toad-stranglin' downpour just as the race started, and the paint a stream down the Judge's face as he crossed the finish line, and the hometowners hollerin' "ringer!" I've seen hangropes in a red-eyed crowd and I've seen losers take off on horseback or go hide in a saloon, so as not to pay, and I've seen guns drawn and the only spark needed to set off a shootout was the wrong word or move. Many times Billy's coolheadedness had prevented a gun battle. You never can tell about a horserace.

The crowd hung around to chat and to gawk at the horses till Young, the fair chairman, came over and said take the horses to the track for the post parade. I put a lead shank on Judge Blair and ponied him and Coyote out to the track, while Billy rode across to the finish line in front of the stands. Parker strolled over. Vic Queen was ahead of us on a pony horse leading High Eagle, who still didn't impress me in any way. Yet here he was shipped in from Kansas City for a big race. He just had to be a runner with all that money bet.

Well, the stands were packed and the railings too. Queen rode to the end of the stands and made a turn, and when the gray gelding lunged a little, Queen jerked on the shank, like the gray was a little rank today. It seemed just another race to Crider, who ignored everything.

As I led Judge Blair past the stands, the crowd started to clap. You may not believe this, but the Judge pricked his ears and picked up his feet and pranced for 'em, the way I've seen circus horses do, though this was on the Judge's own. No reminder from a trainer. I tell you my whole body puffed up with appreciation for my horse.

Coyote had gone conservative in dress for the race. Sometimes he'd paint his face and put an eagle feather in his blue-black hair, which hung straight, cropped at the neck, and he'd strip down to a breech-cloth and beaded moccasins, long-fringed, Comanche style. One time he painted Judge Blair like a Comanche war-horse. White circles around both eyes and white stripes across his face, and a white hand painted on his chest and white lightnin' streaks down his front and hindquarters. As one preacher said, he was like the vengeance of the Lord tearin' down the track. This day the Judge looked like his true dark bay self; and that blaze, which comes to a point between the nostrils, looked like spilled milk, and the four white feet, like clean socks just taken off the wash line.

We moved on to the head of the track where I released my horse and Lawson waited for us. He couldn't have looked any sterner had we all come in broke and needed a loan we couldn't pay on till a year from now.

"I don't want any monkeyshines," he growls. "No jumping ahead at the last second, or back you'll come. You will walk your horses up to the line. When both noses are even, I'll holler 'Go' and drop the flag."

When I explained about the swingin' break, he scowled that over the same as he might if I'd asked for an extension on an overdue loan payment. He says, "That means your horse's head will be turned a little to one side, so how am I gonna tap 'em off with both heads not straight?" and I saw that he was about to rule against it.

"We've used it many times before and never been turned down."

"Wherever that was ain't the Stonewall County Fairgrounds track today."

"Don't tell me," I says, "that as many races as Mr. Jefferson Davis Lawson has tapped off that he can't even up a head turned just a little bit and a straight head? With the swingin' break, you won't have to measure noses."

I could see that he liked the ring of his full "John Henry" because a rare grin, or what I took for a grin, creased his flinty features, painful as it was. "All right," he says at last. "Just no monkeyshines."

At that, I rode back and joined Billy and Parker to watch the race. Not till then did the logical question come looping back to my mind.

Why hadn't Vic Queen protested the swingin' break? It was honest, sure, but it was also an advantage, one of Billy's wrinkles, which I'd never seen nor heard of till he introduced it to me and Coyote. Maybe Queen figured a horse with its head turned wouldn't be set to break? What he didn't know was that short step to pull on for momentum.

The thought left me as I saw the horses turn and approach the line. Suddenly, High Eagle broke ahead and Lawson waved them back. The second time it was Coyote off too soon. I could see Lawson's head bob as he jawed at the riders. They circled back. Again they approached. They looked lapped.

Of a sudden the flag dropped and they were off. Judge Blair in front, but High Eagle close up.

At the hundred-and-ten yard stake the Judge, straight as an arrow, held a half-a-length lead. At the two-twenty marker he was a length in front. Crider was all over his horse and whippin' right-handed. Parker ran to the rail and shouted, "Come on, High Eagle—come on!"

At three hundred yards I knew we had it won. High Eagle had run his race. Crider was layin' on the leather at every jump, but his horse was out of it, overmatched. When they crossed the finish line, with the crowd in full voice, Judge Blair had him by three lengths of Texas daylight.

I turned to Billy and whapped him on the back. "That's the easiest big money we've ever won, Uncle!"

He didn't say anything. His attention was hard on High Eagle. He eyed the gray gelding until Crider reined off the track for the barns. "Almost too easy," Billy says in a puzzled voice.

Parker was shaking his head as he came over to us. His baby face was mournful as he drew a leather wallet and paid me two thousand dollars, a thousand dollar bill and the rest in hundreds.

"I don't understand it," he says. "High Eagle just didn't take to the track. Didn't fire. I believe that's the right term."

Because he was a good loser, I wanted to make him feel better. "It was a pretty good race the first furlong. You never can tell about a horse race, Mr. Parker."

"Call me Pat. I could tell about Judge Blair. Does he always run that fast?"

"When he's on his feed, and he was today. But I've seen him run faster."

He turned to go. "Mr. Vail is gonna be very unhappy with one Patrick C. Parker and Company." He gave that big belly-laugh, like when he poked fun at himself. "Maybe I'd better look around for some good bottom land and plant me some tomato trees." Then we both laughed and shook hands and he went off to the barns. Well, I thought, it's Vail's money, not his.

"High Eagle fired, all right." Billy still had that puzzled look. "He just didn't have much to fire with. I can't believe that horse is unbeaten unless he raced against draft horses. Did you ever hear Coyote whoop?"

"Don't believe I did."

We moved out onto the track where the admiring crowd had Judge Blair and Coyote surrounded. Coyote dismounted and Billy says, "We didn't hear you whoop, Coyote, pardner."

"No need, Grandfather. Easy for the Judge, it was. Like a hard breeze. The gray horse never challenged us."

"That other horse didn't belong on the same track. I don't savvy this unless High Eagle's sick, and they didn't have to run if he was. Beats me."

After all the hubbub at the track, we cooled Judge Blair down and left him in his stall at the fairgrounds with plenty of feed, then met Blossom at the hotel.

"High Eagle didn't run much of a race," she says. "I almost felt sorry for Mr. Vail losing all that money."

"Parker said High Eagle had never lost a race, and don't forget that we bet our money the same as Vail did."

That evening we got all slicked up and took in the awards banquet. Buck Young, who can lay on the molasses after he's had a toddy or two, couldn't say enough about Judge Blair. Said he was "The pride of all Texas . . . the greatest racehorse in Texas history . . . even the entire West . . . even greater than Steel Dust and Shiloh."

Now, that was a considerable statement. Every Texas schoolboy knows that Steel Dust came out of Kentucky before the War Between the States, and that Shiloh, likewise, was brought in from Tennessee about the same time. Both had exceptional speed and became foundation quarter horse sires. Both traced back to Sir Archy. There was rivalry between them, too. Steel Dust and Shiloh were matched to run, but Steel Dust reared up against the starting chute and ran a splinter into his shoulder and never raced again, and the question of which horse was faster was never settled. Even in Texas today, I've run across cowboys eager to peddle a wore-out nag and one will say, "This fine-lookin' horse comes straight down the ladder from Steel Dust on his daddy's side." All I can say is that if Steel Dust had sired what he's credited with, the whole Lone Star State couldn't hold his descendants.

Next, Buck Young introduced the outfit one by one, and I, as the owner of Judge Blair, was asked "to say a few appropriate words." I had Billy take another bow and I called him "Doctor" and said he was the greatest trainer in the history of racing, bar none, and the greatest veterinarian of all time because his savvy of horses went far beyond physical ailments.

Billy, dressed in his favored frock coat, white shirt, string tie, and bench-made boots, looked more like a just-elected U.S. senator than a vet. He bowed and opined that, as a Texan, as usual I had stretched the blanket except in the case of Judge Blair, who, he said, was a great horse in that he could run short or long, thanks to his superior breeding, which Billy recited without a hitch back for three generations on both sides. But the Judge's greatest quality, Billy pointed out, was his desire to run, his heart, which pedigree didn't always pass on to a horse —that heart was what the good Lord had given him.

Billy got a stand-up big hand on that, since Stonewall County folks are strong churchgoers. Then he paid tribute to Coyote as the Judge's jockey and said Coyote's life on the reservation in Oklahoma as the son of the chief of all Comanches, and riding buffalo-runnin' horses bareback, made him the top rider of Billy's experience. Right there I got primed for Billy to shed some light on his own past, but the lovable old codger didn't let slip one little-bitty hint.

Oh, there was more talk and I got off on some of the big races the Judge had won against slippery horsemen and everybody ate that up, though I didn't go into how we had worked the switch. I went on till Blossom gave me the high sign that my "few appropriate words" had run over the rim and it was time to cut the palaver, which I did.

Well, by this time the hour was late, and after we broke up so many folks came by to shake hands, it was close to eleven o'clock when we moseyed back to the hotel, too late to go to the barns to look in on Judge Blair. We felt so good, I and Billy and Coyote hived over to the Lone Wolf for a nightcap. Like always, Coyote passed up the hard stuff for some sarsaparilla, which in Texas is pronounced sassparilla.

Well, there were more horsemen there and we had to go over the race again, step by step, and again and again, and tell more about the Judge and his other races, and that called for our friends to treat us by turns. This went on and on. It was past one o'clock before the Lone Wolf closed and the outfit headed for the hay.

It must have been seven o'clock before I woke up, with a taste in my mouth like I'd had supper with a coyote. I wouldn't have rolled out then if not for Blossom, who said our friends, next door to us, had already gone to breakfast. We joined them. The coffee was bitter and I began to get anxious about my horse.

It was eight o'clock when the outfit reached the barns. The fair-grounds were deserted and there wasn't a body in sight. Over where the carnival had set up was just a field of wind-stirred litter.

We came to High Eagle's stall and it was empty, like the others we'd passed. I had a sharp feeling of guilt as we hurried on to the Judge's stall, guilt because I had neglected my horse while I had a good time; hadn't looked in on him after the banquet or early this morning.

The stall doors were closed, which struck me at once as wrong, unless a fairgrounds worker had done it, because we'd always kept the top half open for ventilation whenever we stalled the Judge. A horse likes to look out and see what's goin' on in his world.

I jerked open the top half and glanced inside and instantly froze, shocked, stricken with disbelief and dismay. Next to when Blossom had double pneumonia and I was afraid I'd lose her for certain, it was the worst moment of my life.

The stall was empty. My horse was gone.

CHAPTER 4

A MEMBER OF THE FAMILY

I just stood there, rooted, eyes on the emptiness, stunned by the reality of the loss, while the wind of a terrible anger whirled up inside me, mixed with self-reproach. Finally I found my voice. "It's my fault. Goes back to what you've always said, Uncle. Never leave a good racehorse unguarded. I did this once. Now he's gone."

I felt Billy's hand on my shoulder. "It's no time to blame yourself, pardner. If anybody's to blame, we all are. But this is the last thing a man would expect to happen in his hometown."

I didn't feel any better. "He's like a member of the family. Blossom will be heartbroken."

"The Judge is a well-known horse. It'll be hard to hide him around here. We'll find him. You bet we will." His words of encouragement couldn't overcome his own dismal tone.

"Look! Here!" Coyote was pointing to the top half of the swung-back stall door and an envelope nailed there, on it one word in big letters: MCQUINN.

I jerked out the nail. My hand shook as I opened the unsealed envelope and took out a folded sheet of paper and began to read the bold, slanting handwriting:

In a few days you will receive a letter at general delivery. If you expect to see your horse again, you will be wise to follow all instructions exactly and no deviations. Do not bring the sheriff or Rangers into this—do, and your horse will be shot. Keep that in mind, McQuinn. Meanwhile, you are being watched.

Deviations. That was a fancy word for a common horsethief to use. Didn't sound like cowboy lingo. More like a schoolteacher.

It was unsigned. Every word burned into my mind like a hot iron, which is why I remember 'em to this day.

My anger was like bitter gall and my hand still shook as I passed the note to my pardners. I'd seen Billy in many tight places, his clear blue eyes steely. Now they turned an icy blue. He and Coyote read it together, Coyote just as grim. Billy handed it back to me. "No mention of ransom."

"Ransom?"

"That's the first reason that comes to my mind. The next is to steal a fast horse and run him under another name in another part of the state, or out of state."

"Guess I've got an enemy I don't know about."

"He wouldn't have to be a personal enemy. Just some crook with a sharp eye for a fast horse. I figure there's more than one in on this."

"Could be revenge. But I can't imagine who it might be. I haven't had any run-ins lately."

"Revenge for what? If I know you, Dude, you're the softest touch in Stonewall County. If it is revenge, why even leave a note? What's more, if the Judge was a stud, I could see some fella on the steal to breed him some good runners. There's no reason to leave a note unless ransom is the main motive. If a thief's gonna run this horse in Texas, however, he'd better be careful, because the Judge is the best-known runner in the Southwest and would be spotted pretty quick."

"Unless they painted him. And I know only one man who's an artist at that." It wasn't meant to be funny and it wasn't likely, another man as handy with a paintbrush as Billy. "What do you think, Coyote?"

"Ransom, this Comanche thinks. Like Grandfather says. Meanest white man did this bad thing." He made motions to scalp, left hand a hold of his scalp lock, right hand under the left to cut. "Maybe Owl Person to me will speak."

Coyote wasn't what I'd call superstitious, but he was still tied to the old tribal ways enough to believe in the power of owl medicine. But I never teased him about it. Neither did Billy. You see, as the outfit traveled around, takin' on all comers, up against all kinds of horsemen slick with the fix, Coyote's Owl Person medicine had been right more than once! That's gospel. You can believe it or not.

A late thought came to me. "Tracks, Coyote. What about tracks? Can they tell us anything?"

He was already ahead of me, eyes on the ground. He pointed and we saw the marks of the Judge's hoofs and we traced them out to the track, where we lost them in a clutter of prints.

From there, we checked all the barns and all were empty, which we expected. I figured most horsemen had taken their horses home soon after the big race. That left us stumped. I hesitated about goin' to the sheriff, contrary to the note's warning, but decided to go anyway, and Billy and Coyote agreed. The Sheriff offered to wire all neighboring county sheriffs, also marshals in the smaller towns, and to send a description of Judge Blair and my thousand-dollar reward.

Monday morning I rode to the office of the Stonewall County Courier and placed a front-page notice about the theft, and the reward for information that would lead to return of my horse. In it, I described the Judge in such detail a kid would recognize him. Next, I moseyed over to the Lone Wolf and passed the word. That put the boys in a horn-tossin' mood almost equal to my own. They wanted to form a posse right then, but I said no. "Where would we search? I don't have a single lead yet. All I ask is that you boys be on the lookout. I'd sure like to pay that thousand-dollar reward." I didn't let on about the letter that was supposed to come. Too, it's common knowledge that posses fortified with the best whiskey in town have been known to make more blunders than a mail-order detective. If this developed into a long chase, and I had a hunch it might, I didn't want anybody but my outfit and maybe the sheriff and some veteran deputies or some Rangers in on the windup. Coyote could read tracks on rock like it was all wrote down in an open book, and Billy was always cool and quick in a showdown.

The letter came Wednesday, postmarked Big Spring, Texas, addressed in that bold hand. It read: Bring $5,000 and go to the post office at Colorado City for further instructions, if you expect to see your horse again. Don't come with any officers. If you do, your horse will be shot. We mean business, McQuinn. Remember, you are being watched.

We. So there was more than one in on it. *Remember you are being watched.* That was hard to believe. Here in my hometown? Yet, anybody could have rustled the Judge while the outfit was at the banquet or at the Lone Wolf h'istin' more than a few. They knew our location all the time. But why bring the ransom to Colorado City? Why not to a nearby town, like Sagerton or Stamford? Wouldn't the thieves want their money as soon as possible? Most would, I reckoned. Except, Colorado City was farther away and maybe they figured safer. Except, too, this was a different passel of horsethieves, I realized by now. Nothin' ordinary about 'em.

But five thousand! Well, I'd pay that and more to get my horse back. Still, I had to gulp a little. "Afraid I'm just a mite short."

"We'll help," Billy says, and Coyote nodded.

Well, we'd just won two thousand and I and Blossom had that thousand put back. Billy wired Nancy Ann in Kansas for a thousand, Coyote put in five hundred, and I borrowed the rest and some to travel on from "No Loan" Lawson, with the cross-my-heart promise to pay off the note within a year, come drought, hell or high water, the good Lord help me. No Loan is just one big cream puff inside when the chips are down and a man's been done wrong. Each one of us packed his own money.

I read the ransom note and felt more discouraged. The thieves were way beyond us by now. Colorado City was a two-day ride on horseback from the ranch, and Big Spring, likewise on the Texas and Pacific Railroad, was another forty or fifty miles horseback southwest from there.

We saddled up at the ranch at daylight next morning, packed on grub, utensils, blankets, and canteens, nosebags and grain for the horses, and made ready to leave. Blossom was close to tears. "Oh, Dude, do you think we'll ever see Judge Blair again?"

I tried to sound hopeful, which I didn't feel. "I believe we will. We have to keep our hopes up. These people want the money and we want our horse back. But I'd sure better see that blazed face before I fork over the dinero. Could be, if things go right, we can get the Judge back and won't have to give up the money."

"Now, Dude, dear, promise me you won't force any gunplay."

"I promise." But I knew in my heart I'd burn powder if I got the chance. There's nothin' lower than a horsethief that's kidnapped a member of your family.

I kissed her good-bye twice, called her sweetheart and hugged her hard. She hugged Billy and Coyote too, and we rode off to the southwest. A neighbor lady would stay with Blossom. You can always count on ranch folks in a pinch.

We cut across rolling country, stopped only to rest our horses and catch a few hours of sleep, build a fire for coffee and eat what Blossom had packed for us. It hadn't occurred to me to go any way but horseback. We could have taken the Fort Worth and Denver line to Sagerton, the Panhandle and Santa Fe to Sweetwater, then caught the Texas and Pacific to Colorado City. But I always feel better with a good horse under me.

Late the afternoon of the second day we drew rein outside Colorado City, the county seat of Mitchell County, just east of the Colorado River. While the red dust settled around us, I looked at my friends. "The post office will be closed by now. What say we scout out the town before we eat supper?"

Billy nodded. "The main source of information in any town is the main saloon. Beats the newspaper."

"The main livery barn is another good bet, Uncle."

"What we have to do, Dude, is try to think like a horsethief. Where would they hide Judge Blair? If they want the money here, they'll have to produce the horse here."

Coyote had his say. "Wise horsethief the Judge out-of-town would keep. A smooth horse like the Judge noticed would be here."

"I want to take a look around first."

We rode into town. I remembered Colorado City through the wide-open eyes of a country boy, in the strict company of a Baptist-cowboy father; it had been a hell-raisin' frontier railroad town sprung up as the Texas and Pacific built to the southwest, a clutter of saloons, dance halls, gamblin' dens, stores, and camps—everything under tents. A place so tough the Rangers had to be called in to restore order, and then cowboys had to shed their six-shooters when they came to town. There was no jail and the Rangers chained lawbreakers to a big mesquite till they sobered up. As we rode by that mesquite, I remember my father remarked, "At least they're in shade and it's cleaner than a 'dobe jail. Not that they deserve it. When they sober up, they'll all be fined. Let that be a lesson to you, son. Stay out of saloons."

"Yes, Papa."

But I can't say that I always followed my father's advice, good as it was.

There was a settled air about the town now, marked by the county courthouse of gray stone, the frame and brick business houses. Several grocery stores, a general merchandise firm that advertised ranch supplies, a bank, a meat market, two hotels—the Southern and the City— the Nip and Tuck Saloon (a carryover name I remembered from the past), a printing office, a feed store, a billiard parlor, a doctor's office, the Three Star Livery Barn, and a wagonyard. The post office was a squat brick building. Few people stirred on the streets at this hour, the hitchin' racks were nigh onto empty, and the red dust blew as of old.

On impulse, I reined into an alley, on the lookout for any shed big enough to hold a horse. My eyes met a scatter of small outbuildings and a litter of boxes and barrels. A pole corral behind the Nip and Tuck held three saddled horses, a gray, a chestnut, and a blue roan. We moved on and out to the street, crossed to the other side and entered another alley. Behind the general merchandise store a shedlike stable and a 'dobe corral took shape. It aroused my suspicion at once. I couldn't see inside the stable, so I dropped reins and hustled around to look inside. It was empty.

As I turned back, a deep voice took me by surprise. "Looking for something, sir?"

The voice belonged to a stern-faced man at the store's rear door. He stared down his long nose at me.

"You bet I am," I says. "For a mighty valuable blaze-faced dark bay with four white socks, stolen last Saturday from the Stonewall County Fairgrounds."

"I daresay you won't find him there, sir."

He was uppity, which irked me. "I daresay I won't find him if I don't look. That's a cinch. Have you seen a horse of that description around town?"

"I have not, sir." He reared back, insulted-like because I'd asked.

"Too bad you can't help. Might save some bloodlettin' that's gonna be redder'n this dust that's in my craw."

He blinked and went inside.

We rode on down the alley and found some more empty sheds. At Main Street I took us on the gallop for the Three Star Livery. By this time I was as tetchy as a teased snake and Billy must have sensed it, because just before we dismounted I heard him say in a low tone, "Take it easy, Dude. Don't bull in here. Let me handle the palaver this time."

"I'm gonna look at every horse in the barn."

"You bet we are. But, first, maybe somebody can tell us something."

We'd made a racket and a man came to the open office door. He had a long, sour face and was round-bellied, with an oxbow mustache stained tobacco-juice brown. Yellowish eyes as sharp as any travelin' horse trader's threw us a look of inquiry. "I'm Cap Bruno. What can I do for you boys?" A toothy smile as yellow as his eyes broke through his crabbed face.

"Good afternoon, Mr. Bruno," Billy opens up. "We need information about a horse. If I'm any kind of judge, you're just the man who can help us."

"Will oblige if I can."

Billy described the Judge in detail, down to his weight. "Have you seen the horse?"

"There's a lot of bay horses around here."

"This one's special. His name is Judge Blair and he was stolen late last Saturday at Aspermont."

The yellowish eyes widened. "Judge Blair? *The* Judge Blair? The fast racehorse? I've heard of him."

"*The* Judge Blair. None other."

"Can't say I've seen him. Can't say I have."

"There's a thousand-dollar reward for his return."

"Well—"

"You won't mind if we look through your barn, will you, Mr. Bruno? Just in case Judge Blair is here and you don't know it?" Billy was all smiles and molasses as he said it, as fraternal as a first-term county commissioner.

Bruno didn't smile. "Don't believe I see any stars on your vests that give you the right to come in here highhanded."

Right then I figured Judge Blair was in the barn, and Billy says, "We have the strongest right of all, Mr. Bruno, next to a search warrant. Mr. McQuinn, here, is the owner of Judge Blair."

Of a sudden Bruno was genial. "I understand. I'm just not used to strangers comin' in here on the prod like this."

"This way we'll have no doubts and neither will you," Billy says, "and you wouldn't want us to have any doubts, would you, Mr. Bruno?"

I'd never seen a man change so fast, from vinegar to honey. Bruno couldn't wait to lead us to the barn's breezeway. "So you won't, I'll show you around myself. The only reason I hesitated is because there's a rough element in Colorado City and around. There's been some hold-ups and horse thievery."

"We understand, Mr. Bruno." Billy slapped him on the back.

Bruno showed us every animal in the barn, but there was no Judge Blair. As we started back, I noticed two sheds in the corral behind the barn where Bruno hadn't taken us. Coyote had noticed, too, and we hotfooted back there. One shed held a sick mule; the other was empty.

Bruno belched and laughed at us. "Didn't think I'd hold out on you boys, did ya?"

We thanked him and as we rode off, his overgenial horse-trader's voice trailed us. "Come back anytime, boys. Meantime, I'll sure keep a sharp lookout for Judge Blair. *Hasta la vista.*"

"What do you make of that hombre?" I says to Billy.

"I wouldn't trust him as far as I could throw a bull by the tail over a ten-foot fence—but he didn't have the Judge."

I was low and showed it and Billy turned to me. "Now, Dude, did you figure you could ride in here and find the Judge right off?"

"Guess I hoped."

His older man's smile was understanding. "Guess we all did. While there's still good daylight, what say let's ride out the whole town for a look-see?"

Colorado City was no place a man could get lost unless he was booze blind and it was nighttime. By just riding along we could see what was in every little corral and shed and small open barn behind the houses. Twice I knocked on the front doors of houses where the barn was closed and told our story, hat in hand; and each time I was invited to see for myself, which I declined, with thanks, because I knew my horse wasn't there.

"I think it's time for a drink," Billy let me know as we headed back.

The Nip and Tuck must have retained some of its old-time railroad honkytonk ways because we could hear the whoops and laughs, an off-key piano and stompin' sounds as we tied up in front. We went in.

Well, the Nip and Tuck wasn't full, but you don't need a roomful of cowboys to make a saloon lively. In all, I remember the head count didn't run more than a handful of buckaroos—one or two of the drug-store variety—a few town hanger-ons and young girls.

We eased up to the bar and ordered our "usual," Old Green River bourbon for me and Billy and a sarsaparilla for Coyote, which brought a grin to the bartender's homely face, and he says to Coyote, "Injun, do you happen to know who John Wesley Hardin was? I say *was*, because he ain't with us anymore."

"Know him I did not."

"Then you don't know his famous sayin'?"

"I do not."

"Well, here it is. He said, and I'm quotin' the *Police Gazette*, 'I'll take no sass but sassparilla.' Ain't that a good 'un?"

Coyote grinned. "It is. Was he ever sassed?"

"I'll put it this way and you can judge for yourself. He had forty-some notches on his guns when shot from behind by Old John Selman in the Acme Saloon down in El Paso. He died with his boots on, with one on the bar rail."

"In that case," says Coyote, his face straight, "my sassparilla without any sass I also will take, but look behind me I will."

"You're all right, Injun. You catch on fast. Here it is, without any sass."

When the piano player gave out and the dancers broke for refreshments, I waved the barkeep over. "I'm buyin' drinks for everybody in the house, then I want to make an important public announcement."

"You bet," he says, all for that. He passed along the good news and everybody bunched up to the bar like cows at a feed trough, and when the drinks had been poured, he calls out to me, "Mister, if you like, get up on that table yonder when you're ready to make your spiel."

I didn't waste any time. "Folks, my name is Dude McQuinn and I ranch on the Salt Fork of the Brazos up in Stonewall County. Last Saturday night my racehorse, Judge Blair, was stolen from the county barns. You've prob'ly all heard of Judge Blair. He's never lost a race and we've campaigned him from Texas to Kentucky. He set the quarter-mile record at Juárez when he beat the great Mexican speed mare, Yolanda, in twenty-one and change."

I could see cowboys nod as I talked.

I went on. "He also holds the mile record set at the old Kentucky Association track in Lexington at Fifth and Race Streets. He burned that mile in one-thirty-four and four fifths."

"That's somethin'!" a cowboy yelled.

"Judge Blair is a dark bay gelding with a blazed face and four white socks, stands a shade over fifteen hands and weighs eleven-fifty."

"Twelve hundred," a voice breaks in, and I don't have to look to know that's Uncle Billy, who never misses a point on horses.

"He's a picture-book runnin' horse," I kept on. "A compact horse for a Thoroughbred. Has a good head with fox ears, wide-set eyes, and a big jaw. Powerful front and hindquarters. Deep of girth. A short back and a long underline. His legs are straight and set square. He's a balanced horse, which helps him change leads goin' into a turn and to change back when he comes out on the straightaway. He's got a beautiful blaze, which comes to a point between his nostrils like a trickle of milk. Remember, he's a dark bay. . . . Now, boys, there's a thousand-dollar reward for his return, and I mean cash in the hand when I see that blazed face. If you've seen a horse like him the past few days, or have any information at all, we'd sure appreciate it if you'd get in touch. If you can lead us to our horse, the money's yours on the spot. As for the thieves, we'll attend to that matter person-al, if you get what I mean? With me to back me up are my two pardners, Dr. William Tecumseh Lockhart and Mr. Coyote Walking, a Comanche Indian who rode Judge Blair in all his big races."

The hum of voices followed as men traded words. I hadn't told them about the letter the thieves had instructed me to pick up in Colorado City, on the chance somebody might let slip a hint that would give us a lead. What's more, I didn't want people hangin' around the post office when we went to get the letter.

I had another Old Green River and waited and nothing happened until a cowboy, his lean, sun-cured face puckered up in sympathy, strolled over and shook hands.

"Sure wish I could help you fellows. I've seen a number of bay horses this past week, but no Judge Blair. Believe I'd know him for sure from your description. A real runnin' horse sticks out. How long you aim to be around?"

"We'll make camp at the river crossing tonight," I says, "and we'll be in town tomorrow for certain. After that . . . depends."

No more was said. The piano player rippled the keys, the dancers sashayed out to the floor, and it was time for us to go. As we turned to leave, I happened to catch sight of a little man at the end of the bar. Maybe he'd just drifted in. There was nothing unusual about him. He wore a gray shirt and a gray felt hat with a medium wide brim. No beard. Just a short, black mustache. While he nursed a mug of beer, he reminded me of a rancher in town on business. His eyes, dark and deep-socketed, gave a shade of melancholy to his face. There was also a kind of self-reliance about him, like he was a quiet man in charge of himself. I said there was nothing unusual or standout about him. Yet, somehow, his face stayed with me as we left to make camp on the river road.

CHAPTER 5

ALL BRAG AND NO BOTTOM

By the time Billy and Coyote rolled out of their blankets next morning, I had watered the horses at the river, fed them grain from nosebags, built a fire, and had the coffee pot on. There was a bite of fall in the crisp air.

Billy was stiff as he moved to the fire and stood backside to it and his voice had a tetchy edge, which I could understand when his joints ached. "Dude," he says, with a straight-on look, "you know they never open the post office till eight o'clock or thereabout, don't you?"

"Yes, Uncle." I knew I was in for a hiding.

"Uncle Sam's minions also need time to read the postcards and catch up on local gossip that's comin' in or goin' out, and time to sort the mail and put it up in the boxes. You know that, too, don't you?"

"Yes, Uncle."

He glared at me. "Then why in thunderation did you have to get us up at daybreak? This is no cow outfit on the trail to a Kansas railhead, and we're not here to send a horse out for an early morning work." A look of pain shot across his face. The last remark, I sensed, had raked up memories of Judge Blair, which only made him feel worse.

"I couldn't sleep, Uncle. Every time I woke up I thought about that letter we're supposed to get. Reckon I did get you up too early. Sorry I broke into your beauty sleep. You'll need an early toddy." That was a mistake about the beauty sleep and the toddy, I knew the instant I spoke.

He bristled some more. "At my age sleep is not for beauty and good whiskey is medicine and not to get drunk on."

"Tell you what I'll do, Uncle. I'll make the biscuits this morning."

"Oh, no, you won't. I'm like Coyote in that respect. Don't think I could stomach a brown-paper cigaret butt in my vittles this early in the morning. I'll make the biscuits."

With a deep scowl, he made a bee-line for his pack, and in a moment I heard the cork on a bottle go *thung*, just like it used to when he kept a jug of sour mash in his "medicine chest" at the rear of the wagon. After a pause, he eased back to the fire and I caught the keen smell of sour-mash bourbon. His scowl was gone, rubbed out as Coyote would say, his tetchiness behind him, a soft smile on his saintly features. "Dude, you know I'm an early riser and you know I appreciate your offer to make the biscuits. It's just that I've had a little more experience than you've had, maybe fifty years or so. Now, hustle me up some more wood, pardner."

I'd have cut down a mesquite with a pocket knife to please him. I'll say this for Billy. On the trail he was never one to let a little early morning camp friction last past the first tin cup of coffee. And as mysterious as his background was, he was always straight as a wagon tongue with his pardners.

It was after nine o'clock when we rode into town. By now word about our purpose had made the rounds for certain. I could tell by the way heads turned and the stares fixed our way. That stop and settin' 'em up at the Nip and Tuck had done it. In Texas, Judge Blair was better known than a state senator; and as an old cowman once told me, with a twinkle in his eye, a good horse was far more honest than a politician.

Eyes still followed us as we drew rein at the post office and I hurried in and asked for mail at the one window.

"McQuinn . . . Dude McQuinn. Let's see." The clerk shuffled through a batch of letters. "Afraid there's not a thing for you, Mr. McQuinn. Sorry."

"Has today's mail come in?"

"Has from the east. Not from the west."

"When will that be in?"

"Around noon, if the train's on time. We close at one on Saturday."

I hadn't thought about it before, but I figured the letter would come from the west or southwest, since the first letter was postmarked Big Spring. I thanked him and headed for the door.

A little man stood at a long table, head bent over a newspaper. It was the black-mustached man in the gray felt hat I'd seen at the Nip and Tuck. The little man with the melancholy eyes.

I was outside and had reported to Billy and Coyote when the thought caught up with me. Was the little gent there to keep an eye on me? Both the note on the stall door and the Big Spring letter had said I was bein' watched. Then it came to me that the whole town of Colorado City had eyes on us today, agog over what might happen, prob'ly in hopes there'd be a gunfight. We'd become a spectacle that broke the monotony of a small town, where entertainment was usually scarce.

Billy's voice broke my line of thought. "Why not pay the sheriff a call while we wait for the mail?"

The sheriff's office was in the basement of the courthouse and the extra big letters on the open door read: SHERIFF C. T. "MOCCASIN" WILEY. At the desk sat a man who at once struck me as heavy on self-importance: all reared back, arms folded, booted feet on the desk, an oversize star on his calf-hide vest. He was heavy-jawed with a stiff mustache, eyes that put you at a distance, and a mouth permanently set in a superior cast. I took him for the undersheriff.

I didn't wait to be acknowledged. "My name's McQuinn. We're from Stonewall County and we're here about a stolen horse. Want to see the sheriff, pronto."

"A stolen horse? You've come all this way about a stolen horse?" He hadn't yet taken his booted feet off the desk.

"This horse is not just an ordinary cowhorse. He's Judge Blair."

"Judge Blair?"

"Judge Blair, the racehorse."

"Oh. . . . I get you now."

He swung to his feet and clumped back to an inner office. I heard voices. Then the undersheriff waved for us to come in. "The sheriff will see you."

Sheriff Wiley met us at the door with a handshake all around. A burly man, he carried a big paunch and was impressive in a loose-lipped, mechanical-smilin', politician's way. He had a mane of white hair worn long in the old frontier style, thick eyebrows, and a great bush of a mustache, its ends like wings across his florid face. He wore a buckskin jacket with long fringes and a pearl-handled six-gun wobbled on each hip in a hand-tooled holster. His paunch overlapped a wide leather belt, on it an oval-shaped buckle the size of a saucer; across the buckle was the single great word: MOCCASIN.

My father's contemptuous title for would-be gunslingers and frontiersmen jumped to my mind: a Daniel Boone.

"I'm Sheriff Wiley," he greets us. "The good people of Mitchell County have placed their trust in me three times. So I aim to ask them for a fourth term." After I introduced us all, he waved us to chairs against the wall while he took up behind a huge desk. "I got your sheriff's wire about the horse. Must say I'm mighty sorry about that. If there's anything lower than a horsethief, it's a rattler. Wish I had some leads for you boys, but I don't."

"Not one?" I says, let down.

"Not one. But believe you me, I've had my deputies on the double prowl. In fact, two of my boys are out right now on the case. One is checkin' off the area ranches. The other one is bird-doggin' the main roads and trails."

"Guess our sheriff told you there's a thousand-dollar reward for return of my horse?"

"That he did, which should be enough to influence some thief to turn in another thief. A thousand dollars is a lot of money these days."

I wanted to make another point. "The reward will be paid on the spot, on the barrelhead, as folks used to say. Be no waitin' around for me to go borrow the money."

"Man couldn't be any fairer than that. I'll pass the word and have the boys do the same when they come in. By the way, is Judge Blair a Thoroughbred?"

"He is, and Kentucky-bred. By Stonewall, a son of the mighty Lexington, and out of Verona, a mighty fast mare by Glencoe, an imported stud who could carry speed over a distance of ground." It made me feel good just to recite my horse's credentials. "Judge Blair is compact for a Thoroughbred, and could be mistaken for a quarter horse, since he's not the rangy type."

It occurred to me now that while travelin' around so much I had never had a picture taken of Judge Blair. Didn't have the time, I suppose I thought back then. That oversight haunted me now for another reason. If our search dragged on and on, I'd want to have reward posters printed and circulated far and wide. But posters without a picture wouldn't mean much. Sometimes a man hurries too fast through life and overlooks little things he wishes later he'd done along the way. Regrets, regrets, which are damn poor comfort. But even if I never saw my horse again, I knew I'd always carry in my mind this clear, bright picture of him that would never fade: a dark bay on the fly, blazed face thrust forward, ears laid back, white-sock feet skimmin' the ground as he shot across the finish line. And never could I forget how he'd throw up his head and come to me when I whistled him over for a handful of feed.

"Speakin' of Thoroughbreds," Wiley went on, "reminds me of what happened some years back. A rancher friend of mine brought in a young Kentucky stud called Red Wing that could burn the breeze. He figured Red Wing would make a lightnin'-fast rope horse." Wiley grinned in a knowing way. "What he soon learned was that a Thoroughbred can't break as fast as our Texas rope horses and, what's more, can't turn on a dime like a cow horse. A Thoroughbred will just go on by a calf that's changed directions before he can get turned. Red Wing was fast, though. He was by Himyar, who won the Kentucky Derby in seventy-eight."

I saw Billy squirm at that and I knew he wouldn't let it go by. "Beg pardon, Sheriff. Himyar didn't win the seventy-eight Derby. He ran second. However, he was favored."

Wiley shrugged. "So it was Solicitor who won it?"

"It was Day Star. He led all the way. But it was Himyar who became a great sire."

Wiley's florid face turned redder. "What was the distance, a mile and a quarter?"

"A mile and a half then. It's since been shortened to a mile and a quarter, like you said." Billy was trying to be civil, but I could see that he had taken a quick dislike to this blowhard sheriff.

"Well, Doctor," says Wiley, givin' ground, but ever the county politician, ready with that election-day smile, "I can see that you are up-to-date on horses. Might add that ol' Red Wing provided some other excitement around here besides his owner's attempt to make a rope horse out of 'im. Some fool cowboy up an' stole Red Wing. I formed a posse soon as I got word and the chase was on. When the whiskey gave out, most of the town boys quit the trail. But me an' my deputies never quit." He rolled his lips and kinda looked around the office. "If I do say so, I reckon if it hadn't been for my years as a government scout we'd have lost the trail in that rough country southwest of here. Finally cornered 'im other side of Morgan's Peak. He put up a stiff fight, too. A heap of lead was slung that day. When we charged in, he gave up. Luckily, Red Wing wasn't hit. . . . That fool cowboy is now a star boarder at the Cross-Bar Hotel in Huntsville."

"That must have been quite a chase," says I to be polite. I started to ask about other racehorse men in the county, on the suspicion that somebody might have stolen the Judge with the idea to match race him in Old Mexico; but before I could speak up, Wiley had the bit in his teeth, so to speak, and was off again:

"Another time there was this Kansas badman that called himself the Dodge City Kid. Packed two forty-fives and had left the Sunflower State in a high lope, they said. Had shot a stage driver and robbed the stage. Well, I was here in my office one afternoon goin' over some new reward posters—I have a knack, folks say, of once I read somethin' I never forget it: such as an outlaw's description, the color of his eyes, and his peculiarities. Maybe the way he rubs his chin or pulls on his earlobe. Little tell-tale things like that which often lead to a man's arrest—I was here in my office when a clerk from the mercantile rushed in and said the Dodge City Kid had just robbed the store. 'Which way'd he go?' I asked him. 'Southwest,' he said and jumped up and down.

"I don't know why criminals around here always seem to head southwest. They will, nine times out of ten, because it's rough country, I guess, and they feel safer out there around Morgan's Peak in the brush." He treated us to a cat-eatin'-the-canary grin. "What they don't know is that Moccasin Wiley knows every water hole and canyon out there. . . . So we mounted up and fogged outa town. The Kid must've been on a fast horse, because all we could see was a streak of dust. But after a long run of some miles he seemed to slow down and we saw him ride into some cedars. Later, we found out that fast horse had gone lame and that was the reason the Kid stopped. We raced up and went in on foot, but we couldn't see him in the cedars—just his horse with the reins down. I told the boys not to rush in too fast. Didn't want nobody hurt, you know. I called for the Kid to come out and surrender, but he didn't answer. Just let his forty-fives do the talkin'. So we hugged the ground and stayed put."

Billy let go a loud cough and started to get up, but Wiley went right on. "It was late in the year and you know how the weather can change in Texas, faster'n a man can say Jack Robinson. Well, the wind came up and pretty soon it was colder'n a banker's stare in a hard year, and I told the boys to drop back a little and build a fire. They's glad to do that, you betcha. But somethin' told me . . . instinct, I reckon, from my old government scout days . . . to slip off to the right and make a little circle and bide my time. A lawman has to be patient. Well, it got colder and colder and before long it was close to dark. I heard somethin' rustle, but I couldn't make out what it was. I moved farther to my right, still on the circle. . . . Then I saw what it was. It was the Kid all hunkered down, shiverin' in his shirt. Didn't even have a brush jacket on. If I do say so, I'm light on my feet, so I just eased up behind him and says, 'Don't move, Kid. You're covered.' He dropped his guns and I took him down to the fire. . . . He got twenty-five years for that foolishness at the mercantile, and when he gets through servin' that, they want him up in Kansas."

It was time to hurry, before Wiley could launch another windy. We had accomplished no good here. I stood. "We'd better get along, Sheriff."

"How long you boys aim to stick around?"

"Depends."

"If the case breaks, where can I find you?"

"That depends, too. At night we're camped at the river crossing. By the way, Sheriff, does your rancher friend still have Red Wing?"

"Red Wing died of colic and my friend has passed away."

"Sorry to hear that. Any other racehorse men in the county?"

"Not a one. But if there's anything I can do for you boys, just give Moccasin Wiley a holler. If I get any hot leads and you're not around, I'll wire your sheriff."

We filed out with relief. As we rode off, Billy shook his head again and again. "That's the biggest bag of wind I've run into since the barn blew down on the ranch."

We idled around town till the Texas and Pacific chuffed in from Big Spring, waited till we figured there'd been time for the mail to be up, then I left my pardners with the horses and made tracks for the post office.

The clerk recognized me and put on a wry face. "Nothing came in for you, Mr. McQuinn. But there's always another day." He hesitated. "I believe you're the man whose racehorse was stolen at Aspermont?"

I nodded. His question told me something more. If the post office clerk knew, everybody in town knew. Good. Not just the Nip and Tuck crowd.

A sort of excitement rose to his face. "I've read about Judge Blair. It was in the El Paso *Times* when he beat the fast Mexican mare, the champion of Chihuahua. Her name escapes me. . . ." Stumped, he snapped his fingers and chewed his lip.

"Yolanda."

"That's it!"

I warmed up to him. "One of the fastest mares I've ever seen. Not big, but she could fly. A lot of fillies and mares are fast breakers. She broke like a shot. My horse just beat her by a head." In that moment I relived the finish, the picture alive in my mind. Then it was gone.

"Well, I sure hope you get your horse back."

I thanked him. I appreciated what he said. Yet, in a way, it was like an expression of sympathy when a member of the family has passed away, and I felt no better.

Outside the post office a man stood by his horse, a leggy, bald-faced bay; the man's hands busy with the saddle cinch. It was the mustached little bird in the gray hat again. I'd come to know him at a glance. Enough to notice that he had changed from a gray to a blue shirt and the hair on the back of his neck looked shorter, like he'd been sheared at a barber shop. This was three times now. First in the Nip and Tuck, this morning both in the post office and out here. Was he campin' on my trail? The letter had said I'd be watched. But as that suspicion rubbed on me, I could see loafers across the street eyeballin' me. I shrugged and crossed downstreet to my pardners.

"No mail."

I guess my face was a map of discouragement, because Billy just shrugged. "I figure we're a day or two ahead of the thieves' mail. We made fast time from the ranch to here. That letter will come in tomorrow or the day after, or the day after that. We have to keep in mind they want the money and they won't get it if they don't keep up the contact. They will."

He made sense. An older man's judgment. Back to the wait-and-see game. Too early now to make camp. If the thieves were having us watched, someone might make a slip and tip his hand, or a word might be dropped in the Nip and Tuck that would lead us to them. Whiskey is a great tongue-loosener. I tried to picture again in my mind what the thieves looked like. The usual images of range thieves formed: bearded, dirty, wearin' slouch hats—packin' guns—in a hurry. But did the men who had taken Judge Blair fit the usual run of cowboy? Hard to say. Cowboys . . . hardcases driftin' through the country . . . would know a good horse and what to do with one. That was it! Just passin' through, they saw the race and took the horse. Well . . . maybe.

With time on our hands, I took Billy and Coyote to the Southern Hotel for a sit-down meal. Afterward, they said they needed some things at the mercantile, and I said I'd get a sack of oats for feed and I'd meet them in front of the Nip and Tuck.

CHAPTER 6

A LEAD OR A SETUP?

Ace Feeds. A long, shedlike structure that had the earthy smell of grains, always pleasant to me.

A man sat on a high stool, pen in hand, eyes intent, fixed on a red-backed ledger. He glanced up and nodded and wiped his pen. When he stepped down, I saw that he was short and roly-poly, which would fit a jolly person; but when he looked at me, I saw a bearded face as stern as an arm-wavin' backwoods preacher hell-bent after sin and the devil. His thin hair was combed straight back. His mouth, though full, was pressed firm and flat. A sure-enough serious individual, I figured, as I told him my need. He called in Spanish and a Mexican boy brought the sack of oats.

After I had paid and he thanked me, he eyed me with more than the expected inquiry a stranger draws. "You must be Mr. McQuinn, come in search of a stolen racehorse."

"I am."

"This is just another example of the lawlessness sweeping Texas these days. Stolen horses, stolen cattle, bank holdups. Attempts have even been made to hold up the Texas and Pacific." His jowls quivered as he talked.

"I'd say there's always been a fair amount of that."

"Your horse stolen, this Judge Blair, this great runner. It's a hard loss to take, I know."

"I hope it's only temporary."

"You are not alone in that, Mr. McQuinn." He thrust out his hand. "Excuse my outburst of indignation. My name is Al Oldham. I'm just tired of all this. We've had our share in this county as well. Now, I'm not one to nose into another man's affairs, but have you had any trace of your horse at all?"

"Mighty little . . . except we think he might have been taken this way."

"You said *we.*"

"My two pardners are with me."

"Have you talked to the authorities?"

"Talked to Sheriff Wiley."

"Moccasin Wiley. Hmmnn."

I could see that he wasn't impressed. "That is, he did most of the talkin'."

"He give you any leads?"

"Said he hadn't picked up any, though our sheriff has been in touch with him and he's on the lookout." I couldn't hold back a grin. "But he did tell us how his experience as a government Indian scout helped him and his deputies track down the cowboy that stole Red Wing, the Thoroughbred racehorse, and the big gunfight they had, and how the cowboy gave up when they all charged in. And how he captured the Dodge City Kid single-handed. Circled in behind him. Caught the Kid unawares. Indianed up on him."

Oldham looked pained and weary. "C.T. tells that to every stranger that comes to his office. In the first place, he never was a government scout. There was a cavalry detail posted here a while in the early eighties, sent to look for a few bronco Comanches believed raiding for horses. C.T. hung around the troopers' camp, rode out with 'em a few times. They sighted a Comanche or two, but never caught up with one. It was about then that he hung 'Moccasin' on his monicker. Has it on all his campaign cards in great big ol' letters with a big ol' picture of himself in his big ol' white hat: Sheriff C.T. 'Moccasin' Wiley, Former Indian Scout with the U.S. Cavalry, Now Serving the People of Mitchell County. Your Vote for Me Is a Vote for Law and Order.

"He was never hired as a scout because they didn't need one and didn't have one. As for the big gunfight C.T. claimed took place with the cowboy that stole Red Wing, that never took place a-tall. The cowboy's only weapon was an ol' beat-up Rigdon revolver, the kind made in Georgia durin' the War Between the States, patterned after the Colt Navy model. He fired one shot and the old gun jammed on him. So he threw up his hands and surrendered. The cowboy told that to the jailer here, and the jailer, Mike Farley, a personal friend of mine and a strong churchgoer, told me. The deputies never let on or disputed C.T.'s story, of course. . . . And C.T. never captured the Dodge City Kid like he claimed. A norther blew in, the Kid got cold, just walked up to the fire and gave himself up. The smartest thing C.T. and his deputies did that night was to build that fire."

"Reckon the jailer told you that, Mr. Oldham?"

"No, one of the deputies, after C.T. fired him for failure to follow orders."

"Orders?"

"Talked too much. C.T. is the only spokesman for the sheriff's office. The deputy's not around anymore. Went to Fort Worth to work in the stockyards."

"But the sheriff's been elected three times," I says. "People must like him."

"C.T. makes a big show. Shakes a lot of hands. Circulates a lot. Stays in the public eye. Let's say a poor family in the country gets burned out. Loses everything and the church folks take up donations for money and clothes and beddin' and food. Why, C.T. will be the first to put in, and I don't mean just a dollar or two. He'll throw in a ten or a twenty. Maybe drop off a sack of groceries for the family."

"But he is generous?"

"For a reason. I don't mean either that he tells around what he's done. Oh, no—that would spoil the effect. He's just careful to do it in public. That way everybody knows. Come election time they'll remember. And don't think that family that got the sack of groceries won't remember! They'll tell everybody. On top of that, he gives the impression he's always in a hurry. Never walks or trots a horse down Main Street. He goes at a hard gallop, with a deputy or two on the prod behind him. C.T. always rides in front. Makes people think he's on the job, in a hurry to investigate a case or on the lookout for trouble."

"But he has caught some lawbreakers?"

"A few chicken thieves. All the general public remembers are cases like the Red Wing theft and the Dodge City Kid, which all got wrote up big in our weekly paper, the *Sentinel*, and the Fort Worth *Star-Telegram*. They don't know about the cow and horsethieves that never get caught. On top of that, the worst has been the series of holdups by two masked men. I don't mean in town. But a teamster, say, camped by the river crossing, or travelers who've stopped in town for supplies, then got held up on the road. Sometimes a horse trader known to have money on him after a good trade."

"Anybody shot?"

"A few wounded. Nobody killed. The two are careful. They strike fast and are gone. Ride good horses."

"How long's this been goin' on?"

"Three years or more. I don't mean it happens all the time. Things'll be quiet for a spell, maybe months, then there'll be a string of holdups. The two always seem to know who's got the money. The victims usually have stopped in town first. I know people who swear by C.T., and some like me who swear at 'im. We have a Citizens' Good Government Committee at work, but so far we haven't been able to beat him on election day. We call C.T.'s organization the Regime. Way it looks, the Regime will go on and on as long as Moccasin Wiley can continue to make big tracks in public."

I tied the sack of oats behind my saddle and joined my pardners in front of the Nip and Tuck, whose hitching rack was about full at this hour.

Billy looked amused. "You'll have to see what Coyote bought at the store," he says, and Coyote, as if pleased with himself, drew a murderous-lookin' knife from a leather sheath at his belt. The blade was curved.

I examined it. "This looks like the kind of curved knife my father said he used to skin buffalo. I believe he said the hunters used straight-bladed knives to rip."

"Comanches used curved knives also."

"But the buffalo's gone, Coyote, no thanks to the hunters. Why the knife?"

"To use on mean white mans who took our horse." He made the sign to scalp. "We Comanches our horses love like family. Without them, starved we would have in buffalo days. Before the horse we used dogs as beasts of burden. The horse off the ground lifted us like a strong wind, made us like gods across the prairie racing. We could go anywhere. My father the chief his favorite buffalo runner outside his lodge would tie. If raiders near, tie he would the horse's rope to his wrist. . . . My father had many fast racehorses. At Fort Sill he would race the pony soldiers' horses. Before a race into his horse's nostrils he would blow powdered medicine. Wolf and fox tails tied in mane made horses long-winded. Antelope horns made them run faster. Tips of tails and short prongs from antelope horns my father would tie around the horse's neck in a medicine bag. Feathers from hawks and falcons tie my father would to the horse's tail."

"Did your father win many races?"

"My answer is this: His medicine was very strong and the horses he won covered the prairie like a cloud and when they ran the sound was like the beating of many drums."

"Coyote, you should've been a poet." I grinned at him with affection and understanding. This young Indian educated in the white man's school, this honor graduate of Carlisle School in Pennsylvania, who hankered for the Bard of Avon's plays, was still a Comanche at heart, unchanged, and I was glad. He would show the thieves no mercy, and neither would I. "By the way, Coyote, did you ever scalp anybody, white man or Indian? If you took a white man's, I know he deserved it."

I've told you what a great play-actor Coyote was when we campaigned the Judge and took on all comers, like when he pretended the Judge had bolted and Coyote couldn't hold him, and he looked so helpless—done to fool the crowd of rubes whose money we'd just taken after we'd pulled the switch and the outfit had to get out of town fast.

At my question he turned stern and proud, on his dignity, and folded his arms and stared at me hard. Had I hurt his feelings? He broke into laughter and grinned like an impish boy. "Too young I was for war and the only enemies I scalped were in games. But my father the chief showed me how and ready I am now to learn on my own."

That called for a drink and we swung inside the Nip and Tuck for our "usuals." Early as it was, the place was crowded along the bar. There's a lot of whoop and holler to county-seat towns at any hour. Just then the piano player, an old bird with gartered sleeves on a striped shirt and with slicked-down hair, stepped to the piano and rippled the keys. The girls appeared like magic. So did the squad of drugstore cowboys. I didn't see more than a few real cowhands. These I figured were either out of work or had been sent to town on errands for the boss.

I could see right off that the barkeep had taken a shine to Coyote. As he sat the bottle of sarsaparilla down, he grinned and says, "My peaceful Injun friend, ever hear the story about the cowboy who went down into Old Mexico to learn Spanish?"

"I have not."

"And the terrible misfortune that overtook him down there?"

Coyote shook his head, wary of the joke.

"This cowboy wasn't too smart. He was a slow learner and he stayed a long time. Now you're supposed to ask me what happened to him?"

Coyote bit. "What happened?"

"What happened was, he never learned Spanish. . . ." The barkeep paused. "But in the meantime doggone if he didn't forget all his English."

We all grinned.

The barkeep looked at Coyote. "Can you top that?"

"In the first place," Coyote says, "that happen never would to a Comanche. We always have the sign language to fall back on. Yes, top it I can. Perchance you heard about the small war party of Comanches who without warning came upon a large column of pony soldiers?"

"Can't say I have."

"The war party leader signaled a young man named Red Hawk to come forward. 'Red Hawk,' he said, 'the pony soldiers are near and too strong for us. You have been hanging around the teamsters and stable guards at the fort and have heard them talk. You are the only one among us who the white man's language knows. So you make the peace sign and ride up to the pony soldiers' chief and tell him we are peaceful, looking for buffalo. Say nothing of the wagon train we attacked yesterday. Tell him he is a great white chief. Make him feel important.'

"Young Red Hawk all puffed up was at being chosen. Holding his hand high in peace, he rode up to the pony soldier chief and his officers and said, 'Sorry damn mule. Gimme chaw.'

"The officers bewildered looked. This surprised Red Hawk. He began to feel arrogant. Strange, these white men didn't savvy their own language. Now flattery he would try. Smiling, he to the white chief went and on the arm patted and said, 'Heap sonabitch. Heap big, nice sonabitch.' Now you ask me what happened?"

"What happened, Injun?"

"The white officers drew their guns and took poor Red Hawk and the other warriors prisoners to Fort Sill. Kept there they were for a long time. To this day Red Hawk feels disgraced, and to this day thinks he spoke fluent English and nothing bad would have happened that day if only the pony soldiers their own language had understood. 'Strange,' he said, 'the ways of the white man.' "

"You'll get no sass on that one, Injun. Your drink's on the house."

We idled away the time, ears tuned to the talk along the long bar, and now and then we watched the lively dancers. A cute little cutup of a gal, accompanied on the piano, sang "The Old Chisholm Trail" and everybody applauded, and she got an even bigger hand when, with winks and twists, she rendered "What Was Your Name Back in the States?" which never fails to draw grins and elbow nudges from oldtime cowboys. In Texas in the early days, it was bad manners to ask a man his name, and sometimes dangerous, since he might be on the dodge, say, from Oklahoma or elsewhere. Many men left their real names behind when they crossed Red River into the Lone Star State. Names didn't matter much then. Most cowboys went by nicknames, anyway. Too, a goodly number of Texas-bred cowboys of a sudden decided the climate was healthier in New Mexico or Arizona. I heard my father say one time about an old acquaintance, "I guess by now Tom has been out of Texas long enough to use his right name."

As the afternoon wore away, I got restless and fretted over how much time we had wasted in the Nip and Tuck without even one lead. I was ready to break for camp when the bartender came from the far end of the bar and leaned in and says to me, "A man said he'd like to see you outside."

I jerked. "He say what for?"

"No. Just said to tell you."

"What does he look like?"

"Like a hundred other cowboys."

I was suspicious. "You know him?"

"Never saw him before."

"How'll I know him?"

"He'll know you. I pointed you out to him. Come to think of it, he's wearin' a dirty, red-checkered shirt."

My pardners hadn't heard. Billy and an older cowhand were talking head to head and I knew the subject was horses. Coyote, his eyes dubious, was watching the dancers. I could almost read his mind: Strange the ways of the white man. How can they dance without drums?

I gave Coyote a little wave and eased through the crowd and outside and looked around. Three men loitered on the plank walk under the overhang. Two talked. The third moved toward me. I thought he was my man till he walked past me and I saw his shirt was blue.

"McQuinn," a voice says in my ear.

I froze with self-disgust. He had come up from behind me, prob'ly from against the saloon wall. Was I alert! I faced him. He wore a red-checkered shirt, dirty all right; and his sunburned face, like the barkeep said, would fit countless southwest Texas cowboys: sandy complexion, days of stubble on his lean face, a thin mouth, and the bloodshot eyes of a man who took a lot of wind and dust and sun.

"What do you want?"

He cleared his throat. "Where can we talk?"

"What's wrong with here?"

"Too open."

"Then where?"

"Follow me." He moved to the end of the plank walk on run-down boot heels and would have turned into the passageway between the saloon and the saddle shop next door. I balked. I didn't like this. A man could get knocked in the head. "This is as far as I go, old stud. You got something to say, say it here."

He pulled up. "Good enough. Word around town is you're lookin' for a stolen horse and there's a thousand-dollar reward."

"That's right."

"Well, I've got some good news for you."

"Like what?"

"Like how you can get your horse."

"That would interest me." But the longer this hombre talked, the less I believed him. "If it's the right horse."

"He's a racehorse, ain't he?"

"He is."

"A blaze-faced bay gelding with four white socks?"

"That fits the description. By now, everybody in Colorado City knows what he looks like. But how do you figure in this?"

"All I know is a man told me to get in touch with you."

"What man?"

"Don't know his name. I'm new to these parts."

"Why you, if you're new around here?"

"Guess I've got an honest face." He grinned, a lopsided confidential grin like we'd been saddle pals for years. One front tooth was gone, two others broken. He rummaged in a shirt pocket for the makin's and rolled a lumpy cigaret one-handed. "The man paid me twenty-five dollars to contact you. I aim to earn my money."

"That all he told you?"

"I ain't finished, mister."

"You haven't told me a thing yet."

He cleared his throat and struck a match on his left thumbnail and his face hardened with the snap. "I will now—plenty. Meet me in front of the Southern Hotel this evening at six o'clock. The man said you'd better be there if you want to see your horse again."

"We'll be there."

"The man said *alone.* Got that—*alone? Alone*—and bring the reward money." He sauntered off, mounted a slab-sided brown gelding that wasn't far from buzzard bait and rode east out of town.

If you want to see your horse again.

I worked that through my mind. The wording was almost identical to the threat in the note nailed to the stall door and in the letter: "If you expect to see your horse again." Had the drifter penned the note and the letter? I chewed on that. Two ways he didn't fit. I couldn't match his talk with that part of the schoolmarm-soundin' lingo in the note, which I'd kept and studied over and over, which read, ". . . you will be wise to follow all instructions and no deviations," and he hadn't said bring the $5,000 ransom as contained in the letter postmarked Big Spring. He'd only said fetch the $1,000 reward. He didn't know about the $5,000, and neither did the man he claimed had hired him, if there was that man. Therefore, this could mean that Judge Blair had changed hands along the way, rustled again, or maybe in a poker game, the same way I'd won him. Whatever had happened, here the drifter was with our first lead. If there was another man, that swung back to the Aspermont thieves. More than one was involved because the Big Spring letter read, "We mean business, McQuinn," which got me madder'n a hornet's nest every time I read it or thought about it, and which didn't jibe with bring only $1,000. Well, come six o'clock, I damn well aimed to find out who laid the chunk.

I figured Billy and Coyote would be all for it when I told them outside the Nip and Tuck, but Billy shook his head. "I don't like it. For the one reason that you go alone."

"There has to be a local connection because the letter directed us to come here with the money."

"That much I see. That one-man stipulation, I don't. Strikes me as a setup, Dude."

"It's the first lead we've had, Uncle."

"It still smells like a setup."

"Grandfather Billy is right."

They were both dead set against it.

CHAPTER 7

THE OWL PERSON COMES

But at six o'clock that evening I rode up to the Southern Hotel and there was the self-styled drifter on the buzzard-bait brown gelding.

"Where to?" I sang out, like it was just a lark.

"Follow me."

He cut a look behind me and, when satisfied that nobody followed us, headed east out of town as he had before. I reined in behind him, my six-shooter stuck inside my belt, covered by my coat, ready for business. After a time, when I rode up alongside him, he motioned me back. "I said follow me, mister."

"What's the matter, don't you like good company?"

For an answer, he just cleared his throat.

It didn't take long to put the outskirts of Colorado City behind us. Early darkness lay over the rolling hills. The farther we rode the less faith I had in this ride. I guess we had covered two miles or more, not another word between us, when he turned off the main road, checked behind us, and took a dim wagon road.

I couldn't let that go by. "For a newcomer, you know these parts right well. Believe you could catch on as a guide for folks comin' out West to settle."

He ignored my byplay.

About half a mile on a little frame farmhouse took shape. There was a stillness here and a loneliness that was all too familiar to me. The place looked abandoned, prob'ly the blasted hopes of some poor cotton farmer. A kid's rope swing dangled from a big live oak. A whip-poor-will called, that lonesome sound of evening. No light in the house. A slat fence, broken in places, surrounded the weedy front yard and a ragged flower garden of stubborn hollyhocks and daisies and roses.

Four-o'clocks stood on each side of the porch steps, just like Blossom's at home.

The drifter tied up to the fence and so did I. "Go on in," he says in an offhand way.

"Where's my horse?"

"The man will bring him along directly."

"No horse, no reward money."

"Works both ways. No money, no horse."

"Why the delay?"

"We ain't runnin' no train station, mister."

He moved as though to follow me in. Instead, I swung around behind him. "You first, old stud."

He cleared his throat, which I had learned to expect when he was irked or nervous. "Better go on in if you aim to get your horse back."

"Don't recall I ever found a horse in a house."

It was a standoff. I could see the line of his lopsided smile in the dimness. "Danged if you ain't a suspicious cuss, McQuinn. Your horse will be brought here any minute. I'll go in and light the lamp to show we're all set."

He walked in ahead of me and some of my doubt left me. The door was open. I waited till I heard him scratch a match and I saw him hold the flame to the wick of a kerosene lamp. I went in then on slow steps, my hand on my gun, my eyes sprung wide to each side in case somebody jumped me. The meager room smelled of dust and old wood smoke and failure, and for a tick of time I thought of the family that had labored hard to make it here and couldn't and the little towheaded kids playin' on the swing under the ancient live oak. Hard times and brave people who deserved better and seldom whimpered. The room held a table made of rough planks, two hard-used cane-bottom chairs, and an orange crate.

"We'll have to wait," the drifter says. He put the lamp on the orange crate and pulled up a chair. When I sat down I saw that he faced me from the side across the table. From where I was I could see the back door that led from the little kitchen. I started to feel mighty restless. I decided to pressure him. "When the man brings my horse, we'll have to go back in town for the money."

He cut me a look. "That's just talk, McQuinn. You want that

racehorse more than anything in the world and you want him back now."

"I want my horse, sure. But you don't figure I'm fool enough to bring that much money with me, do you? Hell, I could get knocked in the head and not get my horse."

"You're pullin' my leg."

"You'll see when the man brings the horse. I left the reward money with my pardners."

He cleared his throat, so I knew I'd made him nervous. Now and then he'd shift his boots. I had $1,000 in my money belt and the rest in wallets in my boots.

Dusk deepened and the night drew on. The wind came up and the old house creaked and groaned like it wailed for its family. Way off I heard a coyote start his song, which was early for a coyote, I thought. The drifter rolled another one-handed cigaret. I craved a smoke, too, but let the need go by. I didn't want anything in my hand that might slow me down if I had to dig for my gun. A little stretch of time passed. Then I heard the mellow *hoom-hoom* of an owl that seemed to come from the live oaks along the road. I turned my head, but the sound wasn't repeated. That owl was likewise early. Generally, I'd hear one late at night when I was in my blankets. A *hoom-hoom* can make a kid cover up his head and it can get to an adult if he's superstitious and out in the country. Plains Indians, in particular, believe in owl medicine. Coyote taught me that. He always spoke of the Owl Person with wonder and respect and a little fear. So never make fun of an owl. It's bad luck. Owls are smart in ways unknown to man and can bring bad news, Coyote said.

The drifter built another cigaret while he fidgeted and watched the back door. To guy him, I says, "Mind tellin' me how the man got hold of my horse?"

He glared at me—that was all.

"Did he steal the horse from the crooks that stole him from me?"

He kept his eyes fixed on the door.

"If he didn't steal the horse from the crooks, maybe he won him in a poker game?"

He glared again.

I had to laugh at him. "Or maybe he found my horse loose?"

"Damn it to hell, McQuinn, will you shut up?"

There followed a run of time broken only by the groans of the old house and the frequent snap of the drifter's match as he lit another hand-rolled smoke.

It was about then that I heard the *hoom-hoom* again, not from the road, but from the back side of the house. In any tight situation, time seems rigid, seems to stand still, which happened often to the outfit when we took on all comers at all distances and the losers balked at payin' off. We used the switch, but we never fixed the other man's horse —that's gospel! Didn't have to to win. Now, it seemed like a long spell, but I don't think it was more than half a minute after I heard the owl again that I heard the horses. I bent my head to catch their cadence: two horses comin'. That meant the man had Judge Blair on a lead shank. I shot up from the chair, charged with anticipation.

"Hold on! Wait!" The drifter was up, too.

The shuffle of hooves, which came from the road, circled around the house and stopped.

"He's here with your horse," the drifter says, as nice as could be.

I watched the back door. My attention was there when I saw a paunchy man with worn range clothes step in, hat pulled down low over his eyes, a red bandanna across his face. That was when I went for my gun, because I knew it was a setup. I heard the drifter yell, "Don't shoot!" and I saw the masked man throw up his hands. At the same time, before I could whip around, I heard somebody run through the front door and the drifter grabbed my gun arm and a voice in my ear said, "Give him your gun, McQuinn, or this thing's gonna go off."

I gave up the gun to the drifter.

"Now, hand over the money, McQuinn." The voice sounded faintly familiar, but I couldn't place it.

I tried to shrug it off. "The reward money's in town."

"It's on you or you wouldn't be here for your horse."

"How about my horse? Where is he?" I wanted to stall for time, time I didn't have. Then, like a voice out of the night, I heard the *hoom-hoom* again behind the house.

"Take his money belt, Lafe. He has to have one on. Nobody'd carry that much in his pocket."

So Lafe was the drifter's name. He tore the belt off me and he and the masked man tied me to a chair while the third man kept me covered. He was masked, too. That done, Lafe ran out the front way and the masked pair plunged through the back doorway. But instead of the rapid clatter of hooves, I heard a yell, "Where's the horses? Where the hell are they?"

I could hear Lafe's horse on the run down the road. There was a pause, an even tighter silence after that, and muffled voices, and the next I knew the masked pair bulged in the back doorway. Startled, I jerked upright. How come? Then, openmouthed, I saw their hands up, Billy and Coyote armed and close behind them, and at sight of Coyote I savvied the owl hoots and the pair's lack of horses.

"Get over there!" Billy ordered the pair and gave the paunchy one a kick in the butt. Coyote ran over to me, and as he cut me loose with the nasty, curve-bladed knife he'd bought in town, I had to eat crow right there because I'd gone against my pardners' judgment. "The Owl Person sure came just in time and I have to say his medicine is mighty powerful." His only response was to hand me a gun and go back to Billy, who told the pair, "Now, unmask!"

They didn't move.

I felt it was my turn. I tore the red bandanna off the paunchy individual and froze, stunned to see Sheriff Moccasin Wiley, his flabby face already screwed up in a hurry of put-on innocence. Jerking the bandanna off the second man, I met the sour features of none other than Cap Bruno, proprietor of the respectable Three Star Livery. He just scowled.

"Well, I'll be damned," was all I could say.

Wiley's mouth worked fast. "I can explain everything. This is a case of mistaken identity. You see, I got a tip that three bank robbers from East Texas would hit Colorado City. That they'd pose to be on the lookout for a stolen racehorse worth *mucho dinero*. Meanwhile, they'd case the town so they could knock off the bank. A little game they'd played more'n once. So while in the line of duty, yours truly, Sheriff Moccasin Wiley, and Special Deputy Cap Bruno have made an honest mistake." He talked faster. "If I do say so, I've always been one to admit any false leads, as in this case. So you boys turn us loose, give us back our guns, ease on out of town, and nothing will be said. Otherwise, you will face mighty serious charges of false arrest of officers while in the line of duty."

"In the line of duty!" I had to howl. "A schoolboy could think up a better story than that. And since when did a sheriff have to put on a mask to make an arrest? And since when did a sheriff in the line of duty rob a man and run out the back door? And if I was a suspect, why didn't you arrest me and take me to jail? Now, where's my money belt?"

Both men shrugged.

Billy glanced in question at Coyote, which told me they hadn't seen it. But even as paunchy as Wiley was, there seemed to be an extra roll around his middle. I yanked up his shirt and unbuckled my money belt.

Wiley looked sick. He commenced to whine. "You boys got this all wrong. You'll be sorry, damned sorry, before it's over."

"The only thing I'm sorry about is that I didn't get my horse back. I'd be glad to fork over a thousand dollars for him."

Wiley's whine changed to a shrill threat. "You'll all stand trial for false arrest. You'll see. I got influence."

"You won't have any after we take you to town, which is where we're headed. Tie their hands, Coyote."

I could see Wiley strain for some of his old law-and-order bravado, but by this time he was just a skim-milk sheriff. His voice sounded desperate. "You boys are about to make the biggest mistake of your lives. You'll be laughed outa town, bringin' in the most popular sheriff Mitchell County's ever had. Nobody will believe you."

"I know one man who will and a bunch more—Al Oldham and the Citizens' Good Government Committee."

Coyote brought up the pair's horses from where he'd hidden them in the live oaks and we struck out for town, Wiley's mouth flappin' all the way, every word a threat. I didn't answer, just let him rave. At the edge of town, he pulled rein, his voice turned as genial as a country peddler's. "Boys, this tomfoolery has gone far enough. Tell you what I'll do. There's five hundred dollars in my office safe. It's all yours if you'll just untie our hands and ride on outa town. Be the easiest dinero you ever made."

"Why, Sheriff," Billy says in a tone of pretended astonishment, "that's bribery by a public official. A penitentiary offense back where I come from. How could you, sir? And if we took the five hundred, you could say we stole it from the safe, and who could doubt the word of Mitchell County's most popular sheriff?"

That was a rare peek into Uncle's mysterious past, before he schooled me on what a man could do with two look-alike racehorses and the switch. I couldn't pass it up. "Just where was that, Uncle?"

"Now, did I say?"

He hadn't changed one whit. Despite the night's unusual events, he was still on guard about his earlier life and I was sure I would never know. Maybe it was just as well. And no more was said about the dinero. Sheriff C.T. "Moccasin" Wiley had fired his last shot and missed.

We halted in front of the Nip and Tuck and I asked a late loafer where Al Oldham lived.

"Two blocks on. It's the house with the iron hitchin' post."

We found the house, but it was all dark; this hour was bedtime for most country and small-town folks. I hallooed the house for "Mr. Oldham," and presently a light winked and a figure in white opened the door. "What is it?"

"It's me, Dude McQuinn, remember? Here with my pardners in search of my stolen racehorse? We've captured the two masked holdup experts you told me about. They robbed me tonight."

"What!"

"That's right. Now, hold on to your nightcap, Mr. Oldham. Our prisoners are Sheriff Wiley and Cap Bruno."

The lamp he held jiggled till I feared he'd drop it on the porch. Like a wraith, he darted across the yard, long nightshirt on the fly. He held the lamp up and peered at the prisoners. "Wiley, by God! And you, Bruno!"

I was all set for Wiley's spiel and sure enough: "It's all a frame-up to discredit law and order in Mitchell County, Al. Me an' Bruno went out there on a false tip, Bruno along as a special deputy." And he launched into a windy outburst until Oldham cut him off. "That's enough, C.T. Save it for court. Next thing you'll be tellin' me about Red Wing, the noble Thoroughbred you rescued, and how you captured the Dodge City Kid. I want your story, McQuinn, and it had better hold water."

Step by step, I told Oldham what had happened from the time Lafe called me outside the Nip and Tuck until my money belt was taken and Billy and Coyote, at gunpoint, forced the masked pair back inside the house, followed by Wiley's attempt to bribe us.

"Lafe . . . Lafe? Years back there was a deputy by that name who worked for Wiley till he left the county on suspicion of horse theft."

"Well, he's makin' far-apart tracks now. Earned his fee and vamoosed."

Oldham lowered the lamp. "I've heard enough. I'll send my boy for the Citizens Committee and the chief of police. You're under arrest, C.T., you and Bruno."

"You can't do that. I'm the sheriff!"

"This is a citizen's arrest. You'll be held in the city jail. There'll be a preliminary hearing Monday morning before the justice of the peace. If he fails to bind you over for district court trial on the evidence I've heard here tonight, we'll run him out of town on a splintery rail. We'd have the hearing tomorrow, but it's Sunday. I reckon one of your local jackleg lawyers can get you out on bail tomorrow. . . . McQuinn, can we count on you and your friends to appear at the hearing first thing Monday morning? The J.P.'s office is right over the Nip and Tuck."

"You can, but don't know how long after that."

"I understand. Then after the preliminary, you and your friends will be expected to make depositions. That agreeable?"

"It is."

Within minutes, the other committeemen and the police chief took over, and as I and my pardners rode off for a bedtime toddy at the Nip and Tuck, I just had to call back to Wiley and Bruno that old see-you-later parting, *"Hasta la vista!"*

Well, at nine o'clock Monday morning we testified at the hearing before a bug-eyed crowd that lined the walls. Others, they said, filled the stairway and out to the street, and though Wiley and Bruno blustered and denied everything and Wiley called it a "political frame-up," the J.P. still held the pair over for trial. After that, we made depositions for use in district court.

Prob'ly Al Oldham had it figured about right. "As popular as Moccasin Wiley is, and as much bullshit as he's fed the public in three terms, we may get only a hung jury. But facts are facts and in view of the truth told here today, I believe Mitchell County people will have an honest sheriff next election. That's improvement. We thank you three for standing up."

"Dude," Billy says as we walked out, "I don't want any more of these lone-wolf sorties like the other night. Few more and you'll make an old man out of William Tecumseh Lockhart."

"Why, you and Coyote made it look easy, Uncle. If it hadn't been for you two . . . well. You pulled me out of another bog hole. You'll never get old."

"Unless you make me old, Dude McQuinn!"

We three hung around the Nip and Tuck, the object of many curious stares and questions, which we answered and which I figured cost Moccasin Wiley more than a handful of votes. A little after high noon, I went to the post office.

Before I could get up to the window and ask for my mail, the clerk shook a letter at me. "Here's one fresh off the train, Mr. McQuinn. Hope it's what you been waitin' for."

I recognized the bold handwriting at once. I thanked him and turned my back and opened the letter and felt myself turn all horns and rattles as I read:

McQuinn—

Go to the Big Spring post office for further instructions. You are being watched in Colorado City, so we know every move you make. We could gun you down any time we please. We warn you again, McQuinn, don't bring any officers or Rangers into this. Try it and your horse will be shot. Keep the $5,000 handy. We'll take it in due time.

My jaw quivered. I seethed. My anger ripped loose like a wagon sheet in a stiff wind. For a while I let it fly. Then, bit by bit, I beat it down and forced myself to think.

The letter was postmarked Midland, Texas, which is on the other side of Big Spring, from where the first letter was sent; so the thieves hadn't widened much distance between us despite our wait in Colorado City. By the same token, I couldn't say we'd gained any ground. And like before, they claimed they were having me watched. Now more further instructions. Why the delay? Why draw us from town to town? I would have handed over the $5,000 ransom in Colorado City for my horse. Why drag this out? There was more at work behind this than the theft of a once-in-a-lifetime runnin' horse, and I didn't have even a glimmer of what it might be.

Fear for the safety of my horse and the raw fury I felt toward the thieves gripped me again. I tore back for the Nip and Tuck and there on the boardwalk, shoulder hiked against a post, was the little mustached man with the sad eyes. Damned if it wasn't! He seemed to stare through me, into the street and beyond. I'd never seen cooler, steadier eyes. My impulse jumped to challenge him, to find out if he was bird-doggin' me for certain, but my hurry about the letter drove me on inside to my pardners. Other loafers eyeballed me as well. No wonder. I'd become a local curiosity, a man not only in search of his famous racehorse, but one of the three strangers who had testified against Moccasin Wiley and Cap Bruno and exposed them as the masked hold-up pair. The way I felt now, I could have done without all the attention.

After Billy and Coyote read the letter, we hit a high lope for Big Spring, about a day and half's hard travel on a good horse.

CHAPTER 8

ANOTHER DEAD END?

Slowed by the rough country southwest of Colorado City, which I hadn't figured on, we didn't reach Big Spring till late the second morning. Another county-seat town, so named for the fine spring that gushed out from under a huge mass of overhanging rock. We rode to the wagonyard, and after I'd bought feed the proprietor warmed to us, gave his name as Jim Dodd, and said we could pen our horses in the corral and sleep in the bunkhouse at two bits a head per night. There was also a cookstove in there we could use. We cottoned to that! So we unsaddled and watered and fed our horses, glad to have bunks instead of the ground, which, Billy pointed out, seems to get harder as a man gets older.

After breakfast, I legged it to the post office and wasn't surprised when the clerk said no mail for Dude McQuinn. Next train from the southwest was around ten o'clock the next morning, so the outfit was in for another day's wait, a delay that galled me. It was too early for a drink and my steps took me back to the wagonyard. I wanted action, I wanted help.

Now, a good wagonyard man has as keen an eye for horseflesh as any stable owner or cowman, because he sees a world of good horses pass by; he also has a good ear for idle rumor or what my father called the "moccasin telegraph," the grapevine system of information on the plains. Sometimes this was also referred to as a special line for cow thieves and horsethieves, bank robbers and train robbers.

Jim Dodd, a small, neat man whose smooth face was touched with a natural desire to oblige his fellow man, was a sympathetic listener as I laid out the whole story before him, detail by detail. Again, I didn't mention my instructions by mail. Just described my horse and said the outfit was on a search, and reminded Dodd of the thousand-dollar reward. You see, I was brought up not to tell all I know to a stranger, even a friendly one. If somebody let drop one little word about a letter and instructions, I'd have my man right there for certain, maybe the one campin' on our trail.

Dodd shook his head in regret. "They took the best you had, didn't they? Don't believe I've seen your horse. Believe I'd remember if I had. Judge Blair's reputation as a runner is well-known around here. I'd say he's even better known than Traveler. He became a marked horse when he beat Yolanda in Juárez. A man would be a fool to match him around Big Spring after you've passed the word here. As fast as he is, and even run under another name, questions would be asked. It would be a good idea if you put a notice in the paper. Would you happen to have a picture of Judge Blair with you?"

I groaned to myself again how oversights come back to haunt a man. "I don't and I should have. Judge Blair looks more like a quarter horse than a Thoroughbred. For certain he looks like a racehorse. More like a compact Thoroughbred. The imported Thoroughbred Janus, the great sire of quarter horses back in colonial times, was a compact horse. Stood about fifteen hands. Horsemen back then said the quarter horse had blinding speed, the Thoroughbred had bottom. Judge Blair has both. Time after time, he's run the quarter mile in twenty-one and change, and he can also go a distance of ground. When he beat Sir Roderick by a head at Lexington, he ran the mile in one thirty-four and four fifths."

My horse, my horse. There I was again. I had to talk about him a little. It was a kind of comfort.

Dodd whistled at the Judge's time for the mile. Then he seemed to reach far back into his memory. Once more he shook his head. "No, I haven't seen the horse." A dry grin wrinkled his face. "I might suspect one of our top county horsethieves, but the best ones have been gathered up and are now makin' little ones out of big ones at the Huntsville pen—that, or they've moved camp to healthier climes."

"Anybody around Big Spring have racehorses?"

"A lot of fast cow horses, but nobody that campaigns horses. Now and then some cowboys will match a race." He leveled me a close look. "I guess you wouldn't be here if you didn't have a lead?"

Did he know about the letter? Horsethieves come in more than one

color. Red, white, and brown, based on my experience. Big Spring could
be another relay station where Judge Blair was passed on, which I now
believed Colorado City was.

"I just figure they came this way with my horse," I says and to smoke
him out added, "I know they passed through Colorado City. Wouldn't
you figure they'd come through Big Spring? What do you think?"

He didn't bat an eye. "Could be. Meantime, you might check with
the sheriff."

"Right now I've had my fill of sheriffs. The Mitchell County sheriff
tried to rob me of the reward money."

"Not Moccasin Wiley!"

"None other. Him and Cap Bruno, who runs the Three Star Livery.
They're under arrest for a series of holdups."

He threw up his hands. A teamster drove up just then and our conversation was over. Did Jim Dodd know anything? I had my doubts,
and I'm not a bad judge of character.

From there I moseyed over to the weekly newspaper office and told
the editor my story. He said he would put it on the front page in a box.
To show my appreciation, I took out an ad that played up the reward
and where to notify me and the sheriff of Stonewall County. At the
sheriff's office a deputy told me the head man was out on a case. The
undersheriff listened to me, took down all the particulars, and said he
would tell the sheriff. He said it would be hard to trace a dark bay horse
unless he was matched in town.

I left there with the thought that none of this would do any good,
that I was just goin' in circles.

That afternoon, while Billy napped in the bunkhouse, I and Coyote
saddled up to scout out the town as we had Colorado City. We checked
the two livery barns and every alley and every street, knocked on doors
and asked questions, stopped to visit with folks and tell them our mission—and came away with nothing but sympathy. If Judge Blair was in
Big Spring, he was stabled in a house.

Riding back, we heard a calliope start up from the direction of the
fairgrounds. We headed that way, more out of boredom than curiosity
while we marked time for the thieves' next letter. A large banner hung
over the entrance to the midway. It read: ADAMS' BROS. SHOWS.

I looked at Coyote. "Same outfit that was at Aspermont."

We tied our horses to a fence and strolled in with the early crowd. In the distance, the Ferris wheel and the merry-go-round took on riders. It appeared the afternoon shows were just under way. Ahead of us a burst of twangy banjo music announced the medicine show. On a plank platform before a painted canvas curtain—which showed a waterfall and blue skies and across it in giant red letters, MIRACULOUS INDIAN SAGWA FROM THE SKY-BLUE WATERS OF THE KICKAPOO—stood the barker, and the man dubbed by Coyote "the white-man Kickapoo," and the black man on the banjo. A fourth member had been added to the show since Aspermont, a distinguished-lookin' gent in a black suit and high collar whose close-cropped black beard covered his face from ears to chin like moss.

The barker—derby, bow tie, checkered suit and pink shirt, a gold chain lapped over his melon-size paunch—lifted a hand for attention, his voice hoarse and solemn. "My friends . . . my purpose as I travel about this great country of ours . . . is to bring aid to suffering humanity . . . to relieve your many ailments. Call it noble, if you choose. Modesty forbids me to so label it. . . . I have not come here merely to try to sell you something, but only to make you feel better and once again be your robust selves." He raised his head higher. "You men standing back there. I can see from here that some of you have backaches, and pain in your neck and shoulders and legs. Well, help is close at hand!" He waggled a bottle of murky liquid at the crowd. "My friends . . . I hold here a bottle of Miraculous Kickapoo Indian Sagwa. Look at it! I won't say that it will cure only the common cold and rheumatism. No . . . because three tablespoons a day, taken before meals, will cure any disease known to suffering humanity—or your money back. I repeat—or your money back. Can you beat that? And what are its miraculous contents?" He lowered his voice and moved to the edge of the platform. "I'll tell you folks now. It contains—"

An outburst of banjo music broke in.

The barker wheeled around. "Alabama, you know better'n to interrupt the professor when he's about to reveal the true contents of Miraculous Kickapoo Indian Sagwa for the good of mankind. Now stop it."

More loud strumming.

"Alabama, I said stop it! Why do you persist? Your mammy brought you up better than that."

"I wants my Sagwa, 'Fessor."

"You can't have it now. Can't you see I'm busy?"

Again the music sounded, louder than before, a catchy rendition of "Dixie." I laughed with the crowd, and some of them shuffled in time to the music.

"Alabama, for the last time I said stop it!"

The black man kneeled and lifted both hands to his chin in prayer. "I wants my Sagwa, 'Fessor. Please, 'Fessor."

"Oh, all right, Alabama. But later—not now. . . . Once more, friends, as I was about to say, before I was so rudely interrupted. Here are the secret contents of Miraculous Kickapoo Indian Sagwa. . . . It contains compounds of the virtues of roots, herbs, barks, gums, and leaves . . . gathered on the pristine Kickapoo Indian Reservation back in Indian Territory by my trusted associate here of many years—Chief Sagwa himself . . . who wants to share this life-saving elixir with his white friends, eh, Chief?"

Chief Sagwa—feathered headdress, fringed buckskin shirt, and buckskin trousers with a beaded belt—unfolded his thick arms, the look on his dark face noble and stern. "Me like white friends. Me friendly, Chief Sagwa. My medicine heap good. Me share."

"Thank you, Chief Sagwa. The tests of Miraculous Kickapoo Indian Sagwa—conducted in the nation's finest medical laboratories—found it to be blood-making, blood-cleansing, and therefore life-extending. The—"

The banjo music struck again.

"Alabama, how dare you interrupt me again!"

"I wants my Sagwa, 'Fessor. I'se feelin' poorly."

"I warn you, that cussed banjo music is gettin' on my nerves."

"Then you needs some Sagwa, 'Fessor. You needs it bad."

We all laughed and Alabama grinned and the barker waved him off. "Be patient, Alabama. You'll get your Sagwa after my lecture is finished."

"But it'll all be gone."

"Chief Sagwa, can you save a bottle for our good friend Alabama?"

With great care, Chief Sagwa took a bottle from a box and presented it to the banjo player. "Me save one bottle for heap good friend Alabama."

"Alabama thanks you, Chief Sagwa. You is a friend indeed. I is saved."

The barker looked relieved. "As I was about to tell you, the sciences of medicine and chemistry have joined forces to produce a remedy to cure all diseases that arise from impure blood. . . . Friends, you don't have to take my word for it or even Chief Sagwa's, honest Indian that he is. . . . Miraculous Kickapoo Indian Sagwa has been endorsed by the nationally accredited gentleman on my left, Dr. Ebenezer Foote. . . . Dr. Foote is a graduate of the North American Medical College of Philadelphia and a longtime practicing physician there and in New York and Boston. . . . Now come to the salubrious Southwest for his health, after years of overwork in the slums of the humid East, he's found his Fountain of Youth in Miraculous Kickapoo Indian Sagwa . . . and as a member of man's noblest profession is assisting me in every possible way to bring it to you, my friends, for only a dollar a bottle . . . and you'll say it's the best dollar you ever spent. But because of the limited supply, only one bottle to a customer. . . . Who will be the first?"

The doctor nodded to all this, as solemn as a stone owl.

The professor held a bottle high and waited. The crowd held back. People looked at each other, maybe embarrassed to be the first. Then I noticed movement. A clean-faced young man—straw hat, overalls, and a white shirt—worked his way from the rear of the crowd up to the platform and spoke in a voice that sounded timid and uncertain. "Sir, will it cure dyspepsia?"

"If it does not, young sir—after you've taken the full bottle—your money will be cheerfully refunded."

"That's fair enough. I'll take one bottle, mister. It's for my dear old grandmother. Here's my dollar."

Bottle in hand, he disappeared in moments, like a wisp of smoke. A few seconds later I saw him hurry to a van and go inside. He was a shill. Almost fooled me.

After that, there was a general push to the platform as the crowd, among them some I took for cotton farmers, held up hard-earned dollars for the miraculous Sagwa.

From there we ambled on to watch the bear dance and his keeper crank the organ. The bear jangled his chain and seemed to keep the same gait from side to side, while the grinder played the same tune over and over. It struck me as hard work and boring. Out of sympathy for the two, we both pitched silver into the box.

Coyote shook his head while we moved on. "My people used to hunt bears mainly for their oil which the men used to oil guns and the women to oil their hair and prepare hides. The old Comanches would eat bear, but buffalo and deer much better, you bet. I never liked bear meat and eat it would not after tasting it once because the bear upright walks like a person. Just the thought of it sick makes me feel."

"There's no substitute for beef."

"There is one: the buffalo, all gone now."

He had me there.

We likewise felt pity for the lean, smelly lion, poor cuss, in the cage. He looked underfed and in need of flea powder or mange cure while he scratched himself and ignored us. An organ grinder would have helped. We drank red soda pop and ate beef *burritos* and played a dart game, but failed to win a prize. I had my eye on a Kewpie doll for Blossom. Coyote wanted a fancy belt buckle that looked like silver, but wasn't, I knew—too shiny. He swore the strong medicine of the fat white man who ran the game made the darts fly crooked, even when I tried to explain it was the way the darts were weighted that caused 'em to go every which way, so that a man couldn't hit a bull in the butt at two feet with the darts, the way they jumped around, let alone a little-bitty cardboard target the size of a postcard set fifteen feet away with the wind blowin' through the patched canvas walls. To win, you had to hit the bull's-eye.

The foghorn barker at the Hawaiian Parade got us next with the "for adults only" show. He winked as he said it. When I paid my dollar to see Princess Matilda, I wondered what Blossom would think and knew the answer mighty quick. Inside the tent, crowded with men and boys, a musician with long greasy hair played a guitar while another look-alike beat a drum and together they chanted and swayed as the heavyset hula girl danced. I couldn't see that her act inside was any different from the way she performed outside. And the closer I and Coyote got, the older and uglier she got, and she still wore the same grassy outfit, no less. But I have to say this: She sure could make the grass rustle.

After a run of this for some minutes, a man hollered, "When's the adult show gonna start?" And the barker he says right back, "This is it, friend. You are witnessing a rare spectacle, seldom performed in the Southwest, an authentic ethnic Polynesian hula. The musicians are chanting the story and Princess Matilda is doing it in pantomine."

"In what?"

"In pantomine. She's acting it out. Very authentic."

"Well, this may be authentic but it sure as hell ain't what you claimed it would be outside before we paid our money. I want my dollar back."

"This is authentic art, my friend."

"Art, hell. I want my money back!"

"Me, too," another voice yells. "This is a gyp. I want my money back." And another joined in, till there was a chorus of wants. Then, "We're gonna get it, too!"

That set 'em off. Everybody seemed to break at the same time. They rushed to get hold of the barker. I guess this had happened before as the carnival traveled around, because he jumped off the platform, mighty agile for a man with his tallow, and darted out a side door as quick as a cuttin' horse.

"Let's get outa here, Coyote!"

We eased back out the front way while the crowd gave chase. In past us charged a couple of carnival toughs with big clubs. "Break it up—break it up!"

"What do you think of them shuckin's, pardner?" I says after we had cleared out.

"Strange are the ways of the white man. Nothing wrong I saw with the woman's dance, as old and fat and ugly as she is. Why complain?"

"It wasn't exactly her dance, Coyote," I started to explain. "It was . . . that she kept too much grass on." I gave up. Comanches are modest people and Coyote was like a country boy at his first county fair.

We idled by the Ferris wheel and the merry-go-round and a game where you threw baseballs at a dummy, and one where you tossed wooden rings at a row of red pegs. We went on with wry grins. We'd been duped enough. Little by little, what had pecked at my mind since we'd come here took hold. "Coyote, this carnival was on the fairgrounds when Judge Blair was taken. Some worker might know something. Let's go over where the wagons and vans are. Besides, I'd like to see the draft horses." Out of desperation, I guess, I'd reached the point where I'd question anybody. Another long shot. The carnival had pulled out that evening or night or early morning like the horsemen, all except one Dude McQuinn, who had left his horse unguarded while he whooped it up. I would always blame myself and only myself.

We passed a freight wagon. Behind it a carnival worker was just in the act of takin' a nip from a darkish bottle. Embarrassed, he grinned and offered the bottle to us. "Have a snort of Sagwa. It kicks like a mule and is smoother than whiskey."

"Much obliged, but guess not." I had to have my little laugh as he stuck the bottle back inside the wagon. "Up in Kansas," I told him, "I've seen temperance workers march into a saloon and bust every whiskey bottle in the place, yet they'll sip patent-medicine cures the way a kid does soda pop, unaware the stuff's loaded with alcohol."

The first big draft team that caught my eye was a pair of Percherons that showed dappled coats and the usual great bone and clean legs. A man poured oats into feed boxes attached to the side of another freight wagon. When he'd finished, I gave my name and Coyote's and told him we'd come to Big Spring in search of our horse, stolen at Aspermont the last night of the fair, and how we'd seen the carnival there at the fairgrounds. Had he noticed anything unusual that evening or heard a ruckus at the barns?

He said his name was Will Reed. He was a spare man with tired gray eyes and iron-gray hair, bushy eyebrows and a slow, deliberate manner that told me he had a necessary quality needed around horses of all breeds: patience and more patience.

He frowned as I told him. "Sorry to hear that. I don't remember anything that night that was out of the ordinary. No ruckus, though as usual the last night some of the boys had their drinks."

"Thought maybe you noticed somebody that evening lead off a dark bay with a blazed face and four white socks? Maybe right by your wagon?"

"I keep my nose out of other folks' business. However, I do recall late that afternoon I saw horses being led from the barns."

"Horsemen takin' their runners home."

"I didn't pay much attention because my outfit was gettin' ready to pull out at first daylight."

"By the way, you did stop in Colorado City, didn't you?"

"Just stopped overnight. Our next fair date after Aspermont was here." He took an abrupt step away. "You boys will have to excuse me. I've got more chores to do."

But I wasn't finished. "These are fine draft horses you have here, Mr. Reed. Hope you've had good luck with 'em?"

He paused, a man who loved horses and understood them and was pleased to tell you about them. I could see that. "I'm one of two team-ster bosses. I've got twenty head of draft horses here, about half part Percherons and part Clydesdales, and half purebreds of each breed. People ask me, 'Why don't you use mules?' I like mules and I've worked mules, and if I had a stagecoach line, I'd use mules. They're tough and they can take the heat better than a horse and they're faster. But my father had draft horses back on the farm in Nebraska, so I grew up with 'em. I enjoy these big horses. You can't beat 'em for pure power and easy handling. All heavy breeds are temperate horses, whereas a mule sometimes will work for you ten years for the one chance to kick you into the hereafter. . . . The Percheron is long-lived and a willing worker and requires less feed than any other breed to keep him in good condition. He runs to gray or black, with a minimum of white in his color. A gray will be gray-white by the time he's ten. They're all honest workers, believe me. They'd pull down a mountain if I asked 'em to. Only I can't say the pay is equal to the work we put out." He squeezed his lips together, and I had the insight he felt he'd said too much. "When this season is over, I'll take my friends back to Nebraska where we belong." He hesitated again, as though he'd vented his feelings too much.

A breathless boy ran up. "Mr. Reed, Big John's sick again."

Reed groaned. "Wish I knew what was wrong with that horse. You men excuse me. I'd better go see about him."

"We'll go with you."

We followed him and the boy to the second row of wagons and a handsome, powerful gray gelding that, to my eye, stood at least sixteen hands and weighed a ton.

Reed patted the gray's muscular neck and stepped back to study him. "Big John's off his feed and I don't like the way he stands. I've treated him for colic, but that's not what ails him. He can't work and I won't leave him here if he can't travel day after tomorrow, when we're sched-uled to pull out for Midland. He's the best young horse I have. Mr. Gus will raise Old Ned if there's a delay."

I was curious. "Who's Mr. Gus?"

"He manages the shows for the Adams Brothers out of Kansas City. Is a stickler for schedules. I'll go along with that as long as there's equal consideration for the stock and reasonable time is allowed between towns. Big John is a purebred Percheron worth a thousand dollars sight unseen. I refuse to work a sick horse and damned if I'll leave him behind to pick up later. He'd die. I've never had a horse before with this ailment, whatever it is."

The eager boy spoke up. "Mr. Reed, maybe you could put Big John in a van and give him a ride to Midland? He'd like that."

The boy got a pat on the head. "I might have to think about that if I can't get him back on his feed." Reed turned to us. "Jimmy wants to be a circus acrobat. Meanwhile, he's learned how to curry and brush and feed draft horses and not to get his toes stepped on, which is the main danger around gentle stock like this. As it is, we've got a minimum of wagons and vans to move the shows, and Mr. Gus might not like it if we had to pile gear on top of a vehicle to make room for a mere horse." He cut himself off all at once, an unhappy man for more reasons than a sick horse.

"Is there a vet in town?"

"There is, but I was told he's out at a ranch where there's a sick stud. Was this morning, when I tried to get hold of him."

"Our pardner is a top vet. I know he'll be glad to help if he can. We're camped at the wagonyard."

"Would you go get him?" Reed was actually pleading. "I'd sure appreciate it and I'll pay him well."

"I'll go." Coyote took off.

While we waited and watched Big John, helpless to aid him, I swung back to the purpose that was never far from my mind. "Mr. Reed, I'll be very much obliged to you if you'll pass the word around about my horse. Maybe one of the carnival hands saw or heard something that night that might help. I figure my horse was taken that night when the outfit was at a banquet. You see, he'd won a big match race that day. Everybody at the fair knew my outfit would be at the banquet because all of us would be honored. What better time to take him, than while the banquet was goin' on?"

Reed just shook his head.

"There's a thousand-dollar reward for the safe return of my horse. I don't mean a promissory note. I mean cash in hand, paid on the spot."

He seemed to listen without any change of expression or much interest.

"We'll be here till late tomorrow morning, maybe longer. Depends on what might turn up."

And then, on instinct, I guess, because I liked the man and how he treated his horses, I let go and told him about the $5,000 ransom demand and the letters, and how the thieves had threatened to shoot Judge Blair if I brought any officers into the case. How although I hadn't called in Rangers, I had asked for sheriff help without any results.

He faced about, a quick move that surprised me, anger hard across his eyes, more than a vague listener now. "The sons of bitches! And they just lead you from town to town. If they want the ransom—if that's all they want—why don't they give up the horse? Why didn't they back in Colorado City? Why not here, if that's what they want?"

"That's what I'm wondering. I don't know any more than I did back in Aspermont. No letter this morning. Maybe tomorrow."

"This is strange, McQuinn. I never heard of a horse being held for ransom before. Strikes me, their idea is to string you along to make you suffer more and more, just to draw you on. It's more than horse theft." He made an abrupt gesture. "It's . . . I'd like to help if I could. I'll tell the crew about the reward money." He lifted his right hand to his chin in an unfinished motion, and, suddenly, picked up a brush, and with short brisk strokes he cleaned Big John's back while we waited for Billy to come.

CHAPTER 9

SOUNDS IN THE NIGHT

Not many minutes had gone by when Billy and Coyote rounded the
wagon at a fast walk. Billy carried a little black bag which I'd never
noticed before. I stared at it.

"Didn't think I'd leave all my medicine chest behind, did you?"

"Uncle, this is Mr. Will Reed, who owns the sick horse, and this is
Dr. William Tecumseh Lockhart, our pardner." They shook hands.
Reed fairly pumped Billy's. "This is the patient, Doctor . . . Big
John."

Billy was all business. He put down the black bag and slowly, step by
step, his eyes intent, circled Big John. "Mr. Reed, I've never seen a finer
individual representative of the Percheron breed, but I can see that he's
a sick horse. Has he refused his feed?"

"He has for two days. Just stands at his feed box. Generally, he
cleans up every grain. Always been a good keeper."

Billy drew out his turnip-shaped pocket watch, placed his right hand
beneath Big John's throat, and checked the horse's pulse. That done, he
put the watch back and looked at Reed. "The pulse in a healthy horse
beats from thirty-six to forty times a minute, a bit more or less, but not
much, and any wide variation from this indicates unusual excitement or
disease or suffering of some kind. Big John's pulse, I regret to report, is
close to seventy-five per minute. He also has a fever. I can feel it with
my hands and I can see it in his watery eyes, which are inflamed. You
say he refuses his feed. There is one rule that never varies: Never drive
or work a horse that declines his feed. This brings us to another approach." Billy continued to eyeball the horse. "Does Big John lie down
carefully and roll, Mr. Reed? I mean as if he hurts and is extremely
sore?"

"Not like that. However, he likes to roll after a hard day's work."

"That is natural. So we can rule out colic." He moved to the patient's head and peered into the nostrils. "The natural color of the inside of the nose is a light pink. Big John's is red." Next, Billy felt of the ears. "His ears are cold, Mr. Reed. How are his bowels and kidneys acting?"

Reed scratched his chin. "Well . . ."

"Would you say the excretions are scanty?"

"Yes, very much."

Billy fell silent, in deep thought, which I took as a bad sign. He circled Big John again. "Mr. Reed, I regret to tell you that this fine representative of his breed has distemper. Some Kentucky vets would call it influenza."

Reed looked shocked. He clamped a hand to his forehead.

"But maybe you've called me in time. There's a chance we can save him if we act fast. And you should keep him isolated. This can be contagious."

Reed was stricken. He paled. "What caused it? I take good care of my horses."

"I know you do. Maybe he got too hot and wasn't cooled down properly. Hard to do when a man has many teams to look after as I can see you have here. And horses will get sick. Don't blame yourself."

Billy opened the black bag and took out two bottles and held each to the sky to measure the contents with his eyes. Satisfied, he stuck a small funnel into the neck of a quart whiskey bottle that had once held Old Green River, Billy's favorite Bourbon, and poured a trickle of powder from both bottles. "Now, bring me a dipper of water, Mr. Reed."

Reed dashed behind the wagon and returned with a dripping dipper, which Billy took and poured into the whiskey bottle and shook it fast. "Now, friend Reed, take a light rope or leather rein and fasten it to this fine fella's upper jaw and gently pull his head back a little. The lower jaw must remain free to move so he can swallow. There—that's good. . . . Don't force him too much. Aw . . . that's just right."

In seconds, Billy poured the contents of the bottle down Big John's throat, clamped the lower jaw tight against the upper, and stroked the gray's throat as he swallowed. "Good—that's good." He drew a memorandum book and scribbled fast and tore out a sheet. "Dude, dash to the drugstore and get this prescription filled. In case the pharmacist can't read good penmanship, I want one ounce of powdered gentian, one ounce of powdered copperas, three ounces of Peruvian bark, three ounces of hops, and two ounces of carbolic acid and an eye dropper. . . . While Dude's gone, Mr. Reed, let's double-blanket Big John and bandage his legs. He must be kept warm."

I left on the run. I found the drugstore and a short time later galloped back, tied my horse, and ran to the wagons.

"Very well, Dude. Sometimes you Alamo Texans do more than talk about your heritage and the Great Rebellion." The old codger had to get that in when he knew the true name was the War Between the States. Bless him. "Now, Mr. Reed, I need two thirds of a bucket of boiling water."

That took some time. Reed had to build a fire. When the boiling water was ready, Billy, count by count, dropped in thirty-three drops of carbolic acid—no more, no less—and three ounces of hops. "Now, friend Reed, put this bucket on a stool or bench and stand Big John over it so he will inhale the vapors. Do this for twenty minutes. Repeat it again this evening, after you've given him a dose of what I'm mixing from the drugstore. I'll write out the amount of the dosage for you and how much water to give with it. All you have to do for the vapors is reheat the water. . . . That will do for today. I'll be back in the morning to check on this fine young gentleman." Billy made ready to leave.

"What do I owe you, Doctor? Can't tell you how much I appreciate this."

"Not one penny, Mr. Reed. Just take good care of your horse. Tomorrow we'll see a change for better or worse. This is all we can do now. There's a chance, just a chance, that we've caught this in time."

"I'd like to offer you a drink, Doctor, if that's all right?"

"Friend Reed, you speak the language of my tribe!"

After supper that evening, Billy sat up late by lantern light in the bunkhouse, spectacles on the tip of his nose, bent over a worn book taken from his saddlebag. At times he would jot down a word or two in his memorandum book. At other times he would scowl and shake his head, like he didn't agree with the book—which I figured, though he never let on, was a horse-doctor book like the ones he called "tomes" back in his medicine chest that we used to haul around in the rear of the wagon when we campaigned the Judge against the field.

Next morning early, Billy hotfooted it over to the drugstore and was gone a long time. Back, he mixed up some powders in a fruit jar and poured that into the empty Old Green River bottle and added half a pint of whiskey, never once saying a word to his pardners about what it all was, while we hung around him and gawked and wondered. That was Billy, always mysterious. I knew if I asked him I'd get, "Now, did I say?"

Around nine o'clock we all rode out to the carnival grounds and the sick horse. Reed was waiting. He wore a worried look and Billy says, "I guess he's no better this morning?"

"Still refuses his feed."

"Uh-huh. I kind of figured he would." Billy took Big John's pulse and examined him as he had the day before. "I can't see any change, but neither is he any worse. We'll do something drastic, take the bull by the horns, as the old saying goes. We're gonna give him a big dose of Epsom salts in warm water that would clean out a canal. Warm up half a gallon, Mr. Reed, and we'll get about this."

When the water was ready, Billy filled a quart fruit jar and mixed in the salts, which foamed, and while Reed held the gray's mouth open, Billy poured in the salts. Big John shook his head. "One more quart," Billy told Reed, and when that was done and some time had passed Billy says, "I have prepared some different medicine, an oldtime potion that book doctors would never give, but that's proved effective time and again in the field, where they separate the doers from the theorists, who wouldn't know bone spavin from the blind staggers." He held up the Green River bottle. "Now, Mr. Reed, if you smell whiskey, don't be alarmed."

"Whiskey, Doctor?"

"Yes, whiskey, but that's not all. The dosage contains other ingredients which I'll not enumerate. The whiskey makes it taste better and act faster on the suffering patient."

"Well, I'll be doggone."

"You might say we are administering horse-sense medicine to a sick horse. I can't tell you why this particular remedy works. All I can tell you is that it does in some bad cases. Not all. It's still a long shot. All right, boys, let's give him his medicine. Dude, you and Coyote stand on each side of Big John to steady him if needed."

Big John rattled his halter at first as Billy poured the whiskey-laced stuff down him, but the patient took it all, hardly a drop wasted.

Reed laughed. "He kinda snorted on that, Doctor."

"Anybody will snort and shake his head the first time he tastes whiskey, good or bad. We'll start the vapor treatment in a little while. I want him to sweat."

I hung around and listened to Billy and Reed talk horses. Uncle was in a mood to lecture, which told me he felt good and his joints didn't hurt, and when the two made a trip to the jug in the wagon, like old cronies, I looked at my watch and found it was time to go.

It was after ten o'clock when I rode up to the post office and tied my horse. The line was long. By the time I reached the window several possibilities tumbled through my thoughts. In the letter the thieves would instruct me to bring the money to a certain place on a lonely road or trail. Or I'd be told to leave the money somewhere and get my horse later, a condition I'd never agree to. I'd have to see my horse. No horse, no money. Or I'd be instructed to go on to another town. And, despite my promise to Blossom, I'd burn powder if the chance came.

"A general delivery letter for Dude McQuinn?"

The clerk shuffled through the stack twice. "Sorry."

I hadn't expected that. Seemed the idea was to let me dangle some more. Will Reed's indignant words jumped to my mind: "If they want the ransom, why don't they give up the horse? They're stringin' you along."

And if a man was campin' on my trail, why was a letter needed at all? Why couldn't he handle the exchange? And if my horse wasn't in or around Big Spring, where did we go from here? Not a thing made sense. At this late time, by no logic could I see that money was the main motive. Yet beyond the money, what was there?

Frustrated and bitter all over again, I talked the clerk out of a sheet of paper and bought a stamped envelope and reined in my scattered thoughts to pen a long overdue letter home:

Dear Blossom,

I got a letter back in Colorado City that told me to come to Big Spring for further instructions, so here we are. Been here two days and still no word from the thieves. Will have to wait. We have no choice. But they'll have to keep in touch with us if they want to get the money. Works both ways.

We are all fine. Billy is doctoring a sick draft horse for a teamster at the carnival, the same carnival that was at Aspermont the night Judge Blair was taken. I talked to the teamster, but he couldn't shed any light on what happened that night. Hope all is well at the ranch. Remember that Texas Jack likes bran mashes. He's spoiled, and I did it on purpose. Don't worry about us. Everything will turn out all right. Will just take some time. I miss you.

Love, Dude

Why tell her about the Moccasin Wiley episode and bein' rescued by my pardners? Why tell her that, in all honesty, I was afraid I'd never see my horse again? Why tell her we were at the mercy and whim of cruel persons whose motive and identities I hadn't the slightest knowledge or suspicion of? Why tell her when she'd only worry?

Thus, I was in a low and prickly mood when I left the post office and went out to my horse. As I started to untie the reins, I happened to glance across the street. My eyes took in a sight that raised my fur even more. Again, it was the little mustached hombre in the white hat, with the melancholy eyes. Enough, by God! This had to stop! Like a dumbjohn, I'd left my six-shooter in my pack at the bunkhouse. But no matter, the time had come!

The sound of hooves and the rattle of a wagon warned me in time to avoid bein' run over. The farmer at the reins threw me a startled and disgusted look, like "Cowboy, don't you come to town very often?" I stepped back to let him pass.

I thought I detected a glint of amusement behind the little man's dark eyes, which rubbed me still more. I made fast tracks for him. The humor faded from his face all at once when I grabbed him by his shirt-front, every bit of my pent-up wrath and frustration of these past days in my grip and in my voice.

"Who the hell are you? What do you want? What's goin' on?"

I expected him to cuss and struggle. Instead, as calm as could be, he says "Young man, I can't answer your questions very well unless you let go of me."

I didn't know why, but I let him go and I felt my anger drop away as well. Maybe it was his matter-of-fact voice.

He pulled his shirt-front down. "Who I am does not matter. It just happens that now and then I am where you happen to be. I get mail at

the post office same as you and others, and like you, maybe, I am
expecting a letter."

"I saw you first at the Nip and Tuck in Colorado City."

"True. Your name is Dude McQuinn. I heard your story as you told
it to the crowd. Your racehorse was stolen. You and your friends are
searching for it. You've offered a thousand-dollar reward."

"So . . . and who are you, mister?"

"That is of no consequence."

"It is to me. The people who stole my horse tell me I'm bein'
watched. You could be the bird dog, because about every time I look
around, there you are eyeballin' me."

"Young man, these are small towns with not many people. Everybody is quite visible." That little hint of amusement surfaced. "If I
camped on your trail, would I be so conspicuous? Would you, if you
followed somebody?" With a nod, he swung away.

Guess he had a point. If he was a manhunter after me, he was too
conspicuous. A smooth way to put it. But he wasn't a manhunter. He
was merely an observer, a watcher to report what Dude McQuinn did.
So I figured. Whatever he was, my suspicions of him refused to die.

I watched him move past his bald-faced bay and enter a store. He had
on a light brown shirt today. Last time he wore a blue one; gray before
that. He sure had a batch of shirts.

I crossed over to his horse, a well-set-up gelding, a rangy saddler.
Nice head. Wide-set eyes, short ears, the good short back, long muscles,
sloping croup, good bone, heavy shoulders, deep heartgirth, with a long
underline and a good slope to his shoulders. I wondered about his
breeding.

I also noted blankets, saddlebags, canteen, grub sack, and a yellow
slicker tied behind the cantle. Mister No-Name was equipped for the
trail, just like us, travelin' light. If he wasn't campin' on our trail, whose
was he on?

I moved on. Now the outfit faced another day's delay. Wait, wait,
wait. How many days had it been since we'd left the ranch? Seven,
eight? I'd lost track. Time seemed frozen. And nothing had been
gained.

With plenty of daylight to burn, I legged it to the weekly newspaper
office again and ordered a dozen posters about my horse. The editor
said he could have the posters ready by early afternoon, and he'd put

the reward notice in extra big black type to catch the eye. His paper was about to go to press with the story he'd promised to run in a box on page one. Would I like to read a galley proof of the story? Would I! The story read mighty nice. Had all the important details. I offered to pay for it, but he grinned and said he didn't charge for news stories. That the story about Judge Blair was the only "hot" news in this issue. Rest of it was mainly who had visited Aunt Abigail and who was on the sick list, and births and a few obituaries of folks who left "a host of friends"; and some stock news, such as the price of steers, which was still low on the Fort Worth Market.

All this made me feel better. I tailed back up the street and had a surprise. The bald-faced horse was gone. I pondered on that. Had I scared him off?

Later, when the posters were printed, I went about town and asked permission to place one in the front windows of the grocery stores, feed stores, saloons, and saddle shops. Everybody obliged, you bet. I had a drink at each saloon, even bought a few rounds, visited with the bartenders and patrons, and yet when the afternoon was over all I had collected was useless palaver.

Billy rode up to the wagonyard just as I did. "How's Big John?"

"I gave him another dose of that oldtime potion and Reed kept him on the vapors most of the afternoon."

"Did the salts work?"

"Like Grant took Richmond."

"Uncle, you know it took Grant a long time to take Richmond."

"Dang it, you know what I mean."

"Well, is he any better?"

"We'll know for sure in the morning. If he's not over the hump by then, Will Reed could lose a fine young Percheron. Any mail?"

"Nope."

Coyote came to the door of the bunkhouse, all grins and pleased with himself. "Grandfather Billy and Dude, I tonight am fixing supper."

"Still can't break you of that grandfather tag, can I?"

Coyote ignored him. "Grandfather, fried bread it will be soon and beans, which all afternoon on the stove have been, for you and white father. Also special treat fixed you I have. It is on the stove."

He waited for us to show our appreciation, for Billy handled most of the cookin'—in self-defense, as he claimed.

"That sounds good, Coyote," I says, but puzzled about the treat.

Billy was suspicious. "That special treat wouldn't be dog meat, would it?"

"To meat market of white mans I have been, Grandfather. Comanches eat dogs do not. Dog is coyote's cousin and coyote is taboo, trickster of the prairie, a demi-god."

"If it's not dog, what is it?"

Coyote grinned like a prankish boy. He could be mysterious, too.

I smelled something strong the instant I entered the bunkhouse, as Coyote stepped to the stove and stirred the contents of a boiling pot with a long fork. He dipped in and came up with a light-colored mass, holding it like a rare prize.

Billy halted in his tracks, hand to nose. "Tripe. It stinks—" Then he caught himself. "But tastes good, if you like tripe."

We didn't want to hurt Coyote's feelings and we said no more. After supper, while Billy studied his horse-doctor book and Coyote read Shakespeare, that English poetry fella, and I fought down the belches from my pardner's "treat," I sat in silence and brooded.

After a while, Billy looked up from his book. "I know what's in your craw. We're no closer to gettin' the Judge back than when we started. It's hard to be patient."

"I've tried to think of all the crooks we ran against that could be capable of stealin' the Judge. Somebody we beat back there and won big money off of with odds. Maybe this is a get-even move, some horseman's revenge?"

"Who, for instance?"

"Take the Honorable Gideon Lightfoot, as he called himself, the crooked banker. Why, he even passed counterfeit bills on us, or tried to, but you caught him at it when he finally paid off. But he didn't pay till we cornered him in his bank. We had to thank the widow Wheeler for breakin' him down, when she said she knew about the two sets of books he kept and would tell the bank examiner if he didn't pay up, her bet included. My, how it pained the old scoundrel. He just couldn't take it when the Judge daylighted his fancy Thoroughbred, Old Dominion. As loaded as Lightfoot is, he could hire a whole gang of slick thieves to steal the Judge."

"Except for one thing, Dude. The Honorable G.L., as we called him, is in the Kansas state pen for embezzlement of bank funds. I read that in the Kansas City *Star* some months ago. Forgot to tell you, we've been so busy. You remember, the widow Wheeler's late husband was part owner of the bank? But when he died, she was left with a pittance. Lightfoot claimed bad loans were responsible. Instead, he had helped himself to his partner's share. I guess the widow finally got all the goods on him and spilled the beans to the examiner."

"Glad to hear it. Couldn't happen to a more deserving swindler. The widow took a shine to you, I remember."

"Er . . . ah . . . all widows are lonely."

"And you stayed late at her house one night and Amos had to bring you home in the buggy, and you did a lightnin' fast fadeout right after the payoff when she was lookin' for *her Billy.*" I made a little face as I said the last.

Billy's face turned a trifle red. "A widow woman can throw a big loop when a poor devil's got a few bucks in his jeans. Just a passin' fancy on her part till a new man comes to town." He shrugged it off, but his face was still red.

I couldn't keep my old pardner on the hook any longer, so I changed the subject to another crook. "Shag Fallon could have a strong motive. I never saw a man so mad when the Judge measured Fallon's Hondo, which had won thirty-three straight. Remember how Fallon conditioned his horse before a race? Worked him over with a chain. He didn't give a damn about Hondo and Hondo was a heck of a horse. So, in a race, all Fallon's jockey had to do was rattle that chain a little and Hondo turned into Flying Hondo, except he couldn't quite take the Judge. Fallon lost a gunnysack full of money that day. He's an outlaw type, if I ever saw one. He could be the one behind this."

"Except for one fact, Dude."

"What do you mean?"

"Fallon got a permanent case of lead poisoning right after a race when he wouldn't pay off. Happened in Weatherford. Tried to claim his horse was fixed, when if ever a crook tried to fix the other man's horse it was Shag Fallon. An old friend of mine from Lone Tree, Texas—Fallon owned the town, remember?—happened to drop by the ranch and told me. The town actually celebrated the event. He was a no-good s.o.b. and cruel to his horse. I'd liked to have had Hondo. Believe he could have made a distance horse. Half Thoroughbred. Rangy. Stood sixteen hands, weighed around fourteen hundred pounds. A big dapple gray. A balanced horse. A little over in the knee, but he could run. As we know, it took a champion to beat him."

I had to admire his memory. "You never forget, do you? I mean the points of a horse? Well, I remember another vulture that could have hired it done. On the outside a sweet ol' Southern gentleman, all manners, and every other word a *sir.* On the inside, he'd cheat a widow woman out of her egg money at the country store on Saturday."

"I take it you mean Colonel C. Travis Bushrod?"

"The self-promoted Colonel C. Travis Bushrod, who was only a forager with General Hood's army in the War Between the States, and had this fast stud called Night Owl. Remember, Bushrod's sister pretended her buggy horse was runnin' away? When Coyote left the Judge and ran out to help and stopped the horse, somebody slipped in and stuck sponges up the Judge's nostrils so he couldn't get his wind. You caught the fix just minutes before the race. Anybody that slick could hire a passel of high-class horsethieves."

"Except the self-made colonel couldn't have hired it done. Not if my information is correct and I believe it is."

"Why not? He had the money and was as sinister as Lightfoot."

"A neighbor of mine sold some two-year-old quarter horses down there in East Texas not long ago to a sleazy bird named Cassius Pyle. Wasn't he Bushrod's son-in-law and they worked together?"

"He was."

"Then it ties in. After the deal was made, Pyle said something about his father-in-law being too feeble to advise him anymore. So . . . there goes your theory."

"Unless Pyle hired the thieves? Consider that."

"As I remember him, he wasn't smart enough. All blowhard with a rich father-in-law, who was the brains of the two."

"Let's not overlook Kate Taggart, the bandit queen of the Cherokee Hills. Was she purty and connivin' and did she have a temper! But could she set a table! I'll never forget: four kinds of pie for dessert. She was a walkin' picture, Uncle. I remember you called her *my Katy girl,* and she called you *my Billy boy.* Guess you'd known her before? Maybe you'd been sweethearts before she married Big Jim and had all them mean, ignorant boys? Can't forget their names—Monte, Tooter, and Lucky." I shook my head at the memory.

"Now, did I say?" Billy had donned his saintly expression.

"I remember the night before the race you painted Texas Jack to look like the Judge and the Judge to look like Texas Jack. You put Texas Jack on picket and that night somebody stole him. We ran the race and the Judge beat Jackpot by a head and we won three thousand dollars. Kate raged at the judges; couldn't understand how her horse got beat. Just then somebody ran up and said the bank'd been robbed by a masked man on a blaze-faced horse with four white feet. Everybody tore out to help. But the bank president had already caught the bank robber—her son, Monte—on the slow Texas Jack."

"True, Dude, I did know Kate back before she got hitched to the late Jim Taggart. She and Big Jim framed an old pardner of mine, stole his horse and rode it in a bank robbery that was blamed on my pardner. I figured she might repeat the pattern. Since she knew about the switch, I painted and switched horses and her boys stole the wrong horse. Katy lost both ways, but she couldn't have had anything to do with stealing Judge Blair."

"Huh? That woman would crawl through hell to get even. She's mean."

"Agreed. But she couldn't have masterminded the Judge's theft because she's still in the Arkansas state pen. Probably runs it."

"How do you know that?"

"She wrote me a letter. Traced me down somehow. Said she was circulating a petition to get herself paroled for good behavior. Would I please write the governor as a character witness of many years and, for old times' sake, sign the petition?"

"Well, did you?"

"Did I, after what she did to my old pardner, who is still behind bars! Oh, I wrote the governor, all right. I told him what she'd done and that I'd sign Kate's petition for a parole in about fifteen years. No sooner."

"She'll come a-gunnin' for you with them mean boys if she ever gets out. What was it the poet fella said about a woman's fury?"

"I believe it was," Coyote says politely, " 'Heaven has no rage like love to hatred turned, nor hell a fury like a woman scorned.' By Mr. William Congreve. Maybe more than one wife he had."

"I was just about to say that, Coyote. Thanks."

Billy only yawned. "In fifteen years remind me to be on guard."

Next morning, just after breakfast, I heard a horse on the run and glanced out the doorway. It was Will Reed, ridin' like a deputy sheriff. He waved and hollered, "You boys come out. I've got news for you." We hurried out. "Big John has passed the crisis. Stepped right up to his feedbox this morning and cleaned up every grain of his breakfast. He's his old self. Kicked up his heels. Maybe still a little weak, but I believe he's over the hump. So your oldtime potion worked, Doctor. It and the vapors—everything. I can't thank you enough and I intend to pay you for your savvy right here and now." He reached toward his pocket.

"Oh, no, friend Reed." Billy protested with both hands. "You don't owe me one red penny. The good news about Big John is payment enough, as fine an individual as he is. Sometimes you win one, sometimes you lose. Just like a country horserace. But cautions, Mr. Reed. Don't work him for several days at least—say four—and give him light hay and warm bran mashes for two days, go easy on the grain, and keep him blanketed at night. It will be all right to let him trail behind on a halter. However, maybe I'd better look at him one more time."

We saddled up and rode out, Billy with his little black bag. After he had examined Big John, he sent Coyote to town with a prescription for what he called "a follow-up potion." Always watchful of a sick horse on the mend, he said he would lead Big John around to see how he tracked and acted.

While Billy was doing that, Reed drew me aside. His voice was hesitant. "McQuinn, you fellows have gone out of your way to help me, and the least I can do, besides thanking you, is try to return the favor." He looked all about before he continued. "Like I told you, I don't stick my nose into other folks' business. This time I'm going to. . . . I did hear a commotion on the carnival grounds the night your horse was stolen."

I jerked and my blood pounded. It was like a cry for help answered. "About what time?"

"About eight o'clock."

"That was the time of the banquet. What did it sound like?"

"Voices. Some cussin'. There was a clatter. Then everything got quiet again. I didn't hear it again."

"Was it around the wagons or over by the barns?"

"It was over by Mr. Gus's vans. He has several."

My hopes began to ebb. "Was that unusual? I know it's noisy around a carnival with the stock you have and when you're fixin' to break camp."

"We'd already made most preparations. Taken down the shows and loaded up. That's why I was surprised when Mr. Gus sent Sagwa around to tell us to leave before daylight, at around four o'clock. Everybody grumbled. That meant we had to start our day at three o'clock. Feed and water the stock, rustle our breakfast, then harness and hook up."

Some of Coyote's contempt barged into my voice. "What time did this Chief Sagwa come around?"

"I'd say it was a little after eight-thirty."

"So of a sudden everything got in a big hurry?"

Reed seemed to hedge a little. "Now, McQuinn, I'm not saying that anything was wrong. The only thing that struck me as unusual was to pull out an hour earlier and before daylight. But I did hear a commotion. What caused it, I can't say."

"Did Sagwa say why the pull-out time was changed?"

"He didn't explain anything. Never does. Just said that was Mr. Gus's order. You don't question Mr. Gus's orders. You can take 'em or quit. Sagwa is his assistant. His troubleshooter and muscle man. If there's any trouble with the hands, he settles it. Was a professional wrestler back East and a circus strong man. He's busted some heads around here."

"Two toughs came on the run when the hula show broke up."

"They work under him."

"Believe I need to have a little visit with Mr. Gus. I won't say where I got the notion."

"Do as you like. I can always take my horses and go home, which I plan to do anyway before long."

"I won't say anything. Where's Mr. Gus's office?"

"The second van. If you have any trouble, watch out for Sagwa. He'll be close by."

The second van had steps and an overhang sign that read: OFFICE. I went in without knocking. I saw a low counter and behind it a desk and behind that a jowly, bald-headed man in a many-colored shirt whose rolls of flesh appeared about to flow over the desk. His pale eyes, like cue balls, sized me up from a mound of pale dough. Rings sparkled on both doughy hands. He took a sip from a bottle of beer, put it down, and nibbled a pretzel from a bowl. That was when I noticed the bell on the desk. He said no word, but the cue-ball eyes were sharp. What did I want? Why was I here? I had the impression that mostly trouble came through the door.

I told him my name and that I was on a search for a stolen racehorse; that maybe he could help me, since the carnival had been on the Aspermont fairgrounds that night.

"How could I help *you?*" He sounded more wheeze than voice. He stirred as he spoke and his dough rolled.

"I understand there was quite a commotion around the vans that Saturday night about eight o'clock."

"Who told you that?"

I got the message. I could see Sagwa or his toughs workin' over slim Will Reed. "I've asked around. Several people told me they heard it."

"This place is noisy at all hours, day or night."

"This was a particular kind of commotion and eight o'clock was the time of the banquet."

"What banquet?"

"The Fair Awards banquet. I was there. My horse was left unguarded. That's when it happened."

"What the hell would the commotion have to do with your horse?" he wheezed. He inched his hand toward the bell, then drew it back.

Some instinct guided me. The words spilled out of my mouth almost before I realized what I'd said. "That maybe my horse made that commotion—that clatter—that maybe he balked."

He didn't answer. He grabbed the bell and shook it and as it rang Chief Sagwa bulged suddenly through a side door. Minus his chief's getup, he wore a workin' man's trousers and a loud shirt that matched Mr. Gus's. The shirt, half open, exposed a vast sweep of chest as hairy as a gorilla's. His rolled-up sleeves showed arms like a blacksmith's.

"Trouble, Mr. Gus?"

I had expected Sagwa's voice to boom; instead, it came out squeezed and high-pitched.

"Throw this man out. He's come to cause trouble."

Now, I'm not a great big man. But I've lived an outdoor life and I've dug a helluva lot of post holes on rocky ground, and I've wrestled steers, and I've baled a lot of hay. I wasn't about to get tossed out, because I already knew the truth. At least the start of it, I thought.

Sagwa moved around the corner of the counter, an eager relish in his droopy brown eyes, his thick arms out in a wrestler's clutch. I didn't give ground. Our bodies banged together like two bulls in a pasture. I bounced back. I threw a punch to Sagwa's ribs and it was the same as if I'd hit a side of beef. He just laughed and picked me up and tossed me toward the door like a sack of feed.

I landed on my side, my wind half gone. But when he charged me, those muscled arms out, I rolled over on my back and kicked him in the belly with both boots. He let out a yell and fell back, and I thought maybe I'd found his soft spot, if he had one.

I pushed up and rushed him and drove both fists to his belly. He grunted and was hurt and showed it, gasping. Before I could slug him again, he clinched. I felt his arms take hold. I couldn't break free. The next I knew he'd pitched me to the floor. Now I figured the boots wrinkle wouldn't work twice, so when he bulled in to fall on me, dazed like a grappler on the mat, I rolled over and he caught only my left arm. I tried to tear loose, but couldn't. Then he picked me up and tossed me past the door against the wall. The van shook. My hat flew off and I tasted blood and the room went round and round. I was weak and sick. I couldn't get up. In my blurred eyes, Sagwa looked unreal, twice as big.

He had me now and knew it. He looked at Mr. Gus for approval. I could see it in his hound-dog eyes. Why, he worshipped the so-and-so, and Sagwa as strong as a stud horse!

I heard the wheezy voice, "Damnit, Sag. I see what you've done. Now, finish the job. Throw him out the door. Out!"

That little run of time gave me back my wind and the room cleared. I jammed my hat back on and swayed to my feet. When Sagwa charged me, his hands low to protect his soft belly, I squared myself. And acting more on savage instinct than on thought, with all the strength I had left, I smashed his wide-open left jaw, and then his right. Behind each swing was the bitterness of my failures so far, my labors in vain to find my horse and the men responsible.

He went down and the van shook again. I bored in to smash him again. I ached to kill him, but was astonished to see that he was out cold, like an axed steer. His eyes rolled. *Hell,* it dawned on me, *he's got a glass jaw.* It was over for the moment.

I ran around the counter and grabbed Mr. Gus, but didn't have enough heft left to throw him out of his chair. It was like a grab on a fat hog. I snarled into his pink flab, "I'd better have the truth! What happened at Aspermont? You hauled my horse away in a van, didn't you?"

When he didn't answer, I shook him till the folds in his face shook like jelly. "Yes . . . yes . . ." His wheezes had turned hoarse and faint.

"Where did you take 'im?"

Again he refused, so pale with fright I feared he might die on my hands. No matter. I had to know. I shook him again. The beer bottle spilled and the bell hit the floor with a clang. His mouth moved: ". . . Colorado City."

"Then they took the horse there?"

He managed a faint "Yes."

"Where did they take 'im from there?"

". . . Don't know."

"The hell you don't!" I shook him again, raised him up and slammed him down hard in the chair.

He gulped for air. "They didn't tell me. . . . I swear."

That made some sense. Why should they tell him?

"Who paid you?"

". . . Don't know. . . . Never saw his face. . . . At night. . . ." He was always in the dark. Never came in the office. Stayed outside."

"How much did he pay you?"

"Five hundred." He was ready to talk now, the way his words came fast.

"Didn't you see his face when he paid you?"

"He left the money in an envelope on the steps. I never saw him."

"When did he first approach you about my horse?"

"Tuesday night before they took your horse on Saturday."

"You keep sayin' *they*. How do you know there was more than one man in on it?"

"I heard voices when they led the horse up to the van. I saw men with the horse."

"How many men?"

"Several. . . . All I could see was figures in the dark."

"You had to see 'em when they took the horse in Colorado City." I gave him another shake.

"They came for him that night. One man came to the office, stayed outside the office while we talked."

"When did you get into Colorado City?"

"Monday evening late."

"On the road from Saturday night till Monday evening late. Who took care of my horse, meantime?" It galled me to think Judge Blair went two days without feed and water.

"They had a man with 'im in the van with water and feed, and some grub for himself. Nobody saw him. That was part of the deal."

"For the last time, where did they take my horse?"

"I tell you I don't know."

Another dead end. I would have beat the hell out of him to get the answer, but my anger weakened when I saw the shape he was in, and I grasped that he had told the truth. In disgust, I plopped him back in the chair and staggered around the counter. Chief Sagwa was still out cold on the floor. That made me feel a little better as I stumbled outside. I hurt all over and my walk was unsteady.

Head down, my eyes on the ground, I almost ran into Billy. He stepped back at sight of my face. "What happened to you? Reed said you'd gone to the office. I thought I'd better come see."

I wiped the blood off my mouth and told him. "That was slick, wasn't it? While we waited in Aspermont for the letter that didn't come till Wednesday, the carnival had plenty of time to reach Colorado City late Monday with the Judge, and for the gang—that's what they are, Uncle, a gang—to take him on. They had to do it by train."

Billy jogged his head. "In a boxcar. How else could they move a horse so fast and stay ahead of us? Too, I can't see a bunch of thieves who'd want to ride as hard as we have."

"Let's go check the mail."

Coyote joined us and we all rode to the post office.

I clenched my jaw when I saw the familiar handwriting on the letter the clerk handed me. I tore it open and read:

McQuinn—

You will receive your next instructions at the Monahans post office. We warn you again, don't bring the Rangers into this or your horse will be shot. One wrong move and your great racehorse will be dead. How would you like that? Keep in mind that you are always watched.

I boiled as I read it over and over, in hopes there might be some little clue there. There wasn't one. I tried to picture what the writer looked like. A series of faces flashed by: long-jawed, beady-eyed, slouched, a sneaky look. Nothing stuck. I was tryin' to make the writer fit a type, when as a matter of fact you can't tell a horsethief by his face or manner. Years ago there was one back home whose face was so smooth and honest you'd trust him with your best short horse, or even with your wife, and he took both from a neighbor, who never got 'em back.

The letter bore a Van Horn, Texas postmark. Monahans, as best as I could estimate, was a good hundred miles southwest by horseback, a hard two days' ride and more, with Midland and Odessa in between. Van Horn was well over another hundred miles beyond Monahans. Both towns were on the Texas and Pacific. So we'd fallen even farther behind the gang, and I dreaded the long stretches ahead.

My head was down as I went out. But when I saw my pardners, the young Comanche and the old man of vague years, both ready to ride and fight, and I thought of all we'd been through together, and that now they were with me like always, I felt my spirits lift.

They read the letter together and neither showed surprise. Then Billy looked at the sky and says, "The longer we wait here the more daylight we burn."

We bought supplies and packed and as we headed down Main Street, some rooted suspicion caused me to glance over my shoulder. At the same time I saw the little hombre in the gray hat step out of a saddle shop. His eyes followed us. Had prob'ly watched us since I went to the post office. His attention was still fixed on us when I looked back again, just before we cleared town and lined out for Monahans.

CHAPTER 10

WHEN FAST HORSES
ALWAYS LOSE

I had told Billy and Coyote about the little man and how I'd challenged him and got nowhere, and the farther we rode the more he took over my thoughts. I pulled rein, my mind made up. "Guess you noticed the little hombre back there who gave us the eyeball once-over. That's the one who seems to show up about every time I go to the post office, who wouldn't even give me his name. Said it wasn't important. Let's pull off here in the brush and see if he bird-dogs after us. If he does, we'll know for certain that he's with the gang."

I don't know how long we sat there on our horses, but it wasn't more than a few minutes before a rangy, bald-faced bay loomed up on the wagon road, the long-legged saddler in the gait I admired to watch, the rockin'-chair, runnin' walk. Our man was in the saddle.

Billy turned to me when the rider had passed. "Now what? You can't shoot him."

"Don't want to shoot 'im, Uncle. Not yet. But I think I've got it all figured out now just how he operates. He telegraphs ahead whenever we make a move. He knows we got the letter and where we'll go. We'll see him in Monahans."

"But before we get all riled up, Dude, remember he has as much right on the road as we do."

"Yes, Uncle."

We waited a while, then tailed along after him. It was all I could do not to run up and challenge him again. Instead, we settled down to a long and tiresome ride. Gradually, the saddler took him out of our sight and we saw him no more that day.

We made camp at dusk, watered our horses at a spring and fed them, cooked supper and rolled in our blankets. The bird-dogger still occupied my mind. I couldn't sleep. I sat up and rolled a smoke, the only sounds the rise and fall of Billy's snores and the horses as they cropped the short grass. The night was cool and clear, speckled with stars. I stood and gazed off southwest, my mind on tomorrow.

A tiny cone of light caught my eye, about where I figured the road ran. He wasn't as far ahead as we'd thought. While I watched, the firelight went out and I was left to brood. Why was my horse stolen? Why were we jerk-lined from town to town? Why all this mystery, when the gang could've had the ransom money days ago? Why any of this? I could only puzzle over it without the inkling of an answer.

But we did not catch sight of the horseman next day, nor did I spot his campfire that evening. The following afternoon we crossed a line of sand dunes and a few miles on found Monahans, a town a little downsize from Big Spring and, as I remembered my father had said, a watering place for stagecoach travel in the early days. We rode straight to the post office as usual and as usual the first day in town there was no letter at general delivery.

In a way, I didn't mind getting no letter today, because our horses were wore down and needed rest and so did we. We camped at the edge of town where there was water and graze, a sort of community campground. After supper I walked up town to the main deadfall, the Sand Hills Saloon.

At that hour the place had a crowd. It was a good time, I figured, to give my spiel, which I had down pat by now, like an eastern drummer when he called on the trade in his territory. I bought a drink and told the bartender my woes. I could see right off that he was a sympathetic cuss. He said his name was Jack Dunn, formerly of Fort Worth. He parted his slicked-down hair in the middle, had a walrus mustache, sported a high collar, even a necktie, and wore a lodge emblem on his checkered vest.

"You say you want to pass the word about your horse and the thousand-dollar reward? I'll take care of that right now." He raised his voice and waved and called out, "Boys, this gentleman here—Mr. Dude Mc-Quinn, who ranches on the Salt Fork of the Brazos—is on the lookout for his racehorse that was stole. Maybe you can help? He'll tell you all about it."

I told them when and where it had happened and described the

Judge, but, as my custom, did not mention the letters or any instructions to come here. Some of the crowd nodded and said they'd heard of Judge Blair, which made me feel good. "There's a thousand-dollar reward, cash on the barrelhead, for anybody who can lead me to my horse or tell me where he is. Maybe you've seen my horse around Monahans?"

All I got was headshakes and shrugs.

"Well, I'll be here another day or so at the campground. If you have any information and can't find me, leave it with Mr. Dunn. I'd sure like to hand over that thousand dollars to somebody." As I said the last, I was reminded that I might be askin' for trouble in a strange town. In Texas, men have been shot or their throats slit for thirty-five cents. And I'd left my six-shooter in camp. I'm bad about that, mainly, I guess, because I'm not real crazy about guns when used to shoot people. To me, gunplay should be used only as a last resort. When we campaigned the Judge, Billy used to get after me for leavin' my gun in the wagon so often. "It's not," he said once, "that you want to salivate anybody. It's just a matter of self-defense and common sense when you're in a town with the hair on, or when some crook who tried to fix your horse the night before won't pay off when he's been beat fair and square."

I'll say this for Billy, he carried his, and there were times when I was glad he did when I hadn't.

A windburned cowboy spoke up. "We got a big match race comin' up day after tomorrow. It's us cow-country folks' Painted Joe against Solomon Handy's Moon Dance. Since your Judge Blair's been a big winner, maybe you can help us? Give us some pointers?"

"Maybe I can—maybe."

"Handy has dusted us twice with other fast horses we've brought in. We've never been able to beat him. We think Painted Joe can do it this time—if things go right."

"*If things go right.* What do you mean? You think your horses were fixed?"

The cowboy seemed to choose his words carefully before he answered. "I'd better put it this way. They just didn't seem to run up to what they had done elsewhere."

"Maybe Moon Dance is just too much horse. Sometimes a mighty fast horse can make a fairly fast horse look bad."

"Maybe you can advise us a little?"

I had to grin. "Bad advice is cheap, boys. Good advice is generally ignored. I'll do what I can, if I'm still here. Where will the race be run?"

"Right here in town. The finish line is in front of the Sand Hills Saloon."

"Then don't bring your horse into town till the day of the race, and never leave your horse unguarded, which is why my horse was stolen. I left him unguarded one night. Where do you have Painted Joe stalled?"

"At my ranch four miles south of town."

"Walk him in, the morning of the race. Won't hurt him. Keep him quiet, away from the noisy crowd. Talk to him and rub on him. Keep him relaxed and put guards around him. Don't let any outsider pet him or feed him anything such as sugar cubes."

"Why not sugar cubes? Ain't they good for energy?"

"Also easy to load with laudanum."

"Oh—"

Was this cowboy a greener at match racin'! "What time's the race?"

"Two-thirty."

"All right, give Painted Joe his regular morning feed at his regular time, but don't overfeed. Nothing more before the race. Then just a few sips of water at noon. No more, no less." I was beginnin' to sound like Billy in one of his lectures to country yokels. "You want your horse lean and a little thirsty and hungry come post time."

The cowboy beamed. "That's already a big help right there. We'll sure do that, Mr. McQuinn, and we'll sure watch out for sugar cubes."

"Call me Dude."

"That's neighborly."

"How far you matched?"

"Three hundred and fifty yards."

"Then you'll have to take the break. The break's everything in these short-horse sprints. Has your jockey worked on that?"

"He's only worked Painted Joe three times, but he seems to know his stuff. We've brought in a boy named Spider Oden from that runnin'-horse country back in Southwest Louisiana."

"Sounds like you boys are tired of gettin' beat."

"We're not only tired, we're plumb tard of it."

"Does Oden bunk at the ranch?"

"He does."

"How long's he been here?"

"A week."

"Does he come to town much?"

"About every afternoon for a game of pool at the Good-Time Parlor. He's a wizard at billiards."

I had no reason to be suspicious, but guess I've seen too many slick fixes. I let it pass. It was my turn to shrug. Prob'ly I was wrong. "What about the starter? Is he trustworthy?"

"Name's Ab Favor. Straight as a wagon tongue. No worry there."

"Did Moon Dance always take the break?"

"Come to think of it, he did both times."

"Were the horses lapped, head to head?"

The cowboy turned his head. "I was at the finish line. Jeff was at the start. How about that, Jeff? The horses lapped?"

"As best as I could tell, yes."

So much for that. At this stage it was hard to say whether the "straight-as-a-wagon-tongue" Ab Favor was honest or not. These cowboys took way too much for granted in human nature. In a match race, you seldom knew who was paid off, and when you did, it was too late.

"Dude," the cowboy says, and took my arm, "I got another favor to ask of you."

"Shoot, cowboy." I wasn't used to all this attention. A little more and I'd buy the crowd drinks, whether "No Loan" Lawson's back-home loan could stand the strain or not.

"Will you act as my finish-line judge? Each horseman picks one and they flip for the third judge. Handy won. Might know. If it's a close call, he's got us outvoted two-to-one."

I'd overlooked that all-important phase of the race. "Will, if I'm here, and prob'ly I will be."

"That's mighty fine, Dude. Now, how about a drink with all of us?"

"Cowboy, you speak the language of my tribe!" There I was, Billy again, but a good line is a good line and, like always, it drew a laugh, and wasn't a man supposed to learn from his mentor and practice what he'd learned?

The crowd streamed to the bar and I learned that the cowboy, an open-faced young man with laughter in his eyes and a carefree manner, fine qualities but the same as a bird-nest on the ground to a slick horseman, carried the handle of Code Cook. He owned a small ranch, a spread recently inherited from an uncle, and had high hopes in the cow business. I didn't have the heart to tell him he'd prob'ly go broke ever' third or fourth year or sooner, but why discourage him when he'd learn soon enough on his own?

Before long he says, "Have another drink, friend Dude. It's a dry year an' gettin' drier."

"Well . . . if you insist, friend Code." Which was another way Billy had. You don't want to appear eager and you don't want to hurt another horseman's feelin's, unless you figure the drink might be fixed and his aim is to get the advantage as you rock back and forth about conditions of the race.

"I insist, friend Dude."

So I had another drink, and another. I'll say this for Code Cook. He appreciated anything I could do to help him win the race.

"Dude, could you ride out to my place in the morning? I'd like for you to see Painted Joe. Like to know what you think of his conformation and such. If you can, I'll hold off his morning work till you get there. My place is the LX, south of here. There's a sign on the road."

"I'll be there, friend Code." The mail wouldn't be in till later.

Later, when the town tipplers had thinned out and most of the cowboys had pulled out, Jack Dunn filled me in on more past details. "Moon Dance has taken the slack out of anything that can run from here to the border. Although he is a fast horse, the cowboys figure Solomon Handy's outslicked 'em somewhere along the line."

"You mean Handy has actually fixed the other horses?"

"Better not say that out loud. I'll lay it out this way. The inside dope is the fix is always on when you go up against Moon Dance. But prove it."

"What about Painted Joe? Can he run?"

"All I know is that Code Cook and others, on the search for a top short horse, brought him in on a lease deal from Carlsbad, where he ran big. But how can you beat the fix, tell me?"

"You can beat it if you guard your horse night and day, and if the jockey's honest, and the starter, and the finish-line judges."

Dunn laughed. "In other words, you can beat it if everybody's honest, which is like askin' the devil to join church. How can a horse be fixed?"

"A horse can be doped in his feed or with doped sugar cubes, or with cotton or sponges stuffed up his nostrils. Or the night before a race, somebody can slip into his stall and beat on his forelegs with a hammer or take a sharp knife and stick the horse and he'll sore up too much to run natural because he hurts. Or a jockey can be bought off to pull the horse. Sometimes all he's got to do is shift his weight in the saddle enough to throw the horse off stride."

"Never was any evidence the cowboys' horses were worked on. There was Bullet Bob, a flashy colt with Rondo blood from around Sweetwater, and a fast filly, Squaw Doll, a sure-enough singed cat that had cleaned out everything around Silver City and Deming, New Mexico. Both got beat by plenty of daylight. The cowboys took a beating, too. They bet everything down to their socks."

"Tell me about this Solomon Handy."

Dunn paused the same way Code Cook had. "He's the most powerful man in town. Owns the Texas House, the mercantile, the one bank, and even the Good-Time Billiards."

Mention of the Good-Time struck a spark inside my horseman's suspicious nature. Again, I shrugged it off. What's wrong with a little game of pool every afternoon?

"And," Dunn went on, "Handy controls all the gambling in town except here. I don't have a house gambler. Don't want one. Don't want to go that big. If the boys want to play poker or dominoes or what have you, there are tables back there. A penny-ante game or a game of checkers is pretty fast for the Sand Hills. I own the place lock, stock, and barrel and I don't water the whiskey like they do at the Texas House. Handy has offered to buy me out so he can expand his gambling, but I'd never sell out to him." Dunn brought out a dark bottle from under the bar and poured me a drink. "Have one on the house. Some of my Private Reserve. You see, Monahans is Jack Dunn's last stand. I came out here three years ago to get away from a woman in Fort Worth."

"Did it work?"

"Like the cowboy said when another man's horse sorta followed him home, I'll have to explain. Distance does not always make the heart grow fonder for somebody else. Sometimes it sheds a keener light on what you left behind. I went back for her and now we have a nice little home and I've got me a youngun, Jack Junior."

"Good for you, Jack."

It was late and the saloon was about empty, so I thanked Dunn for his help and the drink and left. Maybe it was the night, the clouds on a roll like an off-and-on mask over the full moon, and the cold air that cut inside my old brush jacket, and the heaviness in my head from the drinks that caused a kind of gloom to settle over me. I realized now that when I agreed to help Code Cook and the cowboys I had strayed from my main purpose; yet a man ought to help his own kind when he can. There was a wrongness here, the way Handy always won and the way brought-in fast horses always lost, unless he had another Judge Blair in Moon Dance, unless Moon Dance was another once-in-a-lifetime horse. Possible, yet . . . My always-suspicious mind refused to be still. If the fix was always on here, Handy had been mighty slick to cover it up. The more I thought about match races, the gloomier I got. I asked myself, would I ever see my horse again? Would I ever whistle to him again and see him come up to me for a handful of feed?

A gust of sharp wind shouted down the street and rattled grit against the wooden front of the Sand Hills like buckshot against a canyon wall. I pulled my jacket closer; for the first time, I glanced around. As late as it was, a few men still stirred on the street. I didn't move. I didn't want to. My gloom deepened. People who've never owned a good horse prob'ly wouldn't understand the bond between a man and his horse, together day after day, each dependent on the other. When I was barely sixteen I went up the trail with a cow outfit to the northern pastures. That was when I truly learned about horses, and what a horse can mean to a lonely boy or man as a pardner and friend. When we got paid off and I made tracks for home, I rode my night horse, a tough little blue roan called Chigger. At night I'd stake him out. Now and then he'd come in and sniff me, on my saddle blanket under my old yellow slicker, my hat pulled over my face. Sniffed me like he wanted to make sure I was all right. Sometimes he'd nose my hat a little. Then, satisfied, he'd go back and graze. Near morning, he'd bed down and sleep awhile. On that long ride south toward home I thought of that blue roan as the best friend I could have, because I'd never had a better friend, and he never failed me.

I rode Chigger all the way back home to the Salt Fork. He died there when he was twenty-three years old, and he'd always come up to me when I whistled, just like Judge Blair. And just like Judge Blair, he never got his picture made. More regrets.

Well, I thought, *guess I've had a little too much to drink. A big too much. Time to head back for camp.* A man's sure-enough drunk when he admits to himself he is.

The moon dodged behind a covey of clouds and I felt cold again. I struck out at a fast walk, my head down against the sharp wind. I passed the saddle shop where the sign over the boardwalk swung and screeched in the wind, passed the feed store and the wagonyard. No lights anywhere.

I didn't know when I first sensed that I was being followed, when I first caught the scuff of boots back there, it was so gradual. I looked back and all I could see was muddy darkness and the tallow light from the Sand Hills. The sounds dropped off when I stopped. A cold unease cut through me. I moved faster. Then I heard the boots again. Every few steps I'd look back, but I saw nobody. It was too dark.

The rush of boots sounded all at once behind me. I jerked around and saw two figures, and my head cleared for certain. It was too late to run now. I picked the lead man. I swung for his face, felt my fist strike cheekbone. He staggered, surprised, and exploded a "Goddamn you!" and swung at me and missed. The other man charged me before I could turn. Something crashed against my left shoulder, a club that staggered me. Pain shocked me. But I was clear for a bit and I lunged away, down the street at a slow, dead-legged run.

The one with the club caught me with ease. His next swing took me across my upper right arm and glanced off the side of my head. It knocked me off stride. I was hurt. I had to stop. The man I'd slugged ran up, all curses and snarls. Now the two stood between me and camp.

"The thousand dollars—goddamn you—fork it over!"

"Like hell!"

I thought the camp was close, but I couldn't tell for certain in the darkness. Half blind with pain, I found myself running. Not away from the two, but at them. Almost before I knew it, I split the two. The way a one-run horse drives between horses at the head of the stretch, when he starts the sprint for home. I felt a rain of blows, but I kept on. I broke in the clear. Two quick shots crashed, but I felt no pain. The shots not from my attackers, instead from camp. Behind me I could hear the two on the run for town, and then I reeled into camp and heard the voices of my pardners just before I passed out.

CHAPTER 11

ODDS AND A COURTLY MANNER

When I came to, my eyes met a distant glow. I blinked and the glow grew stronger. It was lantern light and beside it two anxious faces peered down at me. One might have been a white-bearded prophet out of the Old Testament; the other, Roman nose, high cheekbones, eyes the color of plug tobacco, could have been carved out of stone. I groaned and moved. I was bruised, but not busted up, I guessed. I started to push up, but fell back.

Billy's voice sounded far away, "Take it easy." He disappeared into the night.

"Mean white mans almost got you they did, white father." Coyote put the lantern down and sat me up. Billy appeared with a small jug. While Coyote steadied me, Billy held the jug to my lips. The whiskey was hot and faintly sweet. It burned as it went down. I had another sip, a longer one. It began to chase the cobwebs from my eyes and clear my throat. Coyote pulled me to my feet, and after some wobbles I could stand on my own.

"When we heard the scuffle, we knew what it was," Billy explained. "They took off when I fired into the air. How many was it?"

"Two. I'd announced at the saloon about the reward money."

"Dude, you're gonna have to be more careful. That's all there is to it. If you'd had your six-shooter tonight, you could've scared 'em off with a warning shot or two, at least defended yourself."

"Believe you're right, Uncle. I figured there might be trouble when I told about the reward. Maybe you and Coyote should carry what I've got on me?"

"We might be held up, too. No, just be careful."

I was stiff and sore when morning came, but after a trip to Billy's jug and a stout breakfast with plenty of black coffee, I said I was ready to ride to Code Cook's ranch to see Painted Joe. It was a promise and I aimed to keep it for a cowboy friend.

Billy shot me a look. "You're not just about to go out there by yourself. By now every crook in town knows about the reward money. Hell, you could get bushwhacked between here and the ranch. We'll all go and hereafter one Dude McQuinn will pack his six-gun. That's an order."

To humor Billy, I made a show when I buckled on my gunbelt under my coat. We saddled out of town, I flanked by my pardners. There'd been no sign of trouble by the time we neared the ranch road and I had to guy Billy a little. " 'Pears like my bushwhack friends took the day off."

"Dude, did it ever occur to you that they could watch our camp and follow you from town? That when they saw Coyote and me, they backed off? You're too easygoin' and trustful. I wouldn't be surprised if the first day you rode into town as a boy from the Salt Fork with a dollar or two in your jeans, if some slick bird didn't sell you the U.S. post office for a dollar down and a dollar a month. Or, if you'd joined the U.S. Cavalry, if some noncom'd sent you to headquarters to get the key to the flagpole—you'd've gone."

"You're not far off about the town. I remember the first time I ever went to the hotel in Aspermont I knocked on the door like it was a house. I didn't know you could go right in. But if there's one thing you've schooled me on and I've learned, it's to be suspicious of the other side in match races. I think Code Cook and these boys have been taken and I aim to find out."

Billy's smile was dry. "That's progress, Dude. I feel better now."

My cowboy friend had fixed up a mighty nice sign over the entrance to the ranch road, prideful for a new owner on the way up, and down later, in the cow business. A rock column on each side supported a wooden sign that arched overhead and read: WELCOME TO CODE COOK'S LX RANCH. It reminded me of the entrance to Colonel Buxton's Old Dominion Stud outside of Lexington, which likewise had stone pillars. The whole horse layout behind white plank fences. Once a man's seen the Bluegrass, he never forgets how it rolls away. The wooded, rounded hills, the long sweeps of pasture, a bluish tint to the grass when it blooms.

Friend Code must have been on the lookout, because he was on hand to meet us before we rode up to the porch. His genial face alone was an invitation to dismount. I introduced my pardners.

"Dr. Lockhart has taken care of Judge Blair for years, and Coyote is the Judge's jockey. From Texas to Kentucky he rode 'im, and when he whooped, the Judge ran all the faster."

Cook gulped, impressed. "You mean, friend Dude, that Dr. Lockhart was Judge Blair's vet all the time he was undefeated?"

"That's right. I don't like to brag on him in public because it might go to his head and it's already gettin' where he can't hardly find a hat to fit. But the doctor knows how to keep a runnin' horse fit and how to make him run."

Billy sent me a put-down look and lifted a modest hand. "It helps if you've got a sound, once-in-a-lifetime horse with plenty of iron and heart. I'm no miracle-worker, Mr. Cook."

Cook, further impressed, turned to Coyote. "And you rode the Judge in all them big races. That's somethin'."

"Judge Blair all the running did. I rode him only and guided him through places tight. Never I did across the finish line carry him. Now for him we search. Sad I am and much angry I am." And he gave the knife on his hip a slap.

"Sure wish I could help. Well, Spider Oden is down at the barn saddlin' Painted Joe for his morning work. I want you to see him."

"I hope you won't work him hard the day before the race?" Billy says. "Too much can make a horse resent to run on race day."

"Just an easy gallop to loosen him up and keep him sharp, Doctor. I've got my own bull-ring track here. You gents come on."

Oden had Painted Joe saddled and ready when we walked down to the barn.

"Take him around once, easy," Cook says, and gave Oden a leg up.

I no more than glanced at the rider. My eyes clung to Painted Joe. If ever a horse was named right, he was. A paint gelding with irregular broad markings of white and patches of blood-red bay. My, how he caught and held the eye! The colors a Plains Indian loved. Coyote just stood there and gaped, a glow in his eyes.

Oden slow-galloped around the half-mile track and walked Painted

Joe up to the barn and dismounted. For the first time, I took full notice of the jockey. He was older than I had expected, not that it mattered, a wizened man whose face, leathery and lined, was a trace of races won and lost, of mud, dust, sharp turns, bumps, whipslashes and Garrison finishes. His jaw was strong and his eyes, slate-gray and cool, reflected a boldness. *Here,* I thought, *is a hard boot who won't give an inch, who won't be afraid to take the advantage. What the cowboys need for a rider against Solomon Handy.*

Cook introduced us, we shook hands, after which Cook, with a gesture, says, "What do you think of this Injun-colored horse?"

Billy walked around Painted Joe, arms clasped behind him, making his usual slow appraisal, then faced the gelding and observed him at length. "I don't like white around a horse's eyes because white does not reflect sunlight, and therefore the eyes are more likely to be sore from taking in light. And I don't like four white feet, pretty as they are, because white feet don't hold the natural oils of the hoof and the walls of the hoof are apt to be soft and to crack on rough ground. But this is not a cow horse used on rough terrain. This is a racehorse, and I am also reminded that Judge Blair has four white feet and seldom has hoof problems. But we know white is no measurement of heart, which this horse must have, as Dude has told me, since he was the top runner at Carlsbad. His legs are straight and he has a powerful forearm, stifle, and gaskin, and that long shoulder I'm always happy to see. All that tells me he's a speed horse. Mr. Cook, I believe you have a runner."

"Code will bring Painted Joe into town in the morning, instead of stablin' him there tonight," I put in.

Cook was just about to bust his buttons over Billy's praise. "You bet we will, and he'll never be left unguarded, Doctor."

Billy wasn't finished, because there was never an end when you talked horses. "Mr. Oden, how did Painted Joe feel on the bit? Was he eager to run?"

"He was."

"I mean, did he take hold of the bit?"

"He did."

"Did he lug in or out?"

"Nope."

"Any bad habits that we might work on to correct today?"

Oden shook his head.

"How is he on the break?"

"Broke straight."

A little more enthusiasm would be appreciated, it seemed to me. I could see that Oden was about as talkative as a cigar-store Indian and sure never gave a readin' at the schoolhouse.

Billy quit at that and we drifted back to the house and Cook invited us in for drinks.

"I can see you're an expert on horses, Dr. Lockhart," Cook says, after all but Coyote had a round. "I appreciate the once-over you gave Painted Joe."

"An expert, Mr. Cook, is a man who's been right once. I am a bit puzzled, though, over what Dude told me in regard to other races you cowboys have matched with this what's-his-name fella."

"Solomon Handy."

"You brought in two fast horses and both horses lost by daylight. If that was the case, this Moon Dance must be the fastest thing since the telegraph."

"He is fast, but our horses, Bullet Bob and Squaw Doll, just didn't seem to run their races. Frankly, I'm still puzzled. They're both far better horses than they showed here, because I've seen 'em run. Squaw Doll is the fastest horse ever seen around Silver City. Them miners have got rich bettin' on her. Not only that, she's outrun everything with hair on it from Tucson to Nogales. She's a scorpion filly. Has Traveler blood on both sides."

"Hmmnn. Yet she lost by daylight. Did Bullet Bob and Squaw Doll seem sick after they ran? Did they act unusual? Seem glassy-eyed or dullheaded and sluggish?"

"Not one bit, and I looked 'em both over good. Squaw Doll ran on for another hundred yards or more before the boy could pull her up. Both horses still had plenty of run left."

Billy leaned back and ran a hand through his beard. "I'd say both horses were fixed. How, of course, could be one of several mysteries. Apparently, they were not doped or they would have shown signs. Dude tells me the saloon-keeper told him the fix is on when you run against this Handy fella."

"That's the story. Another thing to prove it."

"Since we say the horses showed no evidence of being doped, that brings us to the human element. You say Ab Favor, the starter, is honest, so Dude reports?"

"Yes, sir. If Ab's crooked, then we're all bound for hell. Besides, he's an old friend of my daddy's. He's run the saddle shop here for years."

Billy's smile was dry and remembering. "Yet money has made a crook out of many a heretofore honest man. But, for the sake of old friends, we'll say that Ab Favor is honest. Crooks don't go in much for saddle-making. It takes years to learn and is too difficult and skilled. Was there any interference during the race?"

"How do you mean, Doc?"

"Some fella pretends to be drunk, staggers out on the track into the path of your horse, then steps back. He's out there just long enough to startle the horse and make the horse break stride. It's an old stunt. One of the dirtiest."

"There was none of that."

"Nobody threw a whiskey bottle at your horses as they ran by?"

"No, sir."

"Who took the break?"

"Moon Dance took it both times."

"Against two very fast horses." Billy sounded skeptical. "But Dude says you said the horses were evenly lapped at the break?"

"Yes, sir."

"So . . . we'll say the horses were not doped, they were evenly lapped, and there was no interference on the track. That brings us to the jockeys. If a man's horse is evenly lapped, it's his rider's fault if he fails to take the break. Unless he's on a slow breaker and your two horses don't sound like that to me. That leaves Ab Favor in the clear. Now, did you use the same boy in both races?"

"Used a different one both times. Both brought in. Snuffy Brown from El Paso and Flip Lucas from San Antone."

"Why didn't you use local riders, somebody you know and can trust?"

Cook looked disgusted. "The rider we all wanted was in jail in San Angelo. Slim Moore. Shot a man over a woman. The next rider we wanted, Lacey Neff, got hurt. Horse fell with 'im in a match race at Pecos. He's still hurt."

"Did Handy bring in a boy each time?"

"Uses the same for all his races. Lucky Judson. Tends bar at the Texas House. Was leading rider in New Orleans for a number of years."

"Does he ride for anybody else?"

"Just Handy."

"How did you happen to bring Spider Oden in?"

"A neighbor of mine was in Abbeville, Louisiana and saw Spider win a stakes race and was impressed. So we got in touch."

Presently, it was time to go. Cook went with us out to our horses. Billy was in the saddle when he said, "One more thing. Even though you'll stall Painted Joe here tonight, guard him around the clock. Distance is no safeguard against the fix. Guard him yourself, you and a trusted friend or two of many years. The same caliber of friends you'd trust to look after your mother."

The young rancher broke into laughter. "You are mighty suspicious, Doctor."

"You'd better be when you match a race. What I've covered today are just a few of the dirty wrinkles tried on us when we campaigned the Judge. As fast as he is, we'd have lost some races if it hadn't been for Coyote. Other riders have grabbed his saddle cloth, slashed him and the Judge, forced them to the outside—anything to win. I could go on and on. Coyote outsmarted 'em and knew just when to call on his horse for more run. The rider made the difference."

Cook sobered. "I'll do that, Doctor. And thanks. See you all in the morning. Say around eleven."

We loafed around camp till after train-time that afternoon, then I hoofed up town to the post office. I guess I had my hopes too high, but there was no mail for Dude McQuinn.

That left me glum. I told myself that Monahans could be the end of the trail. There was more at stake than money. What did they want from me? Why draw this out from town to town? My horse could be dead, shot as they'd threatened. But always I came back to the five thousand. They had to want that, too, but evidently they wanted more. But no horse, no money. Past that I was in the dark.

Restless, I idled across the street to the Good-Time Billiards and found it crowded with afternoon loafers, a few cowboys prob'ly out of work, a few Mexicans, the rest townsmen, mostly elderly gents. Domino and pool tables full, the air blue with tobacco smoke as thick as a river-bottom fog. As I walked in, I could hear the occasional slap of a domino and the ring of a brass spittoon and the constant click of balls. A game of billiards was under way at the rear. I sat down on a bench to watch and relax and think. My interest picked up when I noticed one player was Spider Oden. He had long, slim fingers when he set his left hand, and a smooth stroke as he lined up the cue ball for a shot.

After noting that Oden was obviously winning, I let my attention wander from the game and the low voices and the click and crash of the balls. Something was missing in Monahans, something I had expected earlier. Of a sudden I realized what it was: the little man in the gray hat who rode the bald-faced bay saddler. I hadn't seen him. *Why,* I said to myself, sarcastic-like, *he should have been around the post office or the saloon or on the street like a bird dog on the scent.* I was plumb tired of that hombre.

Loud voices broke my musing. Oden had won the game and now held out a hand for the payoff, but his opponent seemed reluctant to pay. The noise in the pool hall dropped off, dominoes slap by slap and the click, click of the other games seeming to run down one by one, till there was complete silence.

"Come on, pay off!" That was Oden.

"You've fudged all afternoon."

"You accusin' me o' cheatin'?"

"Savvy plain English, don't you?"

Oden grabbed him by the shirt and they wrestled back and forth till a house man barged through the watchers and tore them apart. "Break it up, you two! Break it up or go outside an' settle it!"

They backed away from each other. They glared.

"I said pay up! You two-bit cheapskate!"

Still loath, the loser paid. "Anyway, you're plain lucky."

"Me?" Oden struck an injured pose. "Luck don't have a thing to do with it, my friend. It's practice and skill. If I'se lucky I'd always draw the top horse like you, Lucky Judson, and ride for a rich man."

So this was Lucky Judson, Solomon Handy's rider. About Oden's age, I judged, in his early forties. The marks of the racetrack on his creased face. Hard, blunt eyes. A slash of a mouth. Lean as a hoe handle. A mite stooped. Drawn down to muscle and bone. Prob'ly a hard finisher. A whip-slasher, a come-from-behind rider and watch out if you try to pass him in the stretch. Both men much alike. Out of the same tough mold of Southwest Louisiana, a wellspring of fast horses, fast talk, and fast fixes, not that the fair state of Louisiana has a corner on the last item.

Judson made to strike Oden, but drew back his arm. "All I can say is watch out tomorrow. Painted Joe will be so far behind Moon Dance you couldn't throw a rock and touch his dust!" He whirled and stomped out.

Oden stood there, cocky as a banty rooster, and grinned at the drawn-in crowd. "We'll see. We'll see. Anybody else want to shoot a game?"

Nobody moved.

I acted on impulse, before I could think, and stood up. "You're too slick at billiards. Simple rotation is more my style."

He stared at me for a moment. I saw a slow recognition come to the bold eyes. "Rotation it is. How much you want to bet?"

"I figured we'd just play a game. Loser pays the house." When I said that I knew he wouldn't play for pleasure alone.

"I never play unless I bet."

"A dollar?" I wanted to draw him out and didn't quite know why. He wouldn't play for a dollar.

"I don't play for less than five bucks, the same I charge when I give lessons to beginners." He was the center of attention in a crowded pool hall and I could see that he ate it up.

I made my voice extra genial. "This reminds me of the jockeys' room back in Louisville. You know, where they run the Derby . . . Churchill Downs. Let's play for five."

"All right. You break."

We moved to another table and the house man racked the balls and I picked up a straight cue stick from the stand on the wall. I broke and nothing fell. Oden, with that smooth stroke, scored and scored. He was deadly. He ran the table while I watched No-Loan Lawson's money shrink and the crowd enjoyed.

"Another game?"

"Why not?" I wanted to feel him out some more, rub on him a little, even if it cost me money.

"For five?"

"For five."

"You can have the break." It came out as more of a show-off gesture than the sportsmanship he intended for the crowd's benefit.

I broke again. Again, no balls fell for me. Again, he ran the table.
"Another game?"

"Believe not, Spider. I just hope Painted Joe's as fast tomorrow as
you're good with a cue stick. You're the best."

He played me a look that said much, that also said nothing. "Moon
Dance has to be favored. He's whipped every horse brought in here."

"So I hear. Since Painted Joe is second choice, maybe I'd better bet
his jockey."

The leathery face didn't even flicker.

I paid him and after stacking my cue left the place, puzzled by the
contradiction I had sensed in the row between the two men I'd just
witnessed. I studied about it while I made for the Sand Hills. I was
almost there when it unraveled. You don't call a man a two-bit cheapskate and not have a fight on your hands. Lucky Judson's pulled-back
punch and how the two wrestled seemed half-hearted now, the more I
pictured it again in my head. But . . . maybe Judson didn't want to
fight. A coward? I couldn't believe that. As hard a customer as he
looked, I'd figured him for a rough-and-tumble fighter, an eye-gouger or
slasher. Strange.

The saloon was crowded even at this early hour. Jack Dunn set down
a bottle of Private Reserve for me. "Folks already comin' in for the big
race tomorrow. Entertainment's hard to come by out here. I believe a
man could draw a crowd in Monahans if he stood on Main Street and
juggled three oranges and never said a word. But there's another reason
for the early crowd." He put on a sly little smile. "Mainly, because they
hope to see Solomon Handy get beat. I hate to say this about a man, but
Handy is about as popular as a polecat at a Sunday School picnic. Any
leads on your horse?"

"Not one."

"Well, I've told everybody that comes in here and I always stress the
reward. If your horse is in this area, somebody will spot him."

"You're more hopeful than I am. I'm afraid I'll never see him again,
dead or alive."

"Cheer up. Spring always follows winter, though sometimes when a
man's luck is bad it won't arrive till late summer, and if he didn't have
bad luck he wouldn't have any. Here . . . have yourself one on the
house. You'll feel better." A kindly man, he changed the subject. "Did
you have time to look at Painted Joe this morning?"

"I did. He looks like a runner."

"So did Bullet Bob and Squaw Doll."

"I'd have to see Moon Dance before I bet much, though."

"You'd be surprised at the money they say's goin' down on Painted Joe."

"Sounds like folks bettin' with their hearts, not their heads."

"One big reason is Handy's gamblers are offerin' two-to-one odds at the Texas House."

That did surprise me. "They must figure they've got the top horse."

"To be more precise, you mean the fix is on again."

"Whatever kind of fix that is. So far, Code Cook has taken every precaution. Tonight Painted Joe will be guarded round the clock."

"I hate to see these cow and farm folks lose their hard-earned money."

"Maybe they won't this time. And although I prob'ly won't get a chance to size up Moon Dance before post time, believe I'll ease down to the Texas House and take me some of that two-to-one money. By the way, what does Moon Dance look like?"

"You won't feel any better when I tell you. Get set. He weighs in the neighborhood of fourteen hundred pounds and stands seventeen hands. Biggest racehorse I've ever seen. He's a dark chestnut, which makes him look bigger than he is. Scares a man. Got a blazed face. Easy to handle, they say. He's a handsome horse, all right."

"How did Handy get hold of him?"

"What would you expect? Story is—this happened before my time—a horse outfit was passin' through the country and the owner unluckily engaged Handy in a game of Spanish monte. Handy not only took all the man's money, but his best horse, Moon Dance."

"Know how he's bred?"

"I've heard he goes back to Cold Deck. That's all I know."

"That's enough. Cold Deck was a boss short horse back in Missouri in the early days. Carried Steel Dust blood. Moon Dance would have to be a grandson, which is enough." I started to leave again, but another question held me. "What's a big gambler like Handy doin' in a little cow town like Monahans?"

"Story is, he came here in a hurry from New Orleans. Was a riverboat gambler on the Mississippi for years. But he went too far in New Orleans. Cheated and was caught and wounded a leading merchant in the fracas. The city fathers suggested Handy leave town for the good of the community and for his own health. When he delayed, he got out of town two jumps ahead of the law. He came here with money and he's added to it. By now he's the richest man in town. Buys up town property, farms and ranches. They say he's got his eye on Code Cook's spread. So . . . we're stuck with him. This used to be a nice little town."

I'd heard enough.

I found the Texas House even livelier than the Sand Hills. I waited till Lucky Judson, behind the bar, had a free moment. "Where can I place a little bet on the race?"

"Right over there."

He nodded toward a man standing at the end of the bar dressed in a black broadcloth coat, flowing black tie, white shirt with ruffles, and wide cuffs, a dandy place to hide extra cards. Pearl buttons and a gold watch-chain set off a flowered vest. A riverboat gambler's garb, black the dominant color. Jack Dunn had the story straight. I'd seen a few such cardsharps when we took the Judge back East to trace his ancestors. Solomon Handy wore a full black beard and a long mane of black hair, both shot with gray. But his dominant feature was his icy stare as his eyes flicked back and forth over the gaming tables.

I bet fifty dollars at two to one and he wrote it down in a little black book with my name. "McQuinn? McQuinn? You must be the gentleman who's come here looking for his stolen racehorse, the celebrated Judge Blair?"

"That's right." I could see he had courtly manners. More riverboat stuff, fancied to impress the unwary.

"If your horse is around Monahans, that thousand-dollar reward should bring about his return forthwith." He was soft-spoken, a voice that tallied with his genteel manner. I figured him to be in his late forties or early fifties.

"Unless I get knocked in the head first. Last night I was jumped on the way to camp. Two of 'em."

"You don't say! I trust you dispatched them?"

"I was unarmed, but I got away." I patted the six-shooter inside my waistband. "Next time I'll be ready."

He had a boisterous laugh. "No doubt you will, Mr. McQuinn. By the way, all bets are due immediately after the race at the finish line. It's the custom here."

"Jake with me. I'll be there for the payoff."

He dug me a glance that brushed ridicule. "You sound exceedingly confident, Mr. McQuinn."

"I've seen Painted Joe. He looks fast. I'd like to see Moon Dance."

"You won't see him till shortly before post time. I've found it wise to keep a horse secluded as much as possible."

"I'm with you there. No doubt you've got him guarded around the clock?"

"Absolutely."

"It's the only way to beat the fix . . . unless the starter is in on it, or the jockey. Then you're up the creek."

"You sound like a horseman who's been up against unlawful means to prearrange the outcome of a race." He spoke with exaggerated dignity.

What a high-soundin' way to describe the fix, I thought. "I have many times. Man, you know, is the only animal that can be skinned more than once." Billy's sayin' leaped to mind because it fit.

"Everything in life is a gamble, Mr. McQuinn. Courting a beautiful woman—ranching, farming, banking—operating a store on the credit as I do here. I am a professional gambler and make no bones about it. I've made fortunes and lost fortunes and I've never complained. If a gambler loses, he becomes an instant pauper; if he wins, he's considered a cheat in the public eye. So you see . . ." He spread his hands and shrugged.

"Except," I says, "every horse is honest and deserves the chance to run his race without the fix."

He said no more and I nodded good-day and walked out, on my mind the unanswered question, *How would the fix be worked tomorrow? Gamblers only bet on a sure thing. What was it?*

I loafed around town for an hour or more, dropped in at the barber shop for a haircut, and made another stop at the Sand Hills before I returned to camp. Billy and Coyote were gone, likely at the store for grub. Still in my downcast mood, I had thrown the horses some hay and moped around some more when I noticed the buggy on the road from town. I paid no more attention till the buggy stopped. A well-dressed woman stepped down and checked the harness on the left side of the smooth buckskin gelding. She shook her head, seemed puzzled, and looked in my direction for aid.

I went out. "What's the trouble, ma'am?"

"There's something wrong with the harness. Smoky keeps shaking his head. Something's bothering him dreadfully."

"Be glad to take a look." I soon discovered the trouble, only a loose throat latch, so obvious I wondered why she hadn't found it. I fastened it, said, "Believe that's what bothered him," and turned to go.

"Thank you very much, sir. I'm sorry to have bothered you."

"No bother at all." I started to leave again.

"Excuse me, sir, but could you be Mr. McQuinn, the racehorse man?"

I nodded. "Except I have no racehorse now. He's been stolen."

She spoke fast, with excitement. "That's exactly what I heard at the Ladies Club this morning. It's all over town about your horse. We all talked about it, our main topic of conversation. How you were camped here, you and the old gentleman and the Indian, on the trail of the thieves who took Judge Blair." The more she talked, the more attractive she seemed. Her hair was dark beneath her feathered hat, her large eyes hazel. She wore a high-necked, wide-skirted blue dress and jacket which did justice to her full-busted figure. I guessed her age to be between thirty-five and forty. In all, a pretty lady and one of means.

"I hope you've found some trace of your horse, Mr. McQuinn?" She sounded sincere and friendly, which helped lift my mood.

"So far, not a thing. But we have certain information that brought us this way."

"I see. Well, I'm very sorry you haven't found him yet."

"Thank you, ma'am."

"The more people who know the better." She gave in to a small embarrassment. "We club members wouldn't have known had not one lady's husband, who frequents the Sand Hills Saloon for what he calls his daily phlegm-cutter, been there when you made your plea for help."

"Proves saloons are not always dens of iniquity."

She smiled nicely. "And also that sometimes gossip can perform a public service, like getting word all around." Her big eyes flashed. "I love horses and I hate horsethieves. I keep Smoky stalled every night, believe me. I fear we are more noted in this section of Texas for thievery than for our citizenry."

I looked at her horse, a rangy trotter with conformation that marked him as well bred. "Believe you have a top buggy horse here."

"Thank you, Mr. McQuinn. I appreciate that, coming from a true horseman. Smoky was bred in East Texas. He's straight down the ladder from Tennessee stock. I've had him since he was a two-year-old."

"You take good care of him. That shows."

She held out a tiny gloved hand. "I must go and finish my drive and I thank you again. Gentlemen-horsemen are not in oversupply around here. I am Mrs. Belle Nolan."

I swept off my hat. "Pleased to meet you, Mrs. Nolan."

I handed her up into the buggy, aware of her delightful scent, like honeysuckle. She thanked me again and as she took the reins, I saw that she was thoughtful. "I am well acquainted here, Mr. McQuinn, and I shall keep my ear to the ground for any information that might prove helpful to you. You would not be here if you did not have some sort of lead, which is a start for me. I'll begin by asking around. I'll even snoop. If I uncover anything at all, I'll let you know at once . . . and I may just uncover something. If it's here, I will."

I liked her determination. She snapped the reins and drove away, and I was left with the image of a very pretty, sweet-smellin' lady, and a fine buckskin trotter, and a loose throat latch that didn't make sense.

CHAPTER 12

RACE AGAINST THE FIX

Race day.

There's no event that compares with it out West, big town or small, unless it's the Fourth of July Rodeo. The anticipation to watch fast horses run, the eagerness to bet, the pure excitement in an entertainment-starved little settlement like Monahans. Wagons, buggies, and tied horses lined Main Street and side streets. Kids romped everywhere, like foals on a spring day in the pasture. From our camp the outfit could see boomtown business at the Sand Hills and likewise at the Texas House, despite the public fact that Solomon Handy watered his whiskey.

At eleven o'clock we spotted a cloud of dust and the dust became a knot of horsemen. Code Cook and his cowboy friends, Cook in front with Painted Joe on a halter rope. Cowboys on both flanks and behind. As they rode closer, I saw the cowboys all packed rifles and side arms. Nobody was about to slip in and fix Painted Joe today!

Cook waved and gave us a loud holler. "Come join us."

We mounted and followed the cavalcade, which turned off Main and cut around to a small barn and corral behind the Sand Hills. There Cook stabled the paint horse and the cowboys took positions all around, grim and determined.

"Want to thank you-all for comin'," Cook greeted us. "Need all the friends we can muster here on Solomon Handy's territory. Jack Dunn keeps his saddler here sometimes and invited us to use it. Doctor Lockhart, is there anything we ought to do for our horse at this time?"

"Just keep him calm and relaxed. No commotion. I'll be glad to look him over again, if you want me to."

"You bet, Doc. Thanks!"

Billy's examination took some minutes. He even checked Painted

Joe's ears and eyes and nostrils. "Wanted to make sure nobody had slipped in and stuffed cotton or sponges up his nose. And there's no heat in his legs from that work you gave him yesterday. He looks all right to me. Is he a stall-walker by any chance? A nervous horse can wash out before a race."

Cook shook his head. "He's not. He's a very quiet horse."

"Even so, I'd keep somebody right outside his stall for company till post time." Billy glanced around with a curious expression. "Where's your rider, that Spider fella?"

"He promised he'd be here by one-thirty. Said he had some big pool games matched this morning at the Good-Time. Post time is two-thirty."

Billy didn't like that, I saw, but he didn't let on.

We all stood around and talked horse and directly a cowboy stuck his head out the back door of the Sand Hills and hollered, "Word just came that Handy's gamblers are offerin' three-to-one on Moon Dance!"

Cook whistled low, worried. "That means Handy knows he's got the fix put in somewhere. Just wish I knew where and how!"

That was when I missed Coyote.

"He went to the store for something," Billy says.

Time seemed stalled, which is always the way it is just before a big horserace. Most of us had run out of talk. Now and then Cook would go in and look at his horse and rub on him and murmur to him, and Billy would nod approval. Code Cook loved horses. That was good to see.

It must have been about noon when I heard a cowboy say suddenly, "Wonder what's up?"

I looked down the alley and it was Coyote on the double. He came straight to me and Billy and, with his eyes, motioned us aside. His dark face was a cloud of anger and concern. His voice was sharp. "Bad thing I see behind Good-Time Billiards in alley. White man handed many green moneys to Spider Oden."

"Code," I called, "better get over here."

He ran from the barn. "What is it?"

"Coyote just saw somebody pass money to Spider Oden behind the Good-Time."

"Maybe it was to pay off a pool bet."

I held my amazement on him. He was so green for such a good

horseman! "If it was a pool bet, Code, why didn't the loser pay off inside, the way a man usually does? Why on the sly in the alley?" I turned to Coyote. "What did the man look like who paid Oden?"

"This white man black hat he wore and dressed in black he was. Black coat, black tie, black beard, long black hair down to shoulders. Everything black except white shirt."

I knew before Cook burst out, "Handy—hell, it was Handy! That's the fix. He's bought off Spider to pull our horse. Same as he did Snuffy Brown and Flip Lucas. How he's always won. By God, I'm gonna shoot that little sneak of a Spider!"

"Hold on." Billy's campaigner's voice of old, cool and steady. "Use this to your advantage, Code." By now the cowboys had bunched around us. "Don't say a word yet—none of you boys. Keep quiet."

Cook swiped a hand across his face. "But now I don't have a rider, and I'll have to pay Handy a five-hundred-dollar forfeit. That was the agreement. Too late to find another rider." He groaned. "Besides, there ain't another rider."

"You don't have to pay Handy a dime," Billy says. "You've got a jockey right here. A natural born one. Coyote Walking, Judge Blair's jockey. He'll ride Painted Joe. He's been aching to all along. If there's any horse a Comanche dotes on, it's a paint. You'll ride Painted Joe, won't you, Coyote?"

Which was like askin' a country kid if he liked red soda pop on a hot afternoon at the county fair.

Coyote nodded, behind his eyes the ghost of a smile.

Billy made a quick gesture. "But wait. . . . Did Handy or Oden see you?"

"No, Grandfather. Both white mans kept their eyes on the green money. Between two buildings I went after Oden took it."

"Good. Now, boys, there are some things we have to do. Don't let Handy or his gamblers know that we know about the payoff to Oden. That way we can get more of that three-to-one money. Next, there's time to work Painted Joe on the old swingin' break, same as we used to work the Judge."

"The swingin' break?" Cook was puzzled. "What's that, and why do we need it today?"

"You need every advantage you can get, Code, and I'm trying to give it to you. The swingin' break is a matter of momentum at the start, which is where many short races are won. A horse can break faster turned a little sideways than he can straight. Let your horse set himself, then turn him a little and he takes a short step and swings into his getaway. He pulls with that one short step, then takes a long stride and he's outa there."

"Don't think Ab Favor will allow that. It's different."

"It shouldn't matter, Code, so long as the horses are even at the break, with one turned a little. However, we'll go see Favor right now. I believe he'll agree after I talk to him. But you always need to tell the starter ahead of time. Otherwise, he might say no or call the horses back."

"What if Oden shows up while we're gone?"

Billy faced the others. "You boys keep quiet. Don't let on that you know anything. If he asks where we are, tell him we went to bet. If he gets suspicious, don't let him leave. Tie him up and keep him out of sight."

Ab Favor was just like Code Cook had pictured him, a no-nonsense type of individual, thick-shouldered, shaggy white eyebrows and a shock of unruly white hair, and stern brown eyes and a firm mouth. His big hands showed the stain of his profession. He was bent over hand-tooled work on a saddle when we entered the shop.

Cook introduced us and Billy explained the swingin' break. Then we waited while Favor drew it back and forth through his honest mind. He frowned and continued to frown. "Never heard of this before. Sounds kind of tricky to me."

Billy smiled with patience. "To be tricky, Mr. Favor, one horse would have to be ahead of the other when the starter says 'Go.' In fact, some horsemen think the swingin' break is a disadvantage because a horse is not set straight and his feet under him—that is, until they've seen a horse swing into his getaway. It sure beats having the owner smack his horse across the butt with a two-by-four at the break, which I regret to say I've seen done in some match races, and which I would not permit as a starter. I've also seen horses go down when hit that way, they're so startled. Not every horse can savvy the swingin' break, Mr. Favor. I believe Painted Joe can. He's intelligent and has a quiet disposition. Judge Blair savvies it. One reason he breaks like a shot. . . . And once we've explained the break to a starter, we've never been turned down."

A broad smile gullied the saddlemaker's strict features. "Judge Blair, you say? Why, I saw him run at Fort Worth on the Fourth of July. Beat a fast South Texas stud called Buckaroo. Won't forget that. Believe Judge Blair won it by a . . ." He didn't finish.

"By a neck," Billy finished, "and we used the swingin' break that day."

A new understanding changed Favor's expression even more. "Why, of course, you're the people who've come here in search of Judge Blair, stolen at Aspermont."

"We are, Mr. Favor, and meanwhile we're just trying to help Code with his horse. He's had a lot of tough luck against Solomon Handy, even though he tells us he always got a fair start."

I knew we had it won right there with the way Billy put it. I knew he had us over the hump.

Ab Favor couldn't have been more cordial. "I understand now. You gentlemen have my permission on the break. Now that you've explained it, no way I could turn you down. It's a new way to start to me and I had to think it over. I just want to be fair to both horses, no advantage to either. You understand my position?"

"We do, sir." Billy had put on his saintly face. "And we thank you. In turn, we didn't want to spring any surprise on you."

"Have you found any trace of Judge Blair?"

"Not yet. Only, from what little we know, it may be he was taken this way. Dude is the owner, Coyote the jockey, and I'm the vet and trainer."

"Glad to meet you fellows. I hope you catch the thieves and hang 'em all to the highest cottonwood!"

We left on that agreeable note.

Outside, Cook turned to Billy. "Doc, why didn't you tell Ab about the fix? How Coyote eyeballed it all?"

"The fewer who know the better, Code. Even friends. Ab might let something drop to a friend who might spill the beans. One word and news of the payoff would be all over town in minutes. But be sure to tell Ab before the start."

Cook was still troubled. "Handy will know something's wrong when he sees Coyote on Painted Joe."

"Sure, but by then it will be too late for him to forfeit. We'll keep Coyote under cover till the very last minute, till you pony Painted Joe to the line."

But I knew also that foremost on Billy's mind was all that three-to-one money at the Texas House, like a bird-nest on the ground—if Painted Joe was the scorpion Cook said he was. If he wasn't, I could see big chunks of No Loan Lawson's money tossed on the breeze.

It was past one o'clock when we hotfooted back to the stable. Spider still hadn't checked in. Billy slung me a look and I looked at him and Coyote looked at us, and we all nodded without a word and each of us handed a cowboy a hundred dollars to place at three-to-one odds. Then Billy, with a peek at his watch, says, "Code, where's a nice quiet place not too far away, out of sight of busybodies, that we can school Painted Joe on the break?"

Cook had to ponder a bit. "A few blocks behind us here the street plays out . . . and there's a little road . . . and no houses."

"That's good enough."

"Oden's gonna show up here any minute."

I knew the answer to that before Billy's eyes flicked my way. "I'd better stick around here for when he does. You-all go ahead."

The three rode out, Coyote on Painted Joe, and I settled down to wait. Time seemed locked. I could hear the murmur of the crowd along Main Street. The noise swelled, like bees swarmin'. Every few minutes I'd look at my watch. What held up Oden? Be better if Painted Joe was back in the barn when he got here. I turned to one of the cowboys. "Pardner, would you mind goin' out to Main Street and run tell us when Handy starts to pony his horse to the line?"

"I'm on my way."

To pass the time, I took my rope off my saddle and played with it, tossin' little loops here and there. More time passed and I commenced to worry.

One-thirty had come and more when at last I saw Oden. He sauntered down the alley dressed in black jockey boots, little jockey cap, and red-and-white jockey's silks. Big-time stuff, as cocky as if he'd won another five-dollar game of rotation off a sucker.

He glanced at the empty barn and around and frowned. "Where's my horse and where's Code?"

"Painted Joe had started to walk his stall, back and forth," I says, "so Code took him out for a little stroll to cool him off. He was startin' to sweat hard. Code was afraid he might wash out before the race. You know how that is."

He couldn't seem to quite swallow that, I gathered, but he had to ride Painted Joe for the fix to stick. He rolled a smoke, but I could see his hands tremble.

"How'd your pool games go today?" I says to keep the talk steady while we waited.

"As usual."

"You're the best, Spider. You oughta open your own pool hall. You'd get rich and have a barrel of fun to boot. Call it the Spider's Web." I laughed big, but he didn't.

"Understand there's a pile of money bein' bet today," I kept on. "Even three to one on Moon Dance."

"Yeah."

"I took me some of that on Painted Joe, chancy as it is. You see, I bet the jockey, though can't say I ever saw a boy tote a slow horse across the finish line." I had to make talk to kill time. "You figure Painted Joe can take the break?"

He clammed up tighter'n a cob stopper on a jug of canyon-run moonshine. I made a little loop with my rope, tossed it at a weed and dragged it in slow. Hell was about to pop. I could feel it.

Spider rolled himself another smoke, took a couple of drags and threw it down. "Believe I'll ease off down to the Texas House for a little drink before the race."

"Believe not, Spider. You're not goin' anywhere."

His face went stiff and he started to run. I had a loop made. I dabbed it on him and yanked hard. He came down like a busted calf. Then the cowboys rushed in and tied him up, left him on his belly with his hands behind him. Mighty uncomfortable and intended to be that way.

Before we could fetch him to the stable, Cook and Coyote trotted up with Billy. Cook's anger got the best of him when he saw Oden.

"Goddamn you! Coyote saw you take the money from Handy! I oughta shoot you!"

"You got it all wrong. Sol was just payin' off on a gamblin' debt."

"Paid off in an alley?"

Oden wouldn't meet Cook's eyes. He was caught and knew it. He argued no more and appeared to accept it as part of the game. Take what you can when you can. I had a hunch he'd been in this situation before.

We hauled him back to the barn, gagged him with a red bandanna, and closed the door. A cowboy volunteered to guard him till after the race.

"Painted Joe did all right when we schooled him on the break," Billy explained when I asked. "It puzzled him at first, because he didn't know what the idea was. But Coyote kept working with him, and I believe he's got it down good enough to help. Coyote will whoop at him when they break. That will put some swing into it!"

We milled around and talked and smoked and watched Painted Joe. Any good runnin' horse senses when a race is near by the little things his keepers do. The way they rub on him and baby him, maybe wrap his legs, and talk to him. Girls like to weave ribbons in a filly's mane. You can tell that a veteran racehorse knows what's up by the look in its eyes, and Painted Joe had a glint in his that made me think of my horse, what Billy called "the look of eagles." Yet the paint was quiet, and except for the sweat he'd worked up goin' to school on the break, he looked unruffled and ready to run.

Cook was the nervous one. He paced back and forth.

"One of the cowboys is on the lookout for when Handy ponies his horse to the line," I says to calm him.

The afternoon dragged. It was after two o'clock when the cowboy on watch ran up. "Handy has just started down the street on his pony horse with Moon Dance. Man, that's a big horse!"

That last observation didn't make my bets feel any more secure, even at three to one. But Painted Joe looked like a runner, and with Coyote in the irons our chances improved.

Billy checked his watch. "Give Handy five minutes, then we'll saddle on out there. But let's not pony Painted Joe past the Sand Hills. Let's go around, so Handy's gamblers won't know about the jockey change and will keep on giving three-to-one odds." He slapped his thigh. "Why not have Coyote wear Oden's jockey shirt and cap? At a distance they'll think it's Oden and so will Handy till we ride up to the line." Billy was on the lead today, just like when we campaigned the Judge.

And we did just that, stripped Oden of his red-and-white silks and took his cap while he cussed and raved through his gag. He sure was a skinny little runt, but as hard-muscled as a stud horse. Reckon he was a stranger to bath water, because when I handed Coyote the shirt he started to put it on, but then made a face and sniffed and held it at arm's length before he squeezed in his nostrils and got into it.

Now it was time to go. Coyote mounted, Cook snapped a lead shank on Painted Joe, and they swung off down the alley with Billy on the lead. I watched till they turned in on Main and made my way through the packed and noisy crowd to the finish line, marked by a pole on each side of the street in front of the Sand Hills, a yellow ribbon stretched between the poles as the finish-line tape. Two men stood in the judges' plank stand erected for the race. I climbed the steps and nodded to them. They looked, but did not nod. One had the earmarks of a gambler, a cheap imitation of Handy, dressed all in black except for the dirty white shirt. The other was burly and flat-nosed, prob'ly the Texas House bouncer, here to back up any argument. If the race was a nose finish, I knew there'd be trouble. But I wasn't packin' my six-gun today just for show.

I turned away to look up the street. It was then that I saw Belle Nolan in her buggy. Her eyes were already on me. She smiled in a friendly way and gave me a little wave. At about the same time a man hurried up the steps of the stand and handed me a sealed envelope. He didn't explain, just made a gesture toward the buggy like I'd understand, and then left. There wasn't time to read it now. I had a horserace to judge. I stuck the envelope inside my coat and looked back at Belle Nolan. She smiled again and nodded, and I wondered if she'd uncovered some information about my horse. She was a looker, I'll say that, all dressed up like she was headed for a ten-o'clock ball. I wasn't the only man whose eyes were on her.

As I turned my attention back to the head of the track, where Ab Favor in a big white hat stood out like a sheriff at a farm auction, a figure in front of the Sand Hills took my eye. Hell, it was the little bird-dogger in the gray hat. Him again! As bold as daylight. And he saw me, but he didn't wave or show recognition. My old anger boiled over like a pan of milk on a hot stove. Shouts from the crowd brought me back to the race.

From my elevated place in the stand, I had a clear view of the starting line. Handy had released Moon Dance and Lucky Judson had him milling about. The big horse even looked big from here. While I watched, Billy rode up and Cook ponied Painted Joe in. Billy and Coyote told me afterward what happened next.

Handy's mouth fell a foot when he saw the Comanche on Painted Joe. "What the hell is this? Where's Spider Oden?"

It was all Cook could do to hold himself in. "Why should you ask? He's not your jockey."

"But you've changed jockeys. This breaks one of the main conditions of the race."

"Like hell it does! The only agreement we had on riders was on catchweights. Not who rode the horse. I could take the saddle off my horse right here, smear molasses on his back, and stick a fifty-pound kid on his back if I wanted to."

"I disagree. I'll have to forfeit. This is a violation of our gentlemen's agreement."

Favor got into it. "It's too late to forfeit, Mr. Handy. You should have done that this morning. I can't see that you have any ground to complain about another man's jockey unless he commits a foul during the race. So let's run this race."

Cook had waited till then to fire his double barrel. "I'll tell you what it's all about, Ab. Coyote Walking saw Handy payin' off Spider Oden, our jockey. Saw the payoff in the alley behind the Good-Time. Paid him to pull our horse, what else? Same as he paid Snuffy Brown to pull Bullet Bob and Flip Lucas to pull Squaw Doll."

Favor froze, taken aback.

"That's a lie," Handy said. "And what's a dirty Indian's word against a white man's?"

Favor moved right up to Handy. "Plenty, if the Indian's honest, and I believe this young man is. I've talked to him and Dr. Lockhart and McQuinn. They've come here to look for their stolen racehorse. Honest men after crooks."

Handy reined to ride off. "Nevertheless, I'll have to forfeit. As the owner, I have that privilege. All bets are off."

Favor grabbed the pony horse's bridle. "There are other rights, too. You're gonna run this race, Mr. Handy, or you won't be able to live in this town. You'll run it fair and square or the decent citizens of Monahans will ride you out of town on a rail. Now, boys, walk your horses back a way and come up to the line. This race is on!"

There was movement behind the starting line as Coyote and Judson rode back to begin their approach. I saw the horses well-lapped. I saw Favor raise his white hat. Suddenly Moon Dance broke ahead, a false start, and the Handy horse ran some thirty yards, fighting the bit, before Judson could bring him around for another walk-up. Coyote hadn't let Painted Joe go at all, just walked him out a few yards. Handy watched from behind the starter.

Once again, the horses approached Favor. Again, well-lapped. This time Favor dropped his hat for a start. With that motion, Coyote swung his horse a little to the left and back and Painted Joe broke on the run, taking the break by half a length.

For the first fifty yards or so the paint had the lead. Had it till Judson went to the whip and the big horse came to the paint and they ran head to head. Two game horses. Two damn good horses. Two bolts of short-horse lightning. Could Coyote and Painted Joe hold off the big horse? Maybe.

I waited for something out of the past, and needed if we were to win: Coyote's familiar whoop. Now I heard it, more screech than whoop, keen on the wind above the roar of the crowd, and of a sudden Painted Joe flattened out and pinned back his ears. He opened up daylight, comin' like a wild horse. But Judson had the big chestnut on the fly again. They closed. Head to head, again. They'd passed the furlong stake by now.

Come on, Coyote, pardner. Come on. Whoop at 'im some more!

I beat the air with both fists and the wildest shouts I heard around me were my own.

It happened as the horses tore past the livery stable some hundred yards from the finish, still head to head. Coyote whooped and whooped again. He wanted more run from his horse, and he got it. Painted Joe broke in front, Coyote after him with whoops at every jump. Moon Dance, under Judson's whip, rallied and drove at the paint, Moon Dance big and powerful and full of heart. He drew up to Painted Joe's saddle girth. There he seemed to hang, unable to get up in the final strides. I could barely see Coyote's head, hatless now, he was so low in the saddle. A Plains Indian on a paint horse. Like a page in a picture book.

They streaked across the finish line like that, the tape a long trail of yellow ribbon behind Painted Joe. Now it was my turn to whoop.

I faced the judges. "Painted Joe took it by half a length. Any argument?" I had my hand on my gun when I said it. The gambler and the bouncer traded looks and said no word and walked down the steps.

Just then somebody yelled, "The gamblers won't pay off! They're headin' for the Texas House!"

Why, this was just like old times, when we campaigned the Judge and the losers balked. I went down there fast. Three birds dressed in cheap black struggled to push through the crowd. I elbowed in front and pulled my gun. "The payoff's here—same as it would be if Moon Dance had won. Where Handy said it would be. It's the custom. Pay up!"

They paid and they paid, till they ran out of three-to-one money. Then we escorted 'em to the Texas House where they paid up in full. Solomon Handy never showed up.

From there we trooped back to the Sand Hills, where Jack Dunn treated us victors to a free round on the house. Before long Billy and Coyote and Cook and the rest of the cowboys joined the celebration. Cook, who had won big, bought a round and somebody hollered, "Speech—speech!" and he mounted a table and waved his hat. "Boys, the real credit for today's win over Solomon Handy should go to our three friends from Aspermont, here in search of Judge Blair. . . . Dr. William Tecumseh Lockhart, who schooled Painted Joe on the swingin' break so he could get away first . . . and Mr. Coyote Walking, who rode like I never saw a horse rode before . . . and Mr. Dude Mc-Quinn, who saw to it that we all got paid our bets. . . . Now, you gents all take a bow."

We did amid a storm of whoops and hollers. Well, that was mighty nice, Texas-nice. Next, somebody asked Coyote to tell about the race, all the details, and he got up on the table and says, "Painted Joe ran the race, I did not. But scared him a little bit, I think I did, when into his ears I whooped. He was scared, that horse. Away from my whoops he wanted to run, that horse. So remember, white mans, my friends, when your horse faster you want to run, into his ears send whoop after whoop. That is all. Thank you."

They laughed and pounded Coyote on the back, and then they asked Billy to speak, and he climbed the table, as nimble as a mountain goat, and after he'd commented on what a great race it was, fair and square for a change, a cowboy spoke up. "Now, Doc, tell us how to pick a good racehorse."

Billy thought that over before he spoke. "Always pick a horse with straight front legs and a long shoulder. Straight legs mean he's less likely to have front end problems, and a long shoulder gives him stride. And whenever you see a horse that has the eye of an eagle and the step of a deer, buy him on the spot. You've got a runner." He paused. "One more little thing. Make sure your jockey's honest."

They ate that up, and a cowboy bought a round, and after that I was asked to say "a few words," which I did and more. "Don't forget that we're still on the lookout for our racehorse, Judge Blair, and there's still a thousand-dollar reward for his return, cash on delivery."

A cowboy waved for attention. "Give us his description again."

"He's a dark bay with a blaze that comes to a point between his nostrils, and he has four white feet, fox ears, a strong jaw, and powerful front and hindquarters. Deep of girth. A short back and a long underline. His legs are straight and set square. And like Billy just said, he's got the eye of an eagle and the step of a deer. You'd know he's a racehorse because he looks and moves like one. . . . We expect to pull out any day now. If we're not here and you see a horse like that, get in touch with Mr. Jack Dunn here. He'd wire the sheriff at Aspermont." I thanked them and stepped down.

On that, I bought a round and Cook bought another and Billy bought a round. When thought of time eventually caught up with me, I had a start. The afternoon was gone and I had failed to check the post office, which was closed by now. That, also, was when I remembered the envelope. I stepped to the end of the bar and even here in the smoke I caught the pleasant scent of honeysuckle when I opened it. The pretty handwriting in the note read;

Dear Mr. McQuinn:

I have information which I believe will be of importance to you in your search for your racehorse, information which I cannot divulge in a note for fear of danger to myself. But no matter, for "right is right." At full dark this evening come to the house at the north end of town with the white picket fence.

In haste and fear, Belle Nolan

In haste and fear? What did that mean? Was her life in danger? What had she found? My excitement took over. At last, maybe—and there'd been plenty of maybes before—some of the smoke around this puzzle was about to blow itself out. Maybe she'd connected the little hombre in the gray hat. He was here, wasn't he? Belle Nolan was a woman of intelligence and well-acquainted in town—that was plain—and she was pretty. Yesterday she said she'd ask a lot of questions and listen, even snoop around, and with her connections and will she might have uncovered a good lead. I remembered what she'd said: "I just may find something about your horse. If it's here, I will."

Along with the note, that was enough for me. I was desperate and tired and on the prod.

I started to tell my pardners, but backed off when I thought about it. After my experience with Moccasin Wiley, I figured they'd warn me not to go. Like Billy said, I was too trustful; true, but I would follow any lead, no matter how thin it might look, that might take me to my horse, and I was armed this time. If we didn't chase down every lead, how would we ever find him? Only one small item bothered me, the loose throat latch. But it was a small thing, and a town lady might overlook it.

CHAPTER 13

THE COWBOY AND THE LADY

The celebration was still in progress and would go on and on, I figured, when I slipped out of the saloon and went to my horse tied behind the Sand Hills. By this hour it was full dark, the time Belle Nolan had asked me to come. I mounted and rode out to Main and turned north, my horse at a trot. The lights of Main soon fell behind me, and after a few blocks of scattered houses, I rode in darkness, a catch-up question on my mind. Was I wrong? Was I off on another wild gamble?

The house with the white picket fence loomed up. A low light burned inside it. The house sat well back on a big lot and some distance from the nearest house, which was dark.

I tied up at the fence and eased up to the house. There was no porch, just a stone step. I rapped lightly on the door. A heavy silence followed. I rapped again. This time I heard steps, the quick, light click of high heels, and the grate of a wooden bar bein' slid back, and then the door opened. Belle Nolan's voice was low, a pleasant murmur. "Come in, Mr. McQuinn."

I went in a few steps and stopped, with me the sweet hint of honeysuckle, while she barred the door again. A lamp burned on a small table. I caught the honeysuckle scent again as she moved about the room and drew the curtains together on the front window.

"Please sit down, Mr. McQuinn." She sure had a pleasant voice.

I took a chair by the unlighted 'dobe fireplace. "I want to thank you for the note, ma'am."

She sat by the lamp. "I wasn't certain where I'd find you on a race day. If I hadn't seen you in the judges' stand, however, I would've gone to your camp."

"That was some race. Maybe you don't know all that happened before it was run?"

Her eyes grew very big. "Just that Mr. Handy lost."

"Too bad, wasn't it? Our jockey saw Handy pay off Spider Oden behind the Good-Time just before the race. Might have been sooner, but I think the Spider was only holdin' out for more, which he got. So *Señor* Oden didn't get to ride Painted Joe. My Comanche friend, who rides Judge Blair, rode the paint, and how he did ride!"

"I did notice an Indian on Painted Joe, which I thought unusual." The shrug of her slim shoulders said it didn't matter to her who won or lost. "Afraid I'm more interested in trotters than racehorses."

"At least, it was an honest race for a change."

"How can you say that when you are a stranger?"

"A whole flock of little birdies told me that Handy also paid off the cowboys' brought-in jockeys in two earlier races. But enough about horseraces, Mrs. Nolan. What is the information you have, and why are you in danger?"

She touched a hand to her throat. "I've learned that a rancher has recently come into possession of a dark bay racehorse." She looked down. "I don't know whether I should tell you this or not."

"But why would that put you in danger?"

She stood up. "May I get you some whiskey, Mr. McQuinn? I myself need something, perhaps a glass of wine. Then we can discuss this more calmly, I hope."

"A little whiskey would be fine, Mrs. Nolan. But why the danger? Have you been threatened? If so, that should be looked into."

She wrung her hands. "I'll get the drinks, then I'll try to explain." She left the room, a distraught and pretty lady.

I didn't know when I first received the impression about the room and the house. There was something amiss here. This, I gathered, was Belle Nolan's home, and obviously she was a woman of means. I judged that by the clothes she wore and the fancy trotter she drove. But the fireplace wasn't used, though this was a cool night, just right for a mesquite fire. In fact, the house felt cool even to me, a man accustomed to blankets on the ground. A woman wouldn't like a house this cool. Neither did I smell any suppertime cookin' odors. The room was also sparse, almost bare, no rugs on the floor, and old odors crawled out of the walls and plank floor like it hadn't been lived in for a long time—

not unlike, it came to me, the abandoned farmhouse where Wiley & Company had lured me and tried to hold me up.

At that moment she brought me a glass of whiskey and a smaller glass of wine for herself and arranged herself again by the lamp.

"Nice little place you have here," I says, just to talk along.

"I bought it only a few days ago. It needs fixing up something dreadful, as you can see, Mr. McQuinn."

So that was it. Well, I wanted to believe her, if I could.

I started to take a sip, but did not. My mind was on her and my horse. "I don't want you to be in any danger over this, Mrs. Nolan. What about this rancher?"

"He hasn't threatened me yet, simply because he doesn't know that I'll tell you. You see, he was in the Sand Hills when you first told everyone about your search for your horse. He knows you are looking and he knows he told me about his new racehorse. So he'd tie the two together if you went to his ranch looking for your horse. He is so powerful and vengeful, I'm afraid to tell you. He would never forgive me, Mr. McQuinn."

Our talk was all on the circle, I saw. "But people other than yourself must know about this racehorse. People who work for him. And he'll want to match the horse. When he does, the secret will out."

She played me a soft smile. She sure had nice white teeth.

"*Then*, Mr. McQuinn, not *now*. I am worried about *now*, the *present.* You are a true gentleman to show concern for me." She gazed down at her empty glass. "I must be upset about all this. I see I've already finished my wine. Believe, I need another." She rose and left the room, and again as the air moved I caught her honeysuckle scent.

That was when, guided by some vague caution, I tossed my drink into the fireplace and held my glass cupped in my hand.

She was gone longer than it takes to fill a wine glass, I thought, and when she came back her eyes sought me with a long look. "How is your drink, Mr. McQuinn?"

"Fine. Never tasted better."

She sat down and seemed to regard me at length. I moved my arm and when I did she saw that my glass was empty. She rose at once. "Let me get you another drink."

"This is over my limit after what I had at the Sand Hills. I'm just a country boy, you know," a comment that I saw her worldly eyes, amused, did not believe. I put the glass on the floor by my chair because the only table in the room was the one that held the lamp. "You still haven't told me the name of the rancher who has the bay racehorse."

"Frankly, I'm afraid to."

"I can't see why he'd blame you any more, say, than some snoopy cowhand who's after that thousand-dollar reward, and plenty are. You could always deny you told me; too, there's more than one fast bay horse in West Texas. Could be this horse is not even Judge Blair."

"But he just came into possession of this fast horse." She took a long sip of her wine. "My position is quite different from the position of what you call a snoopy cowboy who's seen the horse. You see . . . there's something I haven't yet told you. . . . I know this man rather well . . . on an intimate basis . . . very intimate . . . and he told me about the horse the evening after I saw you and you so gentlemanly assisted me. He has promised to marry me. So it would be unfair of me to tell you his name and where his ranch is." She gazed upward. "Yet right is right, as my sainted mother used to say, God rest her sweet soul. Frankly, I'm torn between right and wrong."

By this time I didn't believe a damn word she said, but I says, "Did he tell you how he happened to come into ownership of this fast bay racehorse? Buy 'im, steal 'im?"

She seemed to be staring right through me, so intent was her gaze. "Oh, he wouldn't steal. But, no, he didn't."

"Mind tellin' me what he did say?"

Her eyes never left my face. "Just that he had a new bay racehorse and he'd tried him out and the horse was very fast."

"Did he say the horse has a blazed face and four white-sock feet?"

"He didn't say."

"Did he say the bay is a stud, a gelding, a filly, or a mare?"

"He didn't say and I didn't ask. To me a horse is a horse . . . and . . . when he mentioned the horse we were . . . in a rather intimate position." She bowed her pretty head in modesty.

I didn't believe a word of that, either. Hell, you don't talk about horses when you're makin' love to a woman or about to. But I kept on, like an exercise in conversation. "Just what is the man's name? I'd even buy the horse back for whatever he paid for it, if he did, and it's my horse."

"I'm afraid to tell you, Mr. McQuinn. I can't bring myself to do it. I'm a moral coward, I guess."

I'd heard enough. I came to my feet and moved toward the door. She was there before I could slide back the bar. In the soft light her well-made face looked regretful and appealing, except this close I noticed what I had not at a distance, the pouches under her eyes and the slack mouth. There was a tenseness in her face and the big hazel eyes bored into me and seemed to search and wait. She placed a slim hand on my coat and her fingers began to knead, first my chest, then my shoulder, then my neck. She had a way, all right.

"You're a kind man, Mr. McQuinn. I know you'll understand why I can't give you his name. I'm so afraid. He could be so violent. I don't know what to do." She lifted her face to me and pressed the length of her body against me, and for a moment all I could see were the rich hazel eyes while the honeysuckle scent rose around me.

A noise behind me, faint as it was, jerked at my senses. I started to spin around, but she gripped my shoulders to keep my back turned. I tore loose and thrust her aside barely in time to see a flat-nosed man almost upon me, club raised. Recognition flashed: the finish-line judge for Handy, the Texas House bouncer, and prob'ly one of the two who'd trailed me from the Sand Hills that night. I dodged as he swung. He missed. Belle Nolan screamed and got out of the way. I grabbed my gun and slammed the barrel across his head as he swung around. Blood spurted. She screamed again. He had a head like a bowling ball and he came at me again. I threw up my arm, and the club caught me high on my arm and threw me against the door. I wanted to shoot him and should've, but he was open and I crashed the barrel down on top of his head, then across his broken face. He sank down, his face a bloody mess, his nose flattened more than before. I heaved a sigh of relief. I was free to get out of there.

"Your money, Mr. McQuinn. All of it. The thousand-dollar reward you've been advertising all over town, and what you won today at three-to-one odds." She threw the last at me, I thought, with a particular venom.

My surprise was complete. She blocked the door and she held an ugly little squat-barreled derringer on me. But I still had my six-gun in my hand. We faced each other like that, a standoff, till she said, "You wouldn't dare shoot a woman, would you, Mr. McQuinn? Not you, a true Texas gentleman-horseman?"

"Don't believe I'm exactly up to date on all that a gentleman is supposed to be or do. Get robbed and not resist. Is that one of the rules of conduct? I'm plumb in the dark, Mrs. Nolan."

She raised the derringer higher. "The money, Mr. McQuinn. All of it. Cut out the palaver. It'll get you nowhere."

"Looks like a standoff, Mrs. Nolan. If you shoot me with that mean little popgun, I'll sure as hell shoot you back. You'd better believe me. And this old forty-five will blow a mighty big hole in that purty hide of yours."

"You wouldn't dare!" The derringer shook. She moved closer.

The bouncer groaned and made a clatter. For a tick of time she cut her eyes at him. As she did, I grabbed the derringer and twisted it out of her hand. That hurt and she screamed and flailed at me with both fists.

Then I did something I'd never done before and haven't since: I hit a woman. I slapped her face so hard she reeled across the room and collapsed in a heap by the fireplace.

"You bastard!" she snarled, her eyes wide with hurt and astonishment, her nice white teeth now like fangs in a twisted face. "How could you do that to me? How could you?"

"Because you ain't no lady, Mrs. Nolan. Because you're a bitch and a crook who put knockout drops in my drink, which lucky for me I didn't."

"But how could you strike me?" I expected tears, but I saw not one. She was tougher'n an El Paso boot.

"Because I ain't no gentleman, Mrs. Nolan. That's why. I'm just a dumb cowboy who trusts people too much."

I still had the little derringer. I stuck it in my pocket, freed the door, and saddled on down the road for town, my glum mood gone like a West Texas dust storm. Ol' trustful Dude McQuinn had bumbled out of this and survived without help from Billy and Coyote. I felt kind of proud. I'd done it all on my own, with a little luck. The bouncer wasn't a bright barroom fighter, which accounted for his flattened face. He should've aimed for my head instead of me in general.

I tied up at the Sand Hills and went inside and found my pardners still there and few cowboys still on their feet. Code Cook was among the survivors, still in the flush of victory. Little did he know what the steer market would do to him later. In time he'd make a top cowman, his *compadres* drought, blizzards, and bankers, bless 'em.

Billy threw me a question. "Where've you been? We wondered. You missed a good time."

"Believe I had my own." I drew him and Coyote to the end of the bar and motioned for Cook and Jack Dunn to listen in, too. Detail by detail, I told them all that had happened, from when Belle Nolan had stopped on the road near camp and I fixed the throat latch to when I slapped her down.

Dunn's head snapped up. "Belle . . . Belle Nolan? Why, hell, that's Solomon Handy's woman. Runs a fancy place behind the Texas House."

"Yeah," Cook says, "and she brings in girls from Fort Worth and El Paso, even Kansas City."

"How'd you know that, Code?"

Cook flushed. "Everybody in town knows that, same as everybody knows Handy waters his whiskey."

Dunn rolled his eyes. "Of course, of course."

I had to speak my piece. "Well, I'll say this, boys . . ." and shut up. I could still feel her fingers as they kneaded their way up from my chest to my shoulders and then my neck. She had her way, all right. I didn't say one more word.

"You don't have all the big news," Billy broke in, and pulled a letter from his coat pocket. "The postmaster, who is an obliging cuss and who like everybody else in town knows about Judge Blair by now, brought this over to us after closing hours to give to you. A postmaster can deliver a letter anytime he wants to, you know. Abe Lincoln did that back in Illinois."

I stared at the letter. There was that bold handwriting that just the sight of got me frothy. "You should've opened it, Uncle."

"We don't open other people's mail, do we, Coyote?"

"No, Grandfather."

"When will you ever quit callin' me grandfather?"

I dreaded to open the letter and glanced at the postmark: El Paso. I opened the letter, which read:

McQuinn:

So far you have followed instructions. That's lucky for you, because your horse is still alive. If you want to keep him that way, come to the Wigwam Saloon in El Paso for final instructions. We mean business. You are still being watched.

Still bird-dogged, I thought, *by the little hombre in the gray hat.* I passed the letter to my pardners and then to Dunn and Cook. "We're gettin' closer to the border all the time. El Paso, here we come. But it's one helluva long ride from here."

Billy shook his head. "We're not about to ride a horse to El Paso. That's brutal. I know, I've done it." He hooked his thumbs in his belt and reared back. "We'll travel in style with our horses, in a Texas and Pacific boxcar."

I couldn't hold back when I glimpsed that wee slit in his hazy past. "When was that, Uncle, that you made that long ride?"

"Now, did I say?"

CHAPTER 14

THE MYSTERY HORSE

Billy had said boxcar travel with horses was stylish. What he meant was it was stylish compared to a three-hundred-mile horseback ride across the desert to El Paso. I was glad to lead my horse down out of that jerker and shaker on wheels. Glad for a hot meal and some Mexican beer at a little Mexican restaurant near the tracks. Afterward, outside in the afternoon sun, we pondered our next destination, which was the Wigwam Saloon.

"This is a town with the hair on," Billy told us. "It's wide open and it's skin or be skinned, shoot or be shot, a bad place to have your gun stick. Makes Colorado City and Monahans look like ideal places to hold ice cream socials and Sunday School picnics. So . . ." He paused long in thought. "We might be wise to change our approach. Instead of the three of us together, why not drift over to the Wigwam one by one, why not pretend we're strangers? Maybe we can pick up something. We'll be close enough if one of us gets jumped. We can pass the word on the street later. What do you boys think?"

Coyote nodded, then I nodded. "But this time, Uncle, when I inquire about a letter, believe I'll not make a public announcement about the reward money. Might get knocked in the head right there for certain."

"I agree. And don't leave your gun in your pack. I feel this thing is about to come to a head. One reason, the gang has run out of post offices."

We broke up and I saddled into town. When I asked a man where the Wigwam was, he laid an odd look on me. "Hear that racket? That's it. You can't miss it—and good luck."

Naturally I hadn't expected to find it in the elite part of town, if there was one, and I wasn't disappointed. This was a section of cheap-whiskey saloons and rowdy dance halls, and when a woman in a narrow doorway swished her hips and invited me inside with a little tilt of her head, I knew what else. Not bad lookin', either. I could hear a piano and a racket of voices raised in argument. If the noise hadn't told me it was the saloon, a wigwam painted on a sign that hung over the dirt walk said so.

As I rode closer, the voices hiked louder and suddenly two men busted through the swingin' doors. Two white men. They cussed and slugged till one pulled his gun and shot the other twice just before the victim got his weapon out of the holster. It was a fast draw. The shooter ran. The saloon emptied. Everybody stood around the wounded man, who looked to be hurt bad. Somebody yelled, "Get a doctor!" Still, they all stood around, not much concerned, it seemed. Then somebody yelled, "Don't bother—call the undertaker!"

It was all over in a few minutes; the body was taken away and the crowd trooped back inside. I tied up my horse with the hope he would still be there when I came for him and I entered the saloon. The place smelled bad, even for a saloon, like wind off a low swamp. At the long bar I ordered a glass of beer. "Lively place you have here," I says to the bartender.

"Second killing this week." He was a stout, pot-bellied man whose cynical black eyes glinted above a drooping mustache. His scarred hands were the size of sledgehammers.

I took my time over the beer. Billy and Coyote hadn't come in yet. The tender, who looked bored, worked along the mahogany with his damp rag. "On the drift?"

"I use the same name everywhere I go. It's Dude McQuinn. Is there a letter here for me, or has word been left for me?"

"This ain't no post office."

"So there's nothing here for Dude McQuinn?"

"Not a letter, not a word."

I pushed a twenty-dollar bill across the wet face of the bar toward him. "Would this sharpen your memory if something comes in?"

"Might." The greenback disappeared in a blink.

"Do you enjoy a good horserace?"

"Do I? It's the only pleasure I have. When I can get a day off from this hellhole and there's a race in Juárez, I always go. The Mexicans know how to enjoy life. Anything goes over there and the beer is better than over here."

"Then you'll be interested in this. My racehorse was stolen at Aspermont, Texas, a short time ago. The thieves—it's a gang—have led me this way. A letter here and there. The last one said come to the Wigwam for final instructions. I hope that means my horse is close by. They want five thousand dollars. . . . My horse is Judge Blair. Ever hear of him?"

"Judge Blair!" His face lit up. He whapped the hardwood. "Hell, man, I saw him beat Yolanda in Juárez!"

"The devil you did?"

"I did, and here's one on the house." He pulled a quick beer. "The Mexicans still talk about that race. No wonder, since most of 'em went home broke that day."

"Reckon you won some money?"

He hung his head, his round face sheepish. "Like most everybody else I bet on Yolanda. I'd never heard of Judge Blair till that day. Anyway, it was a great race."

After that, we talked horse and more horse in between his duties. He'd seen some other good runners, like Blue Jacket, Rondo, and Jim Ned. When I filled him in on what my horse had done in Louisville and Lexington, he insisted I describe each race in detail, and just how they do things back there. He said his name was Dave Abbott. We shook hands. I knew I'd made up ground, found an unexpected friend, thanks to my horse. I said nothing about my pardners.

A fight broke out at a card table. With a weary sigh, Abbott ran around the bar and grabbed both men by their shirt collars, tore them apart and sat them down hard in chairs. "I'm tired of this rough stuff. Stop it or out you go!" He left them muttering among themselves, but they settled down.

Abbott took his post behind the bar and poured himself a stiff drink. "There's no law and order in this town anymore. What police we have are fixed by the big gamblers so they can run wide open. Gunmen walk armed in the streets. The reform movement comes and goes like a light snow, which also is seldom seen here."

I was on my third beer when Billy walked in. He had changed to his dress-up frock coat, white shirt, string tie, and flat-topped gray hat, and had shined his boots. He entered with the dignity of a true Kentucky hardboot, a gentleman of the Bluegrass. He placed a foot on the brass rail down from me and ordered an Old Green River.

A smile replaced the fatigue on Abbott's face. "Sir, I am glad to see somebody who appreciates good whiskey."

Billy nodded, and no more, and sipped, for all the world a gentleman of means and high endeavor. He glanced my way, but ignored me like I was beneath him. I kept a straight face. The old codger sure filled the role. He should've been on the stage.

The place seemed to bounce and sway. It grew louder. More men filed in till the bar was crowded. I heard Billy order another Old Green River, saw him pay and return his wallet to an inside pocket. The way he asked for whiskey, genteel-like, set him off from the rough patrons around him. I saw a tough nudge the man next to him and wink, which meant, "Watch me take the old man." I pulled away from the bar to help if Billy needed me.

The tough left the bar and circled in behind Billy, who, as always in a saloon, watched his backside in the mirror. The tough aimed to rob Billy right there in public, which seemed rough to me even for a dive like the Wigwam. But as he moved in and raised his arm to go over Billy's shoulder for the wallet, Billy whirled and stuck his gun in the thief's startled face. "You lookin' for this, Buster?"

This bird swallowed his surprise and tried to sneer it off. "Better be careful, Grandpa, that thing might go off."

Grandpa was the last word the man should have used. Billy's reply was to ram the barrel into the man's gut and force him back step by step.

"Now, dance, damn you—dance!"

The tough sneered again.

Billy fired a shot into the floor. Still, the thief wouldn't dance.

Billy fired again. His shot must have grazed the hombre's foot, because he howled and grasped it high with both hands and hopped on the other foot.

"Dance, damn you—dance!"

By now the crowd was laughing.

The tough dropped his foot and hopped up and down on both feet. Back and forth. Short and sweet, like an old woman's dance. He stopped, eager to throttle the old man.

Billy fired at his feet again. "More! Dance, damn you—dance! Make it purty!"

Hippity-hop, hippity-hop. Somebody started to sing. Shamed, the man dashed outside while the crowd hooted and laughed.

Billy reloaded, reholstered his gun, glanced around for any more takers, saw none, and resumed his Old Green River.

Abbott shook his head in wonderment. "Sir, I want you to know that's the neatest example of self-defense I've ever seen. That was Chug-a-Lug, the meanest character in this end of town. He likes to brag that he lives on Tough Street, the farther you go the tougher it gets—that he lives in a dugout past the last house. What he aimed to do was grab your wallet and run. I was down at the other end of the bar, didn't see him come up behind you or I'd've stepped in. Your next drink is on the house."

Billy yawned. "If you insist, Mr. Bartender. It's indeed a sorry state of affairs when a peaceful old fellow like me comes to El Paso in the market for a good saddle horse, and what happens but some disorderly person tries to rob him. Fortunately, the money I would pay for a good horse is in the bank, not on me."

A cagey remark that might prevent another robbery attempt.

Coyote came in soon after, dressed as I hadn't seen him in a long time, in his Carlisle School clothes: rusty brown suit, now wrinkled and too small for him, the trousers at high-water level above his ankles. Instead of moccasins he wore the box-toed shoes of school issue. I knew they hurt his feet by the gingerly way he stepped, like through a patch of burs. A black tie knotted in the collar of a gray flannel shirt seemed about to choke him, and his black, broad-brimmed hat was rounded at the crown like a chimney pot. That hat, I remembered, was not Carlisle regulation. He'd bought it in a train station on the way home to the reservation. And, I remembered, he'd kept the clothes in honor of his old school, where he'd graduated with honors, a boy Comanche fresh off the Plains, the son of the chief of all Comanches. But now he looked like a country yokel and I was afraid the crowd would badger him.

He edged in politely at the bar not far from Billy, and when Abbott came up to him, Coyote says, "A sassparilla, please."

I knew what that would bring, and it did, a burst of belly laughs. Here was a tenderfoot fresh for the pickin', an Indian at that, which would make the ridicule all the more cruel.

Abbott, who had been too long in the saloon business to be surprised at anything, blinked and blinked again at the order, but did not laugh; he searched behind and below the bar and finally found a bottle, and Coyote paid him politely. They also taught manners at Carlisle, and before that they taught manners in Comanche country.

The sarsaparilla would do it for certain. Trouble was on the way; just a matter of seconds, I knew. The rowdy bunch along the bar winked and nudged, and I saw one big hombre step out, take a hitch at his belt, mosey over to Coyote and slide in beside him and say to Abbott, "A bottle of Old Six-Shooter." When Abbott set out bottle and glass, the tough poured the glass full and plopped it down in front of Coyote. "Drink this, sonny boy."

Coyote regarded it as he might an object of unusual curiosity. "White man, recall I do not ordering whiskey which drink I do not."

"Drink it anyhow. That sassparilla's sissy stuff."

"See it that way I do not. The taste is pleasant."

"I said drink it, sonny boy, whatever you are, Injun or Mex. Besides, you talk funny. I don't like that. Can you talk American?"

Coyote said nothing, in control of himself.

"I said drink! Drink like a man!"

Hell was about to pop. I stepped clear of the bar, ready to rush over there, when Coyote lifted the glass of whiskey as if to drink it and I felt a protest. Then I heard him say, "I'll take no sass but sassparilla," and he whipped around and tossed the whiskey into the face of the white man, who slapped both hands to his eyes. With that motion, Coyote grabbed the bottle of Old Six-Shooter and brought it down on the man's head. Whiskey and blood and broken glass splattered like spring mud and the hombre staggered toward the card tables, Coyote after him like a cat. He picked up a chair and broke it over the white man's head and shoulders. He went down like an empty gunny sack, out colder'n a March norther.

The crowd rushed for Coyote. So did I. I could see Billy ahead of me. I punched some faces. Out of the tail of my eye I saw Abbott draw a big pistol from under the bar and fire two shots into the ceiling. All at once everybody stopped in their tracks.

"That's enough!" Abbott's voice was a shout, and he looked mighty determined behind that young cannon. "Take him out to the water trough and douse him good. Rest of you quiet down. Indian, finish your sassparilla."

I and Billy drifted in closer as Coyote took his place at the bar. Abbott eyed him hard. "Somebody owes the house for one bottle of Old Six-Shooter and one busted chair, Mexican-made, imported from Juárez." He nodded to himself while he tallied it up in his head. Bit by bit, a half grin broke through his tired features. "On second thought, I'll charge it off to entertainment. And that remark you made—'I'll take no sass but sassparilla'—why, that ain't been heard in El Paso since John Welsey Hardin coined it and backed it up. Indian, you must be well-read."

"I listen to bartenders."

"Well, it's the first time anybody liked to've wrecked my saloon just by bein' nice. Maybe the reform movement is on its way back."

After a while, we left the Wigwam as we had come in, one by one, and I was there by our horses when my pardners came up. I spoke first. "The bartender's name is Dave Abbott. I believe he's all right and has no connection with the gang. He said there was no letter or word left for us."

Billy was chipper. "We got here sooner than the thieves expected. May be a few days yet."

I was discouraged and the tone of my voice was low. "Maybe this is where the trail finally peters out. Maybe this has all been for nothing. We're like puppets on a string."

"Don't forget they want the five thousand."

"Judge Blair could make twenty times that much or more in match races on the other side of the river. What's five thousand?"

"You mean an easy five thousand. No crook's gonna pass up what he sees as easy money. Maybe they figure to have the five in hand and keep the horse, too. They'll make their play before long." He slapped me on the shoulder. "So here we are and here we'll stay till we unravel this."

We saddled back to the little Mexican restaurant for supper, and slept that night in a wagonyard. Two days plodded by, one like the other, without news, loaded with self-doubt and fear. Would I ever see my horse again? Each afternoon I'd drop in at the Wigwam and visit with Dave Abbott. I'd told him most of the story by this time because I trusted him and he wanted to help. What's more, he didn't yawn on the glasses to give 'em a polish, and he didn't water his whiskey, which is a pretty good slant on a saloonkeeper's character.

On the third afternoon when I checked in, Abbott held out a copy of the El Paso *Times.* "Take a gander at this. May mean something, maybe not. But I've never heard of this Señor Juan before."

The headline read: Mystery Horse Favored in Fast Derby Field.

The story read:

"Señor Juan, a mystery horse to the border area, heads a fast ten-horse field of quarter sprinters in the $10,000 Río Grande Derby Saturday afternoon at Juárez.

"Other leading contenders include Devil Mountain, Duster, and the speedy filly Miss Calico. But Señor Juan, by virtue of a flashy early-morning sharpener Tuesday, will go as the odds-on favorite in the 400-yard feature, the last race of the afternoon. He covered the distance in twenty seconds flat on a tight hold, railbirds said. Devil Mountain recorded the second best work in 20⅕, with Duster and Calico Miss showing 20½ seconds. Manny Moreno will be in the irons on the favorite, a compact bay gelding with speedy lines. Post time is 1:30.

"Reportedly owned by a group of wealthy Texas cattlemen who have asked to remain anonymous, Señor Juan is said to have won several big match races in South Texas by daylight and was a last-minute surprise entry at the racing secretary's office. His trainer was not listed by individual name, but as the Pecos Ranch, Inc."

Feeling gripped me as the words leaped out at me. *Mystery horse— flashy early-morning sharpener—twenty seconds flat on a tight hold—* That was Judge Blair time, though he had bested that more than once— *Compact bay gelding with speedy lines—last-minute surprise entry.* No trainer listed by name. Just the ranch.

I handed back the paper. "Want to go with us Saturday?"

"Do you have to ask? We can all take the streetcar, have a drink at Deiter and Sauer's Saloon where we get off, and stroll over to the track."

I was impatient to tell my pardners. Billy didn't jump at the news, in his eyes the experience of an older man who'd seen high prospects end up like the steer market in a bad year. "Sure, we'll go for a look-see. But as for this mystery horse, he's probably a South Texas ringer brought in under another name, and keep in mind that there's more than one compact bay gelding that can burn a hole in the wind. Yet I've got to admit that twenty seconds flat on a tight hold could be our horse. I said *could,* Dude."

This was Thursday. I waited out Friday and Saturday as nervous as a cowboy whose mail-order bride was due in any minute on the Texas and Pacific. Just before we left the wagonyard, I took off my belt and slipped my six-shooter inside my waistband for easier gettin' to. I was ready.

Well, the streetcar was packed like a cattle car bound for the Fort Worth stockyards, and when we got off near the saloon, Abbott led us right in and bought drinks and lunch for the outfit and made certain that Coyote got his without any sass.

From there we set out through the crowd for the track and a look at this Señor Juan, the mystery horse. The closer we came to the stables the thicker the racegoers. An overcast sky made the day cooler in that beery and genial crowd. Billy cast an eye skyward. "May need the slickers we left behind, and could be Señor Juan had better be a mudder."

"Aw, it won't rain, Uncle."

"I didn't say that. I speak for my bones. If it rains and the Señor is a little sore after that twenty-second work, he may like a track that's on the slow, soft side. On the other hand, if he breaks late, he may not like mud in his face and will give ground."

We followed the crowd to the backside, where there was a good deal of commotion, with post time near and horses ponied to the saddlin' paddock for the first race. I asked a man where Señor Juan was stalled and he pointed midway down the shedrow. "The Derby runners are along there." When we reached that area, I asked the location from another horseman. He pointed and did not conceal a grin. "Señor Juan's stall is right over there where you see the constabulary."

I trailed his eyes. Four men lounged outside a stall where the door was closed, even the upper half. They were all Texas-lookin' gents in big hats and big belts and they all packed guns. None was familiar.

With Billy on one side of me and Coyote on the other and Abbott behind Billy, I went over and immediately a man moved out to intercept us.

"Sir," I says, "my name is Dude McQuinn and I ranch on the Salt Fork of the Brazos. These are my pardners and we're in the market for a fast racehorse. We've heard a lot about Señor Juan these past days and we'd appreciate it if we could have a look at him."

He was a big, blustery man and like most horsemen, I'd say, rightfully suspicious of any change on race day. "The horse is not for sale, pardner. Right now he's makin' too much money for us to sell him."

"How much do you figure he's worth?"

"Oh, a ranch or two." He had a laugh that went with his size.

"I can understand that, since he's the Derby favorite and knocked off that work this week in twenty flat. But there's a deal for every horse when the price is right. Since we're due to pull out early in the morning, we wonder if we might have a close-up look-see at him now? Check his conformation, shoulder and legs?"

"Pardner, I wouldn't let my own mother get within ten feet of our horse this afternoon, because the word is out that the fix is on. There's a pile of money bein' bet on the Derby. If our horse failed to win, the long shots would win big. Savvy? You'll have to wait for your look-see when he runs. And he's not for sale at any price."

No, pardner, Judge Blair wouldn't be for sale at any price. I was primed to say more when Billy touched my arm, the signal to let up, and I wished the man luck and we left. Billy's tone urged patience as we walked away. "We'll know soon enough."

All I could think of was how we'd stack up against four well-armed horsethieves.

We angled back through the restless crowd toward the stands. The cool air had changed in this short time to the muggy heat that precedes a Southwestern rainstorm. To offset the heat we had another beer, at Abbott's suggestion. There was a roar from the crowd as the first race got off and an even greater roar at the finish. I wasn't interested. I downed my beer and glanced over the crowd, my mind still back at the barns and the horse the guard wouldn't let us see. As usual, Billy was right. I was too quick to suspect. We'd see the horse run. But why the cover-up? Why? Why *not?* Hold off revealing the horse's identity till the last moment to get the odds up. One word that Judge Blair was Señor Juan would change everything. Mexicans don't forget their champions. They'd remember the heartbreak of Yolanda's loss. So these Texans bring in Judge Blair under another name and . . .

Two men crossed my vision, two men engaged in earnest conversation. One was the bird-doggin' little man in the gray hat—hell, yes, it was!—who rode the bald-faced saddler. The man beside him wore a western hat and was tall and rawboned. I nudged Billy and Coyote and when they turned to look, the two had disappeared into the crowd.

I slapped my leg. "How'd the bird-dogger get here so damn fast?"

"I believe the Texas and Pacific still runs on the same track we came in on," Billy says, tongue-in-cheek.

Abbott had noticed. "You talkin' about the little sawed-off gent in the gray hat?"

I nodded.

"He came in for a beer right after you left yesterday. Nice, clean-cut fellow. Only one beer."

"Nice?" I couldn't agree.

I bought a race program and we all scanned it. The Derby was the last of seven races. Abbott took off and when he came back he said he'd found some two-to-one money on the Duster. "If it rains, I don't think a filly has the strength in mud a colt has, and who knows what the Señor will do on a heavy track."

"It all comes down to heart and whim," Billy put in. "If a horse doesn't like an off track, he won't do his best. But a great horse can run on any kind of footing."

We heard the first peal of thunder soon after the fifth race ended. We could see the storm like a dark hedge off to the Southwest. It seemed to boil and roll. Now the wind whipped up, and dust off the track threw a brownish veil over the next horses when they entered the track from the paddock for the sixth race post parade. They made it brief, a fast trot past the stands and on to the backstretch for the getaway.

The first rain hit us like buckshot just as the horses broke. We hurried and took cover with others by the side of the now overcrowded stands. The storm seemed to put wings in the horses' feet. It was a six-furlong Thoroughbred sprint around one turn, and they fairly flew down the backside and into the bend for the homestretch run. From that point they turned into phantoms, almost lost in the greenish curtain of the wind-driven rain. I dashed into the stands to the steps to get a glimpse of the finish, but it was over before I got there. The roar of the crowd and then the sudden way the sounds raveled off told me. A quick ceremony in the winner's circle and it was done; now the steady buzz of voices took over while the crowd settled in for the Derby.

The downpour fell heavier. Directly, through the screen of rain, I could see pony horse riders leading the runners down the backside from the stables. No time today for the ritual of the saddlin' paddock for the crowd to view the horses; they were already saddled and the jockeys mounted. They started around the turn, heads bent against the gale, apparently to make the post parade.

A yellow-slickered rider left the stands and raced toward the runners, now not far from the straightaway. He waved and directed them toward the head of the track, where the four-hundred-yard sprint would start. There would be no post parade for the feature race.

I sheltered the race program against the wind and rain and studied it. Señor Juan had the Number 1 position, Duster was in 2, Devil Mountain in 5, and Calico Miss in 7.

I could tell very little about the horses from here. But when the official in the yellow slicker wheeled back for the stands, and the lead runner and pony horse turned to go to the head of the straightaway for the start, I glimpsed the No. 1 on the saddle cloth of Señor Juan. He was a dark bay with a blazed face. That was all I got, but in that split instant I felt a surge of powerful excitement. Four white socks like Judge Blair's? I couldn't see. Besides, the legs could be wrapped or covered with mud. By then the pony horse blocked my view, but I had seen the blaze. That was enough. The image of my horse formed before me. I swallowed hard, but the lump wouldn't quite go down.

I forced myself to check the other favorites while they passed up-track. Duster, the 2 horse, was a ghostly dapple gray against the misty light. Devil Mountain, the 5 horse, was a big, stout sorrel, and Calico Miss, who would break from the 7 hole, was a feisty black filly with the air of a classy speedster. Her high action would help her in the mud—if, as Billy had said, she had plenty of heart and not much whim; and if she had enough strength for the mud, I added now. An instinct told me that, barring bad luck, she would be up close at the finish.

The next minutes seemed to pass in single file, the horses only vague objects shrunk smaller and smaller in the bleary light at the far end of the track. I caught a glimpse of yellow, the starter also in yellow slicker. No chutes or gates. Instead, a walk-up start. There was little delay now as the horses turned behind the starting line and moved forward.

Suddenly there was a rush of color as the horses broke, dark and small, bobbing through their greenish world. It looked like a clean break, no bumping. The horses bunched so far, too early to find a leader.

At the point where the oval joined the straightaway, a blur of dark horsehide shot out of the pack and became visible all at once. It was Calico Miss, who had speed and the heart to back it up. But Devil Mountain, the stout sorrel, also was on the charge to the filly's left. Where was Señor Juan? There he was not far behind, along the rail, the gray Duster half a length off him. Both the filly and Devil Mountain shut off most of my view of the Señor.

They held those positions till they raced to the end of the stands, when Devil Mountain began to fade. He'd run his race and Señor Juan and Calico Miss took over, the Señor still on the rail. Duster was out of it. I went up the steps to catch the finish and had to shoulder through for a clear view as people jumped up and down and screamed. It looked like a blanket finish, the winner undecided till I heard shouts of "Señor Juan! Señor Juan!" Evidently, the Mexicans had bet big on him because of his name, and apparently he'd won. Calico Miss, that beautiful black filly with so much heart, was a close second.

Still, I wasn't certain. The horses ran on some distance till eased up and all but one headed for the stables. When I saw the jockey on the dark bay Señor turn to come back to the stands, the blazed face like a signal to me in the gray light, the jockey holding high his whip in victory, I made a fast path through the crowd for the winner's circle. Horse and rider were already there by the time I managed to plunge through. Also there was the big, blustery man, rain in a stream off his hat, his wide smile like a slash. Proudly, he took the horse by the bit and turned him for the fans in the stands to see him better.

I knew the instant I looked. The blaze did not come to a point between the nostrils, and he was gotch-eared; one drooped. There were little differences: the eyes, the way he stood. Does a mother know her own child? I slumped back. It wasn't my horse.

The big man remembered me. "Pardner, you still interested in buyin' this horse? If you are, the price just went up another ranch."

I shook his hand. "Don't believe I could afford him now and you'd be a fool to sell him. He sure ran big. I'm glad for you. Good luck down the road."

He put his head to my ear. "Let you in on a little secret. This horse don't speak a word of Spanish, and back home in Alice, Texas, he goes by the name of Hot Iron."

Afterward, I picked my way back through the happy Mexican crowd, the lowest I'd been since we left the ranch. Another dead end.

CHAPTER 15

THE OTHER SIDE OF THE RIVER

I moped around for two more days. We all wrote letters home. The Wigwam was closed on Sunday, believe it or not, but on Monday we returned to our regular beat: from the wagonyard, our headquarters, to the saloon and back, taking our meals at the same little Mexican restaurant where the frijoles and enchiladas, the tamales and beer made life tolerable.

Billy continued to hold to his belief that we had arrived earlier than the gang expected and that before long we'd hear from them. He always came back to the $5,000, that no crook would pass up such easy money. I had to go along with that.

I made my rides to the Wigwam Tuesday morning and late afternoon without results, and had just unsaddled when a bright-eyed Mexican kid came up on the run. "Señor Abbott says come to the Wigwam now. A man is there to see you. Hurry, he said."

I saddled up fast, but not so fast I forgot my gun, which I stuck inside my waistband again under my coat. Just before we rode up to the Wigwam, Billy threw up a hand in caution. "Let's not all bust in there together. You go in alone, Dude, like before. Coyote and I will drift in pretty quick, one by one. Let this man think there's only one. Just you, the owner of the horse. If you leave the saloon, we'll trail you."

"The little hombre in the gray hat knows there's three of us. He saw us in Colorado City. Wouldn't he pass that on?"

"I can't see that it was important then. But it is important now. It could give us an advantage when we get down to horse and money. A show of strength, a surprise at the right moment."

"What if it is the little hombre?"

"Then we haven't lost anything. If it's not, so much the better."

I went in first, primed for bear. Abbott was behind the bar, busy with a towel and glass. If he didn't ease up, that glass was gonna wear out fast. He jogged his head toward one end of the bar.

Standing there was a long reed of a man, ramrod-straight, whose white-blond hair hung almost to his shoulders. His left hand toyed with a jigger of whiskey next to a bottle that was well down. His right hand was loose on the bar, ready, it looked, if trouble blew. All this time he gauged me. I caught the bulge of a gun under his seedy brown coat. But it was his face that held my attention. An old face in a younger body: sallow, lined, the mouth pinched tight. His burned-out pale eyes squinted at me.

"I'm Dude McQuinn. You want to talk about my horse?" Although I boiled inside, I had a grip on myself.

"That's why I'm here."

I moved to the bar, but kept my right hand as free as his. "Just remember this. No horse, no money. I have to see the horse first."

"You sound a mite high-and-mighty for a man who wants his racehorse back." His voice was as reedy as his pole-thin body looked. He was prob'ly thirty-five, but showed the wear and tear of a man fifty.

My banked-up anger was about ready to flare; again, I tight-reined it in. "You come to parley or lock horns? Take your pick."

The burned-out stare took on a pasty hue. "I have news for you. Your horse is on the other side of the river."

"Guess I should've expected that."

He seemed to relax a little. "Have a drink with me."

"I don't drink with horsethieves."

The waxen face didn't change. Deliberately, he tossed his drink down left-handed. "You surprised everybody when you got here so quick."

"I got here from Monahans the same way my horse did from Colorado City to El Paso—in a boxcar. I have to admit that was slick the way Mr. Gus was bribed to haul my horse in a circus van from Aspermont to Colorado City."

"That was." His tone mocked me.

Behind my back I heard Abbott's overloud greeting, "Come in, Doctor. What'll you have today, sir, another Old Green River?" He was letting me know.

"Yes, my usual."

I glanced around, suspicious. "Where's the little hombre in the gray hat your outfit sent to bird-dog me?"

The trap of a mouth seemed about to form a question, but he said nothing. Hell, didn't he know? Again, I heard Abbott's loud voice, "If it ain't my Indian friend of many moons. After what happened the other day, you'll sure get your sassparilla without any sass." That produced a stir of rowdy laughs.

My pardners behind me gave me strength and I itched to get this done. "So my horse is on the other side of the river. Why don't you bring him over here and we'll close the deal?"

"Oh, no. You go over there."

"So I'll get knocked in the head for the money while the gang keeps my horse and gets rich matchin' him in Old Mexico?"

When he was slow on the reply, I came back at him with, "Don't you have anything to say about this? You just a messenger boy for the gang? That all you are—just a messenger boy?"

"Messenger boy, hell!" I'd touched a sensitive spot, even though he was prob'ly no more than a border drifter, a boozer and hanger-on, here to pick up a few bucks. He looked with longing at the bottle, passed it up and says, "The deal is this. You ride with me across the river to the Kentucky Bar. There you'll get your horse when you pay the five-thousand ransom."

"That all?"

"That's all."

"You mean *that's all you know?* That's all the boss man of the gang told you?"

He flung back from the bar. "By God, if you want your horse back alive, that's what you'd better do!" I'd stung what was left of his pride. Good. Maybe he'd been a good man once before the bottle got him and he'd joined the riffraff along the border.

But I wasn't through. "Did the boss man say he'd share a cut of the ransom with you—or did he pass you some pesos, just enough to get you a few tortillas tonight on the other side, and promise you a bottle of rotgut tequila to boot?"

For a breath of time I feared I'd gone too far and it was gonna happen right there. But he didn't drop his hand to open the ball. Color shot up into the sallow mask of his face and he jerked. "You comin' or not?"

"Lead off."

He swung away and I moved with him stride for stride as we passed Billy and Coyote, who ignored us. From the saloon we stepped out into the muddy light of early evening. I'd have preferred daylight for where I was headed. The messenger looked about with a keen attention. At the other end of the crowded hitching rack two men smoked and talked.

I felt a start. One was the bird-dogger, the other the man I'd seen with him at the Juárez track. I knew the messenger saw the bird-dogger, yet he said no word and gave no sign of recognition. Was the little man here to back him up or not? My unease grew as we mounted and rode off for the Río Grande.

We hadn't covered more than a few hundred yards when I heard hoofbeats behind us which I knew meant my pardners followed. Messenger Boy whipped around at me, as edgy as a one-eyed gambler. "Who's that back there?"

"How would I know? It's a public street."

I heard the louder drumming of horses now, but I didn't look back. Soon I picked up a heavier beat and I turned my head a little to listen. More horses now. Maybe four or five. So the bird-dogger and the other man followed, too.

We took the Stanton Street Bridge over the river. In Juárez, my man turned down a narrow street and before long we rode up to the Kentucky Bar. It was all lit up, evidently a major water hole for thirsty *Americanos.*

When we started for the swingin' doors, Messenger Boy would have dropped in behind me, the old familiar gunfighter's ploy for the advantage. I halted. "You go ahead." He obliged without argument, but as we neared the doors, he slowed and angled back to my right. I halted again. "Either stay ahead of me or on my left." On the right side he could grab my gun with his left, draw his gun right-handed, and I'd be a goner.

He eyed me hard, then barged ahead through the doors.

The busy bar and restaurant, where white-jacketed bartenders and waiters labored, lay to our left. He led off past the bar to a patio open to the sky and enclosed on all sides, with flowers and tables and chairs here and there. A pleasant place in the mellow light of lanterns. A little stone fountain babbled in the center.

Again, Messenger Boy dropped back to my right, and again I stopped. "You're out of position, old stud. Stay ahead."

He did, but the burned-out eyes said he would kill me if he got the chance.

As we rounded the fountain, I spotted a short-bodied man seated at a table toward the rear of the patio, head down, chin at rest on his left hand. Little bits began to tug at my memory: the black bowler, the open frock coat over the checkered vest, the heavy gold watch-chain across the paunch. He looked up suddenly and my mind did a flip-flop when I stared into the beardless round face and baby-blue eyes of one Patrick C. Parker III.

His voice was as cheerful as when we'd matched the race at Aspermont. "Good evening, Mr. McQuinn. It's fortunate that you've seen fit to follow our instructions."

I was so astonished that all I could say was, "You . . . you're behind this." And as my temper flared high, I could not hold back a bitter sarcasm. "How's your tomato crop?"

"Tomato crop?"

"You know . . . where you send a small boy up the tree to shake 'em down? Works fine."

He reared up from the chair and I saw the gun wobble on his right hip. "This is no time for levity, sir."

"Sure. And 'Every man a king. A fair trial for every man,' sir. Now, where the hell's my horse?"

"He's nearby."

"Then bring him in."

"Here . . . in the patio?"

I had the insight that he was putting me off. "No horse, no money."

"Did you bring the five thousand?"

"Where's my horse? That comes first."

Parker's baby-pink cheeks reddened, his mouth worked, but he didn't answer me. He shuffled his feet.

I'd had enough delay. I drew my six-gun and waved Messenger Boy over to stand near Parker. "Now, we're gonna march out to my horse, and if you pretend not to know the way, you'll be sorry for certain."

Parker's eyes shifted ever so slightly. At that twitchy movement I yanked around, but was a shade late as a man slipped from the doorway on my right and I felt a gun barrel rammed into my back.

"Take his gun."

Messenger Boy, with a look of relish, couldn't move fast enough. He snatched my gun and shot me a waxen leer.

I could feel the pressure of the gun barrel ease as the voice behind me spoke again. "Turn around, McQuinn. I want you to see who I am. I've waited a long time for this."

I turned around and met snake-glitter eyes I could never forget. It was Si Eckert, it was Rube Vogel, it was Nate Thompson all rolled into one, the outlaw of many aliases who had headed the horse-rustlin' ring which the outfit had helped break up when we went back to Kentucky to trace Judge Blair's breeding. Long-jawed and lean, only leaner and meaner in my eye now, with the same gap-toothed snarl. He looked flush: flashy suit, diamond stickpin, a stud diamond ring on the hand that held the six-shooter. At that moment I was close to death and knew it.

The mean mouth twisted. "I've waited for this from the day your goddamned messin' in sent me to the state pen in Kentucky. When I broke out with Baby-Face Burke, I knew I'd catch up with you if I went back to Texas where everybody knows that fast horse of yours. All I had to do was ask around. Simple, McQuinn. Simple, like you."

I could only wait. Where were my pardners?

He went on, his pleasure pure and deadly. "You're dumb, McQuinn. Plain dumb. We didn't even need to have you watched. Just said you was. All we did was have Baby Face—that's him over there—write dumb letters to you to lure you on and make you sweat. We knew you'd follow your horse to hell to get 'im back, and that's where you've come to, McQuinn . . . on the edge lookin' down into hell, where you'll be in just a few seconds."

He was gonna kill me, I knew for certain.

Some last instinct of survival made me say, "You kill me you won't get the five thousand. It's not on me. It's back in the safe at the Wigwam."

"What! You're lyin'. You wouldn't come here without the money or you couldn't get your horse. Search him, Burke."

I stood with my gaze split between them, Vogel on my right, Burke on my left.

Burke stepped across to me, on his smooth face a distaste for the search. "Unbuckle your money belt, McQuinn."

"I tell you it's not on me. It's back at the Wigwam."

"Search him, I say!"

Still, Burke held back, in his baby-blue eyes the mirror of his intent to avoid any physical combat. He looked pink and flabby. Abruptly, he tore back my coat. His fat hand was slow and tentative. I caught it and swung him into Vogel, who fired at the same time. I felt Burke jerk with the force of the bullet. Mouth open, eyes wide, he looked at me with an awful expression of wonder. He staggered and started to sink to the floor, but I continued to hold him between Vogel and me, using him as a shield.

Vogel hesitated, too surprised to fire again. He moved to cut around me, but I moved with him.

There came a crash of boots across the courtyard behind us from the direction of the bar, and I saw a swarm of Mexican police, among them my pardners and the little hombre in the gray hat and his race track *compadre*. Vogel wheeled to face them, but he was too late. They had him covered as he had covered me.

It was finished in moments, Vogel and Messenger Boy handcuffed. Two waiters from the restaurant took Burke out on a wooden door. He was in agony and in loud mortal terror of the hereafter as he prayed for forgiveness, a long shot at best.

Billy spoke first to me, as out of breath as a windbroken saddler. "This popped faster . . . than we figured it would. We heard the shot just as we came inside. . . . Those other two fellows were right behind us with the police."

"Sometimes a man gets lucky, Uncle. I was. I just grabbed and hung on."

The little gray-hatted man hurried over, his face and voice warm with apology. "Now I can answer the question you asked me back in Big Spring when you jumped me." Held out his hand. "My name is Ben Greer. I'm a Texas Ranger. We've been after Nate Thompson, alias Si Eckert, alias Rube Vogel, and Baby-Face Burke ever since they broke out of the pen in Kentucky and shot down two guards. Been a nationwide manhunt. Thompson drifted back to his old Texas haunts and old habits. Robbed banks—killed a deputy at Abilene. Added gun runnin' to his specialities. Became rich. We got a tip that he and Burke might hit banks in the Colorado City and Big Spring area, so I was assigned there. . . . I didn't link the stolen horse case with them till we learned

they'd lost some big match races in Old Mexico and were on the lookout for a fast horse they could steal."

Billy nodded. "That wasn't all. Their strongest motive when they
stole Judge Blair was for revenge. To lure Dude across the river and
murder him. You see, Mr. Greer, our outfit helped send Vogel to the
Kentucky pen as head of a stolen-horse ring that operated clear into the
Southwest. Their idea was to kill Dude and have the ransom money and
the horse to boot. They almost pulled it off, too. I should never have let
Dude come in here alone."

"If you hadn't, they might not have showed their hands. Might have
backed off. As it was, a shoot-out was avoided."

I was curious about Burke. "How did Burke figure in this?"

"Thompson and Burke got acquainted in the pen. Burke had been a
crooked jockey and horsethief around Louisville. A glib character, he
studied a little law while in prison, and when he broke out with Thompson he put on a front as an attorney to rehabilitate criminals and pretended to be in search of a place to hang out his shingle. He'd come into
a little town, buy drinks, tell some jokes, and case the bank. He'd have
made a great jackleg lawyer. . . . That's Wade Hall, a U.S. Customs
agent, over there with the prisoners. A few nights ago Hall and other
agents confiscated dozens of firearms and some two hundred boxes of
ammunition bound for Mexico when they posed as Mexican revolution-
aries. Seized the shipment on the Texas side of the river. Took a pris-
oner named Vic Queen."

"Queen was Thompson's trainer." Billy nodded.

That sums it up, I thought. *It's over.* But a late meaning crashed
through my mind, with a sense of guilt for my delay and for my forget-
fulness. "Mr. Greer, we've got to look for our horse. Vogel knows
where he is."

I confronted Vogel, now the old Vogel of Lexington, surly, close-
mouthed, spewin' hate.

"Where is my horse?"

All I got was the old Lexington sneer and, "What horse?"

"You tell me or I'll beat it out of you for certain!"

"Go to hell, McQuinn. Where you'd be now if I'd shot you when I
first came up behind you."

I started to grab him, but Billy caught my arm. "No, Dude, no.
Maybe later, if you have to."

Against my will, I pulled back to Messenger Boy. "Where's my horse?"

He just shrugged, a two-bit imitation of Vogel.

Billy's impatient voice jerked at me. "Come on, Dude. We're wasting time. The Judge is around here somewhere."

With Coyote and Greer and others, we dashed out through the rear of the patio and found ourselves in a dark alley. Coyote ran back for a lantern. Now I could see sheds and piles of litter. We looked inside the nearest shed, and it was empty; and another, which held a couple of goats.

As if my mind must ever run behind on this particular night, of all nights, I stood back and thought, *How could I forget?* And I gave the shrill whistle I did at the ranch when I had a handful of feed for my horse. In my inner vision I saw him again, saw him toss his blazed head and look at me but not come up. The little game we played. Then, on the third whistle, he nickered and came up to me on the trot.

Billy and Coyote looked at me, surprised, but with understanding and approval. The three of us froze. . . .

But nothing happened. No nicker on the wind.

I whistled again, a longer call and more shrill. We waited, and we waited some more. . . . Still, no nicker. I looked down and bit my lip. My horse wasn't here.

In a kind of desperation I whistled once more, this time with all my strength, and held it, and waited. . . . What was that? Did I hear right? A nicker? It was. Also a pounding.

I whooped and Coyote whooped and Billy shouted and we ran down the alley to another shed, guided by a pounding and kicking there, of hoofs against wood against the shed door, which was all atremble.

I tore open the door and when Coyote held the lantern up, I saw the hindquarters of a haltered dark bay horse. I couldn't move fast enough as I untied the halter and backed the horse out, but when I looked at his face there was no blaze and no white socks. I sagged at that.

"Hell," Billy says, his eyes like knives, "they've painted his blaze and white socks. But it's Judge Blair. I'd know this horse if they'd painted him purple all over."

Sure, it was Judge Blair.

The three of us closed in to pet and talk nonsense to him. After a while, we stood back. Billy's voice broke a little. "He's a hundred or so pounds under his runnin' weight, and I see rope burns on him, and he's likely sored up. Lead him out a way, Coyote. Let's see how he moves." And when Coyote had done that, "He's all right. Let's take him home."

"I'm all for that," I says. "But the first thing we're gonna do in the morning, after we scrub off all that paint, is to have his picture made. I've waited too long."

About the Author

Fred Grove has written extensively in the field of Western fiction, from the Civil War period to modern quarter-horse racing. He has received the Western Writers of America Spur Award five times—for his novels *Comanche Captives* (which also won the Oklahoma Writing Award and the Levi Golden Saddleman Award), *The Great Horse Race,* and *Match Race;* and for his short stories, "Comanche Woman" and "When the Caballos Came." His novel *The Buffalo Runners* was awarded the Western Heritage Award by the National Cowboy Hall of Fame, as was the short story "Comanche Son." He also has received a Distinguished Service Award from Western New Mexico University for his regional fiction. He is a contributor to anthologies, among them *Spurs West* and *They Opened the West.* This is his nineteenth novel.

For a number of years, Mr. Grove worked on various newspapers in Oklahoma and Texas. Two of his earlier novels, *Warrior Road* and *Drums Without Warriors,* focused on the brutal Osage Indian murders during the Roaring Twenties, a national scandal that brought in the FBI. It was while interviewing Oklahoma pioneers that he became interested in Western fiction. He now resides in Silver City, N.M., with his wife, Lucille.